Up in the Middle of Nowhere

BLAIR BRYAN

Read More By this Author

Use the QR code below to access my current catalogue. **Teal Butterfly Press is the only place to purchase autographed paperbacks and get early access.** Buying direct means you are supporting an artist instead of big business. I appreciate you.

https://tealbutterflypress.com/pages/books

Also available at Barnes and Noble, Kobo, Apple books, Amazon, and many other international book sellers.

Find My Books at your Favorite Bookseller Below.

Books by Ninya

Books By Blair Bryan

To My Mom in Heaven:

I wish we'd taken a trip like this.

I hope you are proud of the mother I've become.

You're my favorite angel.

Inspired by True Events

While their adventure was inspired by a trip that I took with my own child, Tessa and Nova are fictional characters existing only in my imagination and on these pages. The treehouses, however, were very much real! Find out more information about them in the back of this book.

Use the QR Code below to see photos and videos from the real-life Tennessee adventure that inspired this novel.

Part 1

Chapter One

*"*I hate you!"

"You're not too high on my list of favorite people right now, either," Tessa argued as she cranked up the volume on the radio and hummed along as frustration thrummed through her limbs. Taking her rage out on the gas pedal as she drove them home, she slammed her foot down on the accelerator. She wasn't going to fall for it. At seventeen, Nova loved to push her buttons and often had a penchant for the dramatics. Instead, Tessa kept her thoughts to herself, clamping her lips together to prevent a negative torrent of them from escaping. She knew words said in anger cut the deepest scars and could never be taken back, but containing them at the moment was proving a monumental task.

"I'm going to go live with Dad!" Nova shouted to her mother over the music.

Appalled by this declaration, Tessa yanked the steering wheel hard to the right to pull off on the shoulder and slammed on the brakes. Forcing the car into park, she turned toward her daughter's petulant face. Dressed in black from head to toe, wearing six-inch black platform boots and copious amounts of smudged black eyeliner, Nova's recently favored style was gothic punk. Of all the versions of her daughter she'd experienced through the years, it was Tessa's least favorite. During the last few months, Nova's chosen armor was sharp edges and dark colors, a physical look that matched her daughter's often melancholy and combative mood. A spiked choker circled the porcelain skin of Nova's throat, and black fishnet gloves encased her delicate wrists.

As a budding artist, Nova adored theatrical clothing and dramatic makeup that made a statement and turned heads when she was in public. Nova relished the attention from random strangers, their long stares and shy compliments, but Tessa's boyfriend, Jason, did not. He became flat-out embarrassed to be seen with Nova in public when she segued from concert t-shirts and jeans into a full-blown gothic costume. It was one of many bones of contention between Nova and Jason that had made living under the same roof lately an arduous task. Nova and Jason faced off from opposite corners of the ring, reducing Tessa to referee their frequent arguments. It was a draining dynamic Tessa fought her way through daily.

"Let me get this straight. You're talking about going to live with the same dad that moved a thousand miles away last year without so much as a goodbye?"

Nova wrapped her arms around her middle, huffed her displeasure, and stared out the window. There an impenetrable wall that they'd both erected between themselves when Nova turned thirteen. They'd constructed it brick by brick without even realizing they were doing it.

3

Now, it was a hundred feet high and unscalable, and they each stayed on their own sides, firing shots at the other from behind it. No one had ever told Tessa that raising a teenager was like waging a war every day and, after four years, she realized she had been woefully unprepared for the battle.

"He still has half custody of me, you know."

Tessa turned away to roll her eyes so her daughter wouldn't see. It was true; he *did have* fifty percent custody, but she knew he would never exercise the right. It was the only reason she hadn't taken him back to court. Now that Nova was seventeen, it would be pointless to spend thousands of dollars to win a judgment that accomplished nothing. He wasn't a father. He'd deserted his only child without so much as a second thought, leaving Tessa to pick up the pieces when he'd left. Tessa would never admit it to Nova, but she was relieved when he moved several states away. She had hoped his physical distance would help Nova settle down, but she could see now his absence had only increased her desire to spend time with him.

"I'm going. There is nothing you can do about it," Nova declared boldly, her voice level.

"Over my dead body," Tessa finally muttered. "If he'd wanted to see you, he would have made you a priority." Now that she was practically an adult, Tessa was willing to be more forthcoming with the truth where Nova's dad was concerned. She'd locked it away from Nova for almost a decade because that was what the expert told her to do in the Children in the Middle course they forced her to take to earn her freedom when Nova was eight. But now, when her immaturity and innocence accepted the lies he force-

4

fed her to save his own face, she found she couldn't continue to be complicit in it.

"Dad said he was busy getting his affairs in order and ran out of time, but we talk on the phone all the time now, Mom, when you're at work."

Nova's admission was another dart to her heart. "You do?" Tessa was shocked. It was the first time she'd ever mentioned it.

"Yeah," Nova said with a smug smirk lighting up her features, delighted to one-up her mother. "*And* he said I could come visit any time I want. In fact, we've been talking about enrolling me in school out there."

Fresh rage flooded Tessa's entire being, and she saw red. "He had no right to have that conversation with you without me being present."

"I'm going to be eighteen next year anyway, and then I can do whatever I want. You won't get to decide for me anymore." Technically, Nova was right, but Tessa couldn't give up the good fight.

"So, you'd want to start all over your senior year? At a school filled with people you don't know, a *thousand* miles away?"

"Maybe," she answered with a tight shrug.

Tessa wanted to scream in frustration. The tension was building, and she was sick of it. Tired of the combative nature their relationship had devolved into and her patience was wearing thin.

"Running away from your problems will not solve them. What do you think you're going to accomplish out there?"

"He's going to take me to museums, and we're going

5

to tour art schools." Her tone was wistful, filling her blue eyes with naïve hope.

"Right," Tessa said, the word filled with all the sarcasm she couldn't contain anymore. "The man who couldn't be bothered to visit when you lived in the same town is now going to become father of the year four states away? I'll believe it when I see it."

"Oh, you're going to see it," Nova asserted. She leaned forward, and her straight black hair obscured Tessa's view of her pale face. Her roots were just showing. It had been a shock when Nova shunned her strawberry blonde locks two months ago in favor of stark black. As if she couldn't bear sharing a single physical characteristic with her mother. Tessa sat in silence, awash in conflicting emotions. A few seconds later, she heard Nova sniffle. Seeing her daughter's thin body begin to tremble had shame welling up in her center.

"I'm sorry, Nove," Tessa started in, feeling guilty, wishing the harsh truth she'd shared with her daughter didn't have to hurt her so much. Although she always tried to be honest with Nova, Tessa usually tried to keep the more hurtful words to herself. Addressing conflict this way felt dirty and underhanded, but sometimes teenagers were so infuriating and pushed you to the brink of insanity. And Tessa was there, right there, on the brink of it. She reached out a hand to Nova's shoulder, and Nova jerked her body away before Tessa could touch her.

The obvious dis stung, and Tessa sighed. They were at yet another impasse. Tessa waited a few moments in vain, then shifted to drive and eased the car toward the street, heading home. Their argument had sucked all the oxygen out of the confined area, and she knew they both needed space away from each other to breathe.

Ten long minutes of silence later, Tessa pulled into the driveway of their home. She parked in the garage and walked inside, looking for her boyfriend, Jason, leaving a fuming Nova still out in the car.

"Babe?" she called out. In his home office, carved out of their spare bedroom down the hall, she heard him talking to someone on the phone. She paused to listen and give him quiet in case he was on a conference call. It was the tone of his voice that filled her with unease. The timbre was warmer than usual. She couldn't make out the words he was saying, but it was the tenderness she heard that made the hairs on the back of her neck stand up. He chuckled and continued to croon softly into the phone with the deep voice she'd fallen in love with two years prior. Warm and engaging, it was one of the many characteristics she found attractive about him. Her insecurities were cueing up as waves of panic and fear crashed over her. Who was on the other end of that phone?

She tiptoed down the hallway, closer to his office. Standing outside the door, just out of his line of sight, she focused on his words, holding her breath as her heartbeat hammered in her ears. A deluge of guilt crashed over her. This wasn't the woman she thought she was. A weak, untrusting shrew who listened in on her boyfriend's private conversations. Yet there she was, pressed up against the wall, listening in, unable to stop herself.

"It was great to hear from you, too," he murmured into the phone, and Tessa's heart dropped. She rifled through the list of options of who could be on the other end. His mother passed away over ten years ago. His sister? She

7

couldn't remember the last time he had anything nice to say about her. "I have to go. Tessa just pulled in."

Hearing her name, Tessa slid down the hallway silently, desperate to put space between them. She would die of mortification on the spot if he caught her stooping low enough to eavesdrop on his conversation. On stockinged feet, she rushed to the kitchen. Behind her, Jason whistled as he walked down the hall, every step bringing him closer. To hide her momentary lapse of judgment, Tessa turned toward the refrigerator and tugged the doors open, glancing through the meager ingredients, trying to come up with a plan for dinner.

"You're home early," Jason said over the expanse of granite separating them.

"The principal called. I had to go to the high school for a meeting. Nova got in-school suspension," Tessa admitted, needing to vent and unburden herself. She shut the doors and turned to face him, hugging her arms around her middle.

"Again?" His eyes were wide. "Isn't that some sort of record?"

"Not the kind any mother wants her kid to break." Still exhausted from the conversation in the car with Nova, she changed the subject. "Who was that on the phone?" she asked, unable to help herself. Frustrated, she needed answers to soothe her fears and push down the insecurities that welled up during the call.

"The help desk. They're struggling to get my new phone on the network," he answered, running one hand through his dark hair that was trimmed close to the back of his head but full on top. At almost fifty, he was a catch. She knew it the second she laid eyes on him. His bald-faced lie made her eyes sting with tears.

"And then she dropped another bombshell on the way home," Tessa added.

"What now?" His expression morphed into complete exasperation that matched hers.

"She wants to go live with her dad."

He was silent for a long moment as he considered it, but then his next words stunned Tessa. "Maybe you should let her."

"Are you serious?" Tessa's voice pinched, and she couldn't keep her shock at the absurdity out of it. "You want me to *willingly* deposit her into the arms of the man who deserted her last year?"

"Come on, Tess. Would it be the worst thing?" he asked. "We could use a break around here. I know I sure could."

Tessa didn't disagree. Parenting Nova had been getting increasingly difficult as she acted out at school and balked at household rules. She often left bowls of milk in her room, drawing ants and growing mold. Nova refused to keep her bathroom clean and left streaks of black hair dye in the sink and on their shared towels without a care in the world. Her typical teenage laziness infuriated Jason, and Tessa often found herself wedged in-between them as the peacemaker.

"I'm sick of all the drama that seems to swirl around her life. She invites it in, snuggles with it, and makes everyone around her miserable."

Tessa took a seat at the island, hoping to close both the physical and the emotional distance between them, and asked, "Is that it? Are you miserable?"

"We both are!" He swiped his hands over his face and

let out a long, exasperated sigh. His frustration was palpable. It was a recycled exchange they seemed to have nightly, where nothing ever got resolved. The dynamic was draining them both. He pulled out a chair and sat down next to her. "I haven't been happy in a long time, and if you're honest with yourself, you have to admit you haven't been, either." His voice was softer, barely above a whisper.

She turned toward him. It was a conversation they'd been avoiding for months, skirting around it, and pushing it away to the corners of the room. Now that they were acknowledging the facts, an alarm went off in her heart. It was like walking on a frozen lake in the early spring. She'd been hearing the hairline cracks for months, but the plunge into those icy depths now felt inevitable. Tessa slowly brought her blue eyes over to meet his brown ones.

"That wasn't the help desk, was it?" Her voice barely registered over a whisper, and he recoiled like someone had slapped him. "I heard you." It wasn't an accusation; it was just a painful statement of facts.

Caught in a lie, he was taken aback. His eyes dropped to the floor, and his firm jaw clenched. She saw the beginning of his five o'clock shadow darkening his cheekbones and chin. He scratched his long fingers at the emerging whiskers as a hot breath escaped his lips.

"I don't know if this works between us anymore. I'm sorry, Tessa." His voice cracked, and her heart followed suit.

Tessa's eyes darted around the townhouse they'd rented together. There were still nine months left on the lease. "She's almost an adult. I know the last two years have been hard, but it's almost over. We're almost free."

"Are we?" he asked sadly, his words tinged with regret. "I don't know if I see it the same way. She's going to need your focused support and attention for the next several years."

"She's my daughter. I can't just pack her bags and change the locks when she turns eighteen."

"I understand that. Believe me, I do." Resolved, he stood to his full six foot four inches. His eyes met hers. "I think we both could use some time apart. Don't worry, I'll help with the lease since I made the commitment."

"Gee, thanks." She wanted to tell him to take the lease and shove it, but she was stuck. She couldn't afford the townhouse without him. His minor concession made her heart hurt. After a multitude of short-term relationships, she'd pinned all her hopes on Jason. She thought she was done dating, that she'd found her person. If she was honest, she'd admit to herself he'd been pulling away and taking on more business trips in the last two quarters. Now, she saw the last few months as they truly were, a long goodbye. She brushed away warm tears, squared her shoulders, and stood.

"I'm going to stay at the corporate townhouse for a while. Give you guys some space." It was all so easy for him. To turn his back on the two years they'd spent together and all the plans they'd made. She wanted the hate to come in, but at that moment, she felt alone and unlovable. He tried to take her in his arms, the place she always went for comfort, but this time she refused.

"Don't," she said, holding up her hand as a barrier between them. She knew if he pulled her to his chest and she breathed in the scent of his aftershave for the last time, she would fall apart. She knew little, at that moment, standing in their shared kitchen, but she knew he didn't deserve a gateway to her heart anymore.

A few moments later, he left, shutting the door behind him quietly. That's when the tears flowed. She made popcorn for dinner and chased it with a margarita and was grateful that even Nova knew enough to stay away.

Chapter Two

The next day, Tessa walked through her life like a zombie. She felt detached from it, like she was a balloon floating above herself. Bobbing in the wind and tightly clutched in her daughter's fist. She carried out her routine, dropping Nova off at school, then heading downtown to the firm where she'd been an accountant in Omaha, Nebraska, for almost ten years.

She sat in her car for a long moment, contemplating whether she should turn around and head home to dive under her comforter, when a moment later, her best friend, Kristie, pulled her SUV into the space next to Tessa.

Reluctantly, Tessa opened her door and pulled out her bag with a sigh. She pushed her curtain of long, strawberry-blonde hair behind her shoulder and pasted a smile on her face.

"Well, sheesh. That's the fake one," Kristie called out as she stepped closer to her friend. "Let's grab lunch together. You can tell me what's got you so blue."

"How about a raincheck? I don't think I'll be great company today."

"Lucky for you, I don't expect you to be." Kristi reached up to squeeze her shoulder with a serene smile. "But I happen to know it's impossible to be sad inside a Mexican restaurant. I mean… hello, tacos."

Tessa smiled despite herself. "They *are* the world's most efficient food."

"That's the spirit!" Kristie cheered. She rocked a jet-black pixie cut and a body that had the long lines of a dancer. Having lost both her breasts to a double mastectomy, she'd refused the reconstruction and opted for tattoos instead. Kristie was an unstoppable force, a great sounding board, and Tessa's closest friend. Tessa was an introvert who usually kept to herself, but when Kristie started at the firm six years ago, she wouldn't let her. She dragged Tessa out of the office to great new restaurants and even persuaded her to go on several blind dates. The last blind date she'd been on, Tessa met Jason.

It was impossible to tell Kristie no. She was a diminutive drill sergeant, and when she got an idea in her head, it was easy to get swept up and taken along for the ride.

They walked into the bustling office and went their separate ways. Tessa rounded the corner to the cubicle they had given her when she started at the firm a decade ago. On her tidy desk was a family photo she'd taken with Nova where they looked like twins with their long hair, bright blue eyes, and coordinated clothing. It had been taken the prior summer and was a drastic departure from Nova's current look. In the far left corner of the desk sat a money tree, its placement dictated by a Feng Shui article she'd read. It was supposed to increase the flow of wealth. With her annual evaluation right around the corner, and her partnership offer practically guaranteed, it was finally going to pay off.

She pulled out her chair and settled in at her desk, grateful it was the end of the month. She'd be able to bury her busy brain in credits and debits for the entire next week. On spreadsheets, all the entries added up, and every transaction was accounted for in neat rows. It was a world where she excelled and understood. A tranquil world that was far removed from the emotional outbursts and daily challenges life had become with Nova. After going through her emails, she switched gears to filing sales tax for several of her clients.

The first half of the day sailed by, and when she glanced at her watch, it was already lunchtime. Tugging on her jacket, she logged off her computer and waited for Kristie at the elevator.

A few minutes later, a beaming Kristie bopped down the hall in her high heels that only called more attention to her small stature when she stood next to Tessa. At six feet tall, Tessa was used to being the tallest woman in the room, a fact that intimidated most men. Jason had been a welcome exception.

They rode down the elevator quietly. Kristie tapped out a few texts, then turned toward her friend when the doors opened. "Sorry about that. I got an SOS text from Ollie. His toilet was overflowing." She laughed. "He actually poured *more* water in the bowl thinking it would help! I might have left out a few critical life lessons with that one."

"A mother's job is never done," Tessa remarked, then

repeated, "Never." She slid into the driver's seat and headed toward their favorite Mexican restaurant.

"Okay, spill it. What's got you so glum?"

Tessa sighed, not sure where to begin. "Nova's on another self-destructive streak, first an in-school suspension and then, out of the blue, declared she was going to move in with her dad."

"Deadbeat Donny?"

Tessa nodded. "Yep. Apparently, they have been talking on the phone."

"Whoa. I bet that felt like a betrayal." Kristie inhaled air between the lips of her clenched jaw.

"It was totally out of left field," Tessa continued. "And do you want to know the craziest part?"

"Always."

"Jason said I should let her."

"Okay. That's a no. It's a terrible idea."

"Right? I was stunned."

"You have every right to be."

"I've literally been paying thousands of dollars for intensive therapy addressing her father's abandonment. Her therapist thinks it's a terrible idea. *I* think it's dangerous. Even Nova's *friends* think it's stupid, and yet she is still demanding to go live with the man who has done nothing but destroy her. It's insanity." Tessa paused and then continued, "And if that wasn't bad enough, Jason told me he thinks we should take a break."

"Oh, sweetie. That sucks." Kristie's empathy broke her heart. Tessa swiped at the tears welling at the corners of her eyes, frustrated he had that effect on her. She wasn't one to show emotion in public. Kristie reached inside her bag and pulled out a pack of tissues and offered it to Tessa.

She laughed uncomfortably and mumbled, "Thanks." After taking a moment to collect herself, they walked inside and were seated at their favorite table with two margaritas on the way. When they arrived, Tessa hoisted hers to Kristie. "To the medicinal properties of margaritas."

She tasted the salted rim and felt the tequila warm her insides. "He's decided to stay at the corporate townhouse." Jason's desire for physical space was painful to admit.

Kristie nodded thoughtfully, then offered, "Maybe that isn't the worst thing."

"It sure feels like it is." Tessa picked at the paper tab that wrapped around her silverware, trying to gather her thoughts. "I feel like I never get to relax, like I'm always waiting for the other shoe to drop. With Nova, with Jason. It's draining."

"I know it might not seem like it, but maybe this is an opportunity," Kristie offered, reaching out to squeeze Tessa's hand. "Now you will have the space you need to truly evaluate your relationship."

Tessa nodded, trying to see the good Kristie was offering, but argued, "I don't think I'll find another one like him. No one is perfect, but he's a solid ninety-eight percenter." Tessa shared her calculated assessment after another sip of her drink. It was a habit to distill everything in her life down to a number.

"I'm curious. What is the other two percent that is missing?"

"Well, if I'm nitpicking and being critical, then I wish he was a little more forthcoming with compliments and a little more affectionate."

"Do you hear what you're saying? You just used the

word little twice in the same sentence, all the while mini-mizing *your* wants and needs." Kristie's eyes drilled into hers as she continued, "Distilling your relationship into a mathematical equation is very telling. I hear you rational-izing your feelings and explaining away the lack, but isn't the two percent as important as the other ninety-eight?"

Tessa was stunned as she dipped a crispy chip through the spicy, smokey salsa, considering her friend's words. She chewed thoughtfully and then declared, "I guess I don't think a perfect partner exists. I mean, ninety-eight is as close to perfect as I have found, and I was good with that."

"Were you though?" Kristie questioned. "Do you hear the precise words you've so beautifully chosen? 'A little more... As close to perfect...'"

Getting defensive, Tessa asked, "Do *you* think there is a perfect person out there? Where you line up one hundred percent on every relationship criterion? Because I don't." Tessa continued, "And *I'm* far from perfect. I try to extend the same grace and understanding of shortcomings I would want a partner to extend to me."

Kristie nodded, commiserating. "Relationships are hard. You have two different people with two different sets of needs trying to create a meaningful life together. People make agreements and concessions with themselves to stay coupled all the time."

"Do you think that's what I'm doing?" Tessa asked, truly wanting to know the answer.

"Oh, honey, the only person who can answer that is you."

The distinct sizzle of pan-seared fajitas rounded the corner as their server brought their entrees to the table.

Tessa pointed to a young man eyeing the fajitas like a lover. "See that? All I want is for someone to look at me the way that guy looked at our fajitas."

"Girl, that's what everyone wants." Kristie giggled and sipped on her margarita. "But the bigger question is, do you look at *yourself* like that?"

"Lusty and ravenous?" Tessa joked, placing slices of steak onto a warmed tortilla. "No, because that would be weird."

Kristie laughed. "Not exactly. I was thinking more like 'here comes the most beautiful thing in the world.' "

"Hmmm." Tessa considered it as she swiped fresh guacamole onto the steak and rolled it up for her first bite. "Have you looked at me?" She said, "I know who I am. Practical, unassuming. I'm in halfway decent shape for my age, but not exactly rocking the kind of exceptional beauty that starts wars and inspires sonnets, if you know what I mean."

Kristie laughed. "You know what I see? A woman who exudes grace and strength. A mother who has always put the needs of her child above her own. You are regal like a queen, with that long hair, strong aristocratic nose, and high cheekbones." Kristie lavished praise on Tessa while she loaded up her own tortilla.

"This is why we're friends," Tessa joked and took another bite.

Kristie grinned. "Seriously, you have to be blind not to see what I see. As women, we are always cutting ourselves short, refusing to acknowledge our greatness, our strength, and our contributions."

"Let me guess; I am woman, hear me roar?"

"Something like that, you joker." Kristie went on,

"Look, the longest relationship you will ever have is the one you have with yourself. When are you going to start doting on that girl? You should buy her a dress and take her out on the town! Look her in the mirror and tell her how beautiful she is!"

Tessa sighed, considering the tough love Kristie was so naturally skilled at serving up, then finally admitted, "You're right. I always waited for Jason to dazzle me with compliments and fill me up with sweetness when it was my job all along." She took another sip and continued, "The truth is, he could have had an easier life with almost anyone else on the planet, but he chose me and I always felt I had to overcompensate for it, especially when Nova started acting out." Tessa wiped her mouth with a napkin as the revelation she'd just made stunned her. "Wow. I never articulated that out loud before. I've turned into exactly the kind of weak woman I used to loathe in college." She took another long swig of her margarita. "How did I erode into this pathetic version of myself, worn down by the expectations of other people? It is not attractive."

"It happens to everyone," Kristie commiserated. "You are going to be okay. I promise you, with or without Jason."

"I know." Tessa nodded. "I think I'm most upset about the time I lost. Two years. I keep getting pushed back to the starting line. How many false starts does one woman get?"

"As many as it takes." Kristie shrugged. "It wasn't time wasted. Nothing is ever wasted. You learned more about yourself with him. It's all a journey."

"So wise," Tessa praised as she ate a few more bites,

considering Kristie's words. They finished their entrees while chatting about their weekend plans, and Tessa felt lighter, like she always did after an hour with Kristie.

"Fried ice cream?" Kristie asked with a wink. "I think we deserve it."

"Yes! It sounds like a great first lesson on how to love myself." Tessa grinned and placed the order with their server.

* * *

Back at the office, the rest of the day flew by. Tessa scheduled back-to-back meetings with clients. She enjoyed working with small business owners the most and approached it with a team mindset. Understanding her clients' financial goals and minimizing their tax burden was a worthwhile project that gave her immense personal satisfaction. Spreadsheets reconciled. Bank statements didn't lie. Exercising all the tax loopholes she could find to guarantee the maximum allowed deductions was a game she was a champion at playing. She was an exceptional accountant, and she let herself wallow luxuriously in the sense of purpose it gave her.

After work, Tessa drove to the townhouse with Nova chattering about her day at school. She was digesting her conversation with Kristie. It brought up a lot of lingering feelings she tried to avoid but knew she would have to face head-on and resolve. Walking into their dark dwelling, Nova glanced around, her forehead knotted in concern, then asked, "Where's Jason?"

Tessa hesitated, unsure how much to share, but she always chose the truth, even when it was difficult.

21

"We're taking a break."

"What?" Nova was panicked and Tessa tried to explain.

"It's just for a little while." Tessa wasn't sure if that was the case, but secretly, it was her greatest hope.

Nova's eyes widened, and Tessa saw her swallow hard.

"It's going to be okay, you know," she said, trying to adopt a lighter tone. "I have a proven track record of keeping you alive for the last seventeen years."

"Why does everyone leave us?" Nova whispered in a voice so small it took Tessa's breath away. She reached out to pull Nova into her arms and Nova shrugged her off.

"It's not like that, honey," Tessa said. "It was mutual. We both think some time apart might be beneficial. We have some problems to sort out."

"Did he leave because of me?"

"What would make you say that?"

"He stopped talking to me when we were in the same room. It's like I'm invisible," she admitted as she picked at a piece of dried cheese on the island. "I know I've been doing dumb stuff."

"Then quit doing dumb stuff!" Tessa joked, and Nova smiled weakly.

"He's mad. He hates me."

"Hate is a strong word, sweetheart. He doesn't hate you. He's frustrated. Just think, he's been able to live his life footloose and fancy-free for half a century without children *or* a wife. An instant family requires a huge adjustment."

"It's all my fault."

"Darling, I promise you are not that powerful," Tessa teased. "Besides, I need to decide if he's the right partner

22

for me. When you feel uncertain, it's not the worst decision in the world to take a beat. The worst decision you can make is to stay with a partner out of obligation. Inside a dead relationship is where you die. Promise me you'll never do that."

"Okay, okay." Nova bristled at forced life lessons like most teenagers do, but it never deterred Tessa from trying to teach them.

"How about some pasta tonight for dinner?'

"Are we talking real pasta? No zoodles?" Nova had to clarify ever since Tessa served her a flat slab of grilled cauliflower and tried to call it a steak.

Tessa laughed. "Fine. Real noodles it is. Sometimes you need to indulge yourself. I've been told it's called self-care."

A few minutes later, Nova disappeared into her bedroom, giving Tessa the time to consider her revelation. She always thought Nova was the one who'd chosen to disengage. It surprised Tessa to hear that Jason was just as responsible for the breakdown in their relationship, and she hated herself for not noticing earlier. She set a pan filled with water on the stove, waiting for it to boil, and a single moment of clarity rushed in. She deserved a partner who would make more of an effort with her daughter, and for the first time, she wasn't sure Jason could.

Chapter Three

A few days later, Tessa was in a client meeting in the conference room when the secretary gently knocked on the door.

"There's a call for you on line one. It's your daughter's school, and it's urgent." The secretary hovered by the door, awaiting further instructions.

Hearing the news, Tessa's stomach dropped to the floor. She flipped her phone over and saw notifications for four missed calls. Forcing a professional, calm expression on her face, she answered, "I think we were just wrapping up here. Can you tell them I will call them right back?" Tessa turned back to her clients and feigned a rigid smile. "I'll get our legal department to draw up the articles of incorporation, and then we can save you some significant money on your next tax bill."

"I guess the only thing worse than paying taxes is not making enough to have to pay them at all." Her clients ran a mom-and-pop pet store that experienced explosive growth during the pandemic when housebound people added pets to their families. There was even talk on the horizon of potential franchising opportunities, and they relied on Tessa's sound advice to help them transition to the next level.

Tessa smiled. "You got that right! I am thrilled about your success, and I'll help you navigate the next steps of your growth." Her mind was preoccupied, wandering back to the phone call from the school. Midday phone calls from the high school were never a good sign, but she held it together. Inside, she was a churning sea of fear and frustration, but outside, she was cool and collected.

"You're the best, Tessa." They shook her hand and filed out of her office. She walked them out to say goodbye and then hurried back and shut the conference room door. Eagerly, she punched in the number to Nova's school, where she was quickly connected with the principal.

"Ms. Donahue, we need you to come and get Nova. She's been suspended."

"What? Again?" Tessa asked. "What happened?"

"The hall monitor reported Nova for engaging in sexual activity in the boy's bathroom." The principal's matter-of-fact delivery of the salacious news hovered just above judgmental scorn.

"Oh, God, Nova," Tessa mumbled in shame, her fair skin flushing red. She was heartsick at the discovery.

"We need you to come pick her up now. She needs to remain home for the next seven days, and then she can return and serve her in-school suspension."

"I understand." But she didn't understand at all. In a

daze, she grabbed her purse and car keys and drove to the high school, lost in her thoughts. She sat down in the principal's office while the torrid details were shared. In shock, hearing the word fellatio spilling from the lips of a school official made her nauseous. She squirmed in the chair, assaulted by the onslaught of offensive terms.

Tessa turned to glance at Nova, stunned that she didn't exhibit even an inkling of embarrassment. Instead, Nova looked bored, her eyes fixed on a scratch on the front of the principal's desk. Dressed head to toe in black, down to her black Converse sneakers, her hair was gathered in pigtails and a girlish contrast to the face full of makeup and the smoky eye she'd been favoring lately. After suffering the brunt of full humiliation by the principal, Tessa vaguely remembered responding, "I'm so sorry. This is not how I have raised my daughter." Her words came out in a rush of red-faced apologies. Tessa stood, itching to leave and desperate to flee. Finally, the man stopped speaking, and she said a hasty goodbye, unable to exit his office fast enough.

She checked Nova out and then began the drive home without a word, her outrage seething as she struggled to understand her daughter's actions. In the seat next to her, Nova sat still and sullen like a statue breathing in air that was heavy and oppressive.

"Nothing?" Tessa finally asked. "You have nothing to say?" She darted angry glances over at her and slammed on the gas when the light finally turned green. Adrenaline coursed through her, making her foot heavy on the gas pedal. She rocketed through an intersection and, glimpsing a police cruiser tucked away, glanced down at the odometer. Fifteen over. "Shit." She stomped on the brake and prayed the cruiser would stay in place. Stealing glances in the rear-view mirror, her heartbeat didn't return to the normal range until she couldn't see him anymore.

"Nothing?!" Tessa's voice now had a harder edge that she couldn't bring herself to soften.

"No." Nova stared straight ahead.

"What were you thinking?"

"I think we can both agree I wasn't thinking at all."

Exasperated that she was the only one who seemed to be concerned about the suspension, Tessa blustered her frustration aloud, "You're grounded."

"I know." Nova's voice was even.

"Why did you do it?"

She shrugged, a defiant act that was the straw that broke the camel's back.

"Did he talk you into it?"

"No. It was my idea."

"Your idea? What the hell, Nova? Where is your self-respect?" Tessa pinched her nose to quell the tension headache forming behind her eyes. "You've risked your reputation. Some bells you can't unring. Who was the boy?"

"Brendan."

"Brendan who?" Tessa shot back, not giving her a chance to answer. "This is the first I have ever heard you utter the name Brendan. Are you dating him or something?"

"No."

"No?" Tessa was taken aback in complete shock. "How long have you been sexually active?"

"It was a blow job, Mom."

"You can catch a disease from *any* form of intimate contact. We need to have you tested. I'm calling the doctor when we get home. Have you had intercourse?"

"No!" Nova shouted in the seat next to her, and Tessa had to force her next breath through her nostrils to contain the rage growing inside her.

"You know better than that! We've talked about making safe decisions and respecting your body." She grasped for understanding and it was like sand falling through her fingers.

"I know!"

"You don't know!" Tessa snapped back. "If you had, you wouldn't have debased yourself in the boy's bathroom. I don't understand you at all. I'm so ashamed, and you should be, too. "

The word cracked Nova's hard veneer, and she began to whimper.

"Why? Why would you disrespect yourself like this? There has to be a reason," Tessa cried. She was reaching her breaking point.

"Haven't you ever done anything stupid before?"

"Not like this, and definitely *not* in a public place." Tessa was frustrated. "Why can't you just stop? It's like you want to be miserable, looking for ways to destroy your life before it even gets started."

"Don't you think I wish I could?" Anger made her jaw tight and unyielding, but hurt made her eyes glossy. Fat tears rolled down her cheeks, making black tracks from mascara.

Two words hung like lead between them, two words that were the most logical explanation for her actions.

Daddy issues. It was often the phrase that cued up first in Tessa's mind in a crisis with Nova, always lingering on the tip of her tongue. She didn't say them aloud, knowing they would do more harm than good. Silently, Tessa drove the rest of the way home and sent Nova into the house. Sitting in her car for a long moment, her head ached at the base of her skull, and she twisted her head from side to side, grateful when her neck cracked to dispel some of the built-up tension.

Two hours later, after a quiet dinner that was mostly the clattering of forks, Nova disappeared into her bedroom. Tessa was at the island scraping the remnants of a meal she didn't even taste into the disposal when Nova emerged all smiles. She held out her phone over to a confused Tessa. "Dad's on the phone. He wants to talk to you."

Tessa groaned. Having a conversation with her ex-husband was the very last thing she wanted to do.

"What do you need, Donny?" she muttered into the phone, already annoyed.

"It's been awhile, Tess." His voice sent bolts of fury to her core. Tessa's nostrils flared as she tried to keep her cool, knowing no reaction was the best reaction in this case.

"Nova wants to come to stay with me over spring break."

"Is that right?" Tessa asked. "Did she happen to fill you in on the latest events in her life?"

"She did," he confirmed, plain as day. "Come on, Tessa, chalk it up to teenage hormones. That's all it is. She did something dumb. You were young once, too." Tessa rolled her eyes, scrubbing dishes at the sink so hard the glass broke in her hand, and a straight crimson line emerged from the suds across three of her fingers.

"She's been a handful lately. I'm not sure you're equipped to handle her for any length of time."

"And you're doing such a bang-up job?" he asked. Tessa recoiled. Donny's words stung.

"How dare you judge me! You left her and moved a thousand miles away without so much as a phone call! That was unforgivable and led to abandonment issues she's had to process in therapy for months."

He brushed her criticism aside. "There was a lot going on. I was busy."

"Too busy to say goodbye to your only child?"

"You always make me out to be the villain."

"You always make it so easy," Tessa responded and then was silent. She was tired of fighting, so mentally exhausted and depleted, she pulled out the white flag of surrender. "You know what? Sure, she can come for spring break. You buy her a ticket and forward me the details."

There was a long pause on the other end of the phone.

"Hello?" Tessa asked.

"I'm here," he said, adding, "I was hoping you could split the cost with me. I haven't sold any commissions lately."

"You're not serious?" Tessa's voice was strung tight and pitchy. She couldn't stand his weakness any longer. "You haven't paid a penny of child support in years."

"You make a good living. Don't you think you're being greedy?"

"Wow." Tessa wanted to punch him in the face. "It's a little thing called responsibility. Ever hear of it?"

He brushed the accusations off like crumbs from

morning toast. "Well, I'm glad we could work it out. Nova will be so happy."

"We'll see." She hung up the phone and Nova appeared.

"So?" Nova was smiling and rocking side to side on the balls of her stockinged feet.

"Looks like you're spending spring break with your dad."

Nova let out a whoop of joy and began to chatter. "We're going to go to museums, and he's going to teach me how to play the guitar."

"What fun! Sounds like you two have it all planned out," Tessa remarked, the snark barely concealed. "Are you going to talk to him about the pain he's caused you, or are you going to let him sweep it under the rug again?"

Nova bristled at the criticism.

"His new girlfriend is going to teach me how to cook," Nova gushed. "I love Ashley."

Self-righteous frustration welled up in Tessa, but she bit it back. She'd tried to teach her how to make a pot roast once, but Nova showed no interest at all. The idea of the tramp Donny was currently banging, giving her daughter cooking lessons was infuriating. She wanted to say as much but knew it would fall on deaf ears, so she changed tactics. "I'm concerned that you're romanticizing this visit in your head. He's hurt you and he needs to acknowledge that truthfully."

Nova's shoulders tensed.

"Look, Nova, I want you to have a great time with your dad, I do. But he has a long history of hurting you and letting you down."

"God, Mom, I knoooow." Nova was irritated. "Why

31

can't you ever be happy for me?" Her dramatics were grating on Tessa's nerves.

"I *am* happy for you, but you give too many chances to people who don't deserve them. My only concern in all of this is you."

"It's going to be fine," Nova declared. "Actually, it's going to be better than fine." She wandered back to her bedroom and Tessa scrolled through her text messages with a brief glimmer of hope that was quickly dashed. Nothing from Jason. There had been no communication for over a week. Then she pulled up her bank statement, seeing the deposit he'd made yesterday for his half of their living expenses. The fact that he kept his promise made the sting of his lack of communication hurt even more. She wanted to reach out and thank him, but she shut her phone down, resolved to not be the one to make the first contact.

Instead, she browsed through vacation destinations on her iPad, saving pins on Pinterest to Greece, Iceland, and Bora Bora. All were exotic places she yearned to see with her own eyes. Soon, Nova would graduate and she'd have an empty nest. Then all the traveling she'd put on hold would be back within her reach.

The beauty of beginning the next chapter of her life alone was she would only have to take her own desires into account. No more 'vacations' to theme parks Nova loved as a child, which were pure torture for Tessa. No more all-inclusive resorts Jason preferred where they would sit on chairs by the pool and drink all day. She could spend time in the mountains, hiking like she had fresh out of college when the world was ripe with possibilities and her regrets were fewer.

The life she'd always envisioned after Nova's graduation included Jason. The possibility of facing the next stage of her life alone had never occurred to her, and at that moment, she wasn't sure if she was terrified or excited, so she made the bold decision to embrace them both.

Chapter Four

A month later, Nova got the phone call Tessa saw coming a mile away. Typical Donny waited until the last minute to buy an airline ticket, and since the price skyrocketed, he told Nova he decided to drive instead. Nova spent most of the prior week doing her laundry without being asked and packing her clothing and makeup essentials into Tessa's well-worn suitcases. When Tessa pulled them out of storage, she looked at her luggage longingly, wishing she was the one jetting off.

Soon, she promised herself. She had acquired a wanderlust streak that developed in her twenties, but it had been years since she'd indulged it.

Two days before Donny was due to arrive, his plan fell apart. After a long day at work, deep in the throes of a busy tax season, she arrived home to a dark townhouse. At the door, she'd tripped on the pile of shoes and Nova's backpack that had been flung to the ground. Irritated, she kicked them to the side and flipped on the light switch.

"Nova!" Tessa shouted into the silence. Nova had

gotten a ride home from a friend, at least that's what she claimed in the text she'd sent her mother after school. "Where are you?" The silence broke, and Tessa followed the sound of her daughter's murmurs coming through the ceiling. She climbed the stairs, straining to hear the conversation, but drywall muffled it.

At the closed door, she heard something ricochet against the wall and then a strangled howl came from her daughter that made her pulse quicken.

"Nova?" She turned the knob and slowly opened the door. In the center of her messy bedroom, Nova yanked open her suitcase and dumped the contents onto her bed. Unmatched socks and palettes of eye shadows tumbled from the bed to the floor, along with combat boots and the tulle skirt she loved to pair with them.

"Agh!" Nova slammed the suitcase to the ground and collapsed face down on the bed, ignoring her mother.

"What happened?" Tessa began softly as she walked closer to the bed.

"Spring break. Dad can't make it work." The pillow she laid on muffled Nova's voice. Morose, she flipped to her side and stared out the window. Uneasy, Tessa sat on the edge of the bed, smoothing Nova's hair away from her tear-stained cheeks.

"What do you mean?"

"He's got work to do," she muttered under her breath.

"Work?" Tessa was stunned. Inside, she seethed with rage. She wanted to scream, "I knew it! You do this to her every time! I knew she couldn't count on you!" But she stayed silent, knowing it wouldn't help the situation at all.

Nova continued, "He got a museum show. He said it's the first one in forever and he needs to spend the next month framing his pieces." Nova pulled away and sat up, her posture hunched in defeat. Finally, she pulled her gaze up to meet her mother's. "I could have helped him," she whispered, her eyes two pale blue ponds of despair. "I am an artist, too. It would have been good for me to see this side of the business, that way I'd have a fallback if I decide teaching isn't for me."

Nova was a talented artist like her father. Tessa considered it a victory when she convinced Nova to become an art teacher last year. It was a respectable career in the arts that came with health insurance and a retirement fund. Tessa was desperate to help Nova avoid the pitfalls of Donny's feast-or-famine reality.

She picked at the rip in her jeans. "I know it's silly, but I just wanted to see my dad."

"I know, sweetheart." She wrapped her arm around Nova's waist and pulled her closer as Nova began to cry.

"Why doesn't he ever choose me?" Nova asked wistfully. The tender desperation in her voice broke Tessa's heart. "I sit here like a dog in the corner, waiting for him to come and play with me, and he never does." She wiped her cheeks with the back of her hand and straightened her shoulders. "He's a selfish prick. That was his last chance. I'm done." She seesawed between intense emotions, swinging from one extreme to the other like only teenagers can.

It shocked Tessa to see the absolute clarity in her daughter's assessment of the situation. Nova usually had blinders on when it came to her father, but hearing her articulate the truth as she now saw it was liberating. Tessa hated to see Nova suffer, but in order for her to move on, she had to acknowledge and accept the truth. It was the only way for her to heal and move past it.

Nova tried to act tough when it came to her father, but it was just an act. Deep inside, she was desperate for him to pay attention to her. To see her as valuable, and time and time again, Donny disappointed her.

"I know you were looking forward to seeing him," Tessa said. "One of the hardest things to do, even as an adult, is to believe people the first time when they show you who they are."

Nova grunted in annoyance.

"He's the one missing out, and he doesn't even know it." Tessa tried to smooth her hurt feelings.

The phone rang, and Nova bolted upright as hope sprung eternal on her face. "Maybe he changed his mind." Nova rushed over to where it rested on the ground. Her hopes dashed the second she registered the caller ID and threw the phone back to the bed, where it landed face-up next to Tessa's thigh, still ringing.

"Is it scam? Mr. Scam Likely?" Tessa tried to joke, and it fell on deaf ears. She turned the phone over. "Honey, your screen." Tessa's smile vanished when she saw it was cracked into a million pieces. "We just had it repaired, and it cost over a hundred dollars!" Her frustration was build-ing. "I'm not paying for another one."

"It doesn't matter," Nova mumbled and flopped back down dramatically on the bed. "Nothing matters anymore." Her apathy was in full effect, and she was throwing herself a pity party.

"What do you want for dinner?" Tessa asked, trying to change the subject. "How about a taco pizza?"

"Whatever," Nova said.

"Want to come pick it up with me?"

"Do I have to?" she asked from her nest of clothing on the bed.

"I guess not."

Nova flipped over on her side, inconsolable, and resumed staring out the window. Tessa let herself out and walked back down the stairs into the living room. In her pocket, her phone rang. She pulled it out to see Jason's handsome face fill the screen.

"Hey," she answered, not trusting herself to say another word. Tucking it into her shoulder, she grabbed her purse and settled herself in the car for some privacy, in case she needed it.

"Hey." Jason's voice was cheery. "You've been on my mind. How have you been?"

Against her will, Tessa rejoiced at the news, but instead of brushing her feelings under the rug, she decided to share them with Jason. "It's been a day."

"How so?"

"Nova's dad backed out of his plans for spring break."

"And you're surprised by that?" he asked, and her hopes dashed again. They were right back to having the same fight they always had.

"Your sarcasm, it's not appreciated right now," Tessa said.

"Donny's always been worthless. Did you suddenly think he was going to change tactics?"

"No, but I *hoped* he would. I could use a break from the insanity."

"I bet."

With nothing left to lose, Tessa decided to risk it all. "There aren't very many men who can step up and father a child that is not biologically theirs. Nova craves a father figure. I always hoped you'd be able to give Nova the dad energy she's been missing. "

He was quiet on the other end. "She's made it so difficult. I *wanted* to, I even *tried* to, but it's hard to connect with someone who can't seem to respect the house rules or complete basic tasks. Even getting her to put her dishes in the dishwasher or clean her bathroom is impossible. Not to mention the constant running up to the school for disciplinary meetings with the principal." He paused, and his voice became exasperated as he admitted, "I don't understand her at all. Every day, she is out there actively making poor decisions and our lives more difficult. Her life could be amazing if she'd get out of her own way."

"I know, but she's seventeen. Teenagers are self-destructive and melodramatic by nature."

He continued, "Nova's sucking up all your time and attention. You are so preoccupied with having to dole out and enforce punishments that I only get half a girlfriend. I thought kids were supposed to become more independent as they got older, but that doesn't seem to be the case with Nova."

It took a long time for Tessa to answer. Even though his criticism stung, she had to acknowledge its accuracy. "I can see why you would say that, but Jason, I'm the only solid support system she has ever had." Tessa rubbed her fingers up and down her forehead to quell the tension building there. "I'm frustrated, too. I was looking forward to a break. I wanted us to have some quality time alone together."

"Me too," he breathed. "God knows you deserve a break."

39

"I do," Tessa acknowledged with a long sigh. "But it's not going to happen right now."

"Yeah," he agreed. The line went silent, stretching the distance between them further and further apart.

"Timing is everything," Tessa said to fill the void. "And ours seems to be off."

"Yeah," he admitted, making fresh tears gather at Tessa's lashes.

"If we'd have met in a year or two, things would have been easier." She sighed sadly.

"Perhaps."

His one-word answers were breaking her heart over and over again. In the silence, her fears clamored to the surface, condensing into two words she couldn't bring herself to say out loud.

It's over.

She wasn't ready to say them yet, and she was relieved when he wasn't either. She clutched the phone in her hand, afraid to break the connection.

"I should go," she finally stated. "But I love you," Tessa whispered into the phone, and if she was honest, she knew it was a desperate attempt to cling to the past and the promises they had made to each other.

"Yep," he answered with one word that spoke volumes. She ended the call before he could hear her heart break in two. Though his words were few, they revealed with stunning clarity she was holding on in vain. Promises only worked when both parties kept up their end of the bargain, and now, Tessa saw she was the only one.

Chapter Five

A week later, at three o'clock in the morning, Tessa was dead to the world, tucked into her bed, wearing a weighted sleep mask as puffs of lavender and chamomile-scented vapor diffused into the surrounding air. She was fast asleep when the phone on her nightstand trilled, then vibrated so loudly she bolted straight up in her bed. Disoriented, she pulled the mask from her eyes and glanced down.

What time was it?

3:17 a.m.?

Caller ID Unknown.

Nothing good ever happened after midnight, and she'd learned unknown numbers were usually hospitals when her father had a massive heart attack last year. Certain she'd been called in an emergency, Tessa tensed. Her belly filled with dread as she tapped to answer the call.

"Hello?" she said tentatively. Tessa's heart accelerated, and she tightened her grip on the phone, pressing it tighter against her ear and bracing for bad news.

"Ms. Donahue? I'm Officer Rodriguez with the Omaha Police Department, and I am calling because we have your daughter, Nova, here at the station."

"What?" Stunned, she had a hard time accepting the information she was hearing. First, relief flooded in that it wasn't her father, but then confusion quickly followed. Tessa was in shock. Finding her feet, she padded down the hallway to Nova's bedroom to confirm what the officer was stating with her own eyes. She pressed the door open with her palm, seeing Nova's bed still scattered with the contents of the suitcase she'd dumped on it a week before. On the wall, an oil pastel self-portrait was pinned with thumbtacks, but Nova was nowhere to be found.

In her mind, she ran over the events of the previous night. She'd said goodnight to Nova and then, after reading a bit, had gone to sleep like any normal Tuesday night.

The officer continued, "She was under the influence when we found her and another underage minor vandalizing the Bob Kerrey Pedestrian Bridge." He stopped just long enough for Tessa to grasp the severity of the situation. "She's been charged with minor in possession of alcohol, criminal mischief, and destruction of property."

Criminal.

The word sucked the air out of Tessa's lungs.

"We don't know which class of misdemeanor she's being charged with yet, as the damage has to be assessed, but she'll have to make a court appearance."

"Oh my God." Tessa exhaled a long, hot breath. She leaned against the wall in the hallway for support, then sagged down it to land on the floor, her legs trembling after the rush of adrenaline passed. What in the hell was happening? How had Nova spiraled so far out-of-control right under her nose?

"We can release her to a parent since she's a minor." He offered the devastating information in such a matter-of-fact way, Tessa understood he was required to make similar phone calls to other parents regularly.

"Is she in a safe place? I mean, is she separated from the adult offenders?" Tessa asked.

"Yes."

"I know most parents would rush up and try to fix this, but I need her to understand her actions have consequences," Tessa explained. "How long can I leave her in the clink?"

"Ma'am?" The officer was confused.

"I want to teach her a lesson. She's going to be eighteen next year, and then a stunt like this can do actual damage to her record."

"You're right." She heard the officer chuckle on the other end of the phone.

"Do you guys offer the Scared Straight program? The one where they get to experience real life as an inmate?"

"I'm sorry, ma'am, we do not."

"I know this sounds unorthodox, but she's been on a tear lately and I need to get her attention, so I think I'm going to let her sit until morning. I hope she'll take this time to think about what she's done and where her life is headed."

"In the long run, this could be a real turning point for her," the officer said.

"God, I hope so. I'll come by in the morning before work," she offered and then hung up the phone. Tessa was

43

grateful Jason hadn't been asleep in the bed next to her, bearing witness to her shame.

After the call, Tessa stared at the ceiling for hours, tossing and turning, noticing the cobweb that had taken up residence in the corner of the room. The anger welled up in her gut, making it hard to relax, churning her insides as the minutes dragged on. The house creaked, then shuddered every time the furnace started, then was engulfed by a heavy silence. It was an eerie sensation, knowing she was alone that contributed to her feeling of unease. It occurred to her this was a taste of the empty nest that was looming, a glimpse of Nova's impending passage into adulthood she thought she'd been yearning for, but now, the resounding loneliness was palpable.

Seventeen. Nova was seventeen. Less than three hundred days remained of her childhood. Tessa had heard ad nauseam when Nova was an infant that the days were long but the years were short. Now that Nova was on the brink of adulthood, she worried that she'd squandered it. The years that once seemed endless had whipped by feverishly and were mostly in the rear-view mirror now. In the hourglass of Nova's childhood, only a few grains of sand remained, and it cued up panic in her heart.

"She's not ready!" Tessa said aloud in the empty house.

There was still so much to do. Nova didn't know how to cook a proper meal or balance a checkbook. Tessa felt the brunt of shame about the checkbook especially, since she counseled her clients on being fiscally responsible with the patience of Job. But for some reason, when she sat down with Nova to have the same conversation, it became a battle of wills that ended in an argument. Nova did her own laundry, but many times left it in the washer until it went sour, the mildewy scent clinging to the cotton fibers long after they were dry. Her refusal to separate her whites from her darks stained every one of her t-shirts a dingy blue. Tessa refused to swoop in and fix the situation, hoping it would motivate Nova to make a change, but it backfired.

While Tessa preferred to keep the house organized and clutter-free, Nova's room always looked like a bomb went off, even on the days she finally broke down and cleaned it. The wedge between them widened every day. In her head, Tessa knew she needed to change the destructive dynamic; she just didn't know how.

She didn't sleep a wink that night. Tessa tossed and turned and grabbed her keys more than once to run up to the station on a mission to save her daughter, but then came to her senses and set them back down again. To make the time pass more quickly, she slapped on rubber gloves and decided to deep clean the bathroom. Cleaning was a Zen-like task that gave her control over her world again and a strange sense of domestic accomplishment that she would never admit to any male. Scrubbing at a hard water stain with an old toothbrush dipped in vinegar gave her a chance to clear her mind.

At seven a.m., she dressed for work, drove to the police station, and paid the bond. The door buzzed and a wrinkled Nova walked through it, blinking in the bright light. Seeing her mother, she burst into tears and accepted the hug Tessa forced herself to give her. Pushing past the anger and frustration, Tessa embraced her self-destructive teenager who seemed hell-bent on destroying her life. Nova clung to her mother, her thin frame shaking in relief.

"Once we've completed the full investigation, you'll be notified of her official charges by mail," Officer Rodriguez said. He handed her copies of the documents to sign. "The case is headed over to juvenile court. An officer will be in contact with you."

Juvenile court. Another ugly parenting hurdle to clear.

Tessa eyed Nova to see if the idea of a court appearance affected her, but she was sullen and unresponsive. After several long minutes of explaining the next steps, Tessa tucked the sheath of paperwork into her purse and steered Nova outside and to the Jeep without saying a word. There was a small ash tree planted in the embankment next to the vehicle that Nova rushed over to and promptly vomited on. Tessa's eyes darted around the parking lot, praying they didn't have an audience, and fought back her own gag reflex when the sour scent hit her nostrils.

Bent over at the tree with her stomach now empty, Nova wiped her mouth with the back of her hand and then glanced over at her mother.

"Here." Tessa handed her a bottle of water and some napkins from the glove compartment of her Jeep. "Rinse out your mouth, then chug this. You're probably dehydrated."

"Thanks," she mumbled. Tessa stole glances at her daughter as she walked back to the car. Nova sat down in the passenger seat and fell back with a moan. Tessa slid into the seat next to her and turned toward her daughter. Tears tracked down Nova's cheeks, and she made no move to brush them away. She was a deflated version of the defiant girl that had taken up residence in her daughter over the last eighteen months. Nova reached around on the

46

side and lowered the seat into a more horizontal position with a thump. "Well, that was the worst night of my life," Nova finally admitted.

"I bet it was."

"It was pure hell. People were screaming and crying all night long. I didn't get any sleep at all." Tessa struggled to muster up empathy, taking a small measure of righteous satisfaction in Nova's rough night.

"You know, I didn't get very much sleep, either. It's hard to rest when you receive a phone call at three a.m. from the police who've arrested your daughter," Tessa explained, then asked the questions that had been swirling in her mind since she'd been awakened. "Why would you sneak out of the house in the middle of the night? Who were you with?"

"It doesn't matter."

"It does matter!" Tessa protested. "You can't seem to get out of your own way lately. Now we have to appear in court *and* I have to find a lawyer to represent you. If you have a criminal record, this one mistake could follow you forever. It can make it difficult to pass a background check and challenging to get a job or rent an apartment."

"I can't do this with you right now." Nova sighed, then turned her head away and closed her eyes, still reclined in the seat, not taking Tessa seriously.

Infuriated, Tessa let out a loud huff, blowing hot breath through her teeth to exhale some of the building tension from Nova's apathy. She saw red and couldn't let it go. "Too bad. Suck it up, Buttercup!" She snapped, "Sit your ass up because we are having this conversation right now."

Having no choice but to comply, Nova's seat jerked

back up into an upright position, and she folded her arms across her chest, waiting for her mother to speak.

"Here's the thing, Nove, the self-destruction has to stop. I honestly don't even know if you are capable of making a good decision at all."

"Thanks for the vote of confidence." Nova turned away, pressing herself into the door as far away from Tessa as possible inside the tight confines of the Jeep.

"Is this about your dad?" Tessa asked, already knowing the answer to the question but wondering if Nova was self-aware enough to understand her own motives.

"I don't know." She folded her arms across her chest, defensively protecting her middle. "Maybe I'm just trying to live up to my fullest potential and be the complete and total screw-up you think I am." Her words were coated in the thickest layer of sarcasm her hungover state could command.

"I don't think you're a screw-up. I think you are trying to get your father's attention, and *any* attention, even negative, feels better than none." Fresh tears rolled down her cheeks, and Tessa knew she hit a nerve whether Nova would acknowledge it or not. "Your dad is selfish. You know Donny always does what is best for Donny."

"Yeah, I learned that lesson last week," she admitted bitterly, staring out the window for a long moment before she continued. "That's the reason I became an artist," Nova mumbled, her voice barely above a whisper, and Tessa had to strain to hear it. "I thought if we could talk about art, then he might actually see me."

"Oh, honey." Her vulnerable confession broke Tessa's heart. She turned toward Nova and continued, the anger in her voice softening. "Sweetheart, the truth is, you deserved better. You deserved a dad who doted on you, spent time with you, and made you a priority. I am sorry that he is unwilling to do so, but you need to understand it is *his* loss, not yours. Someday, when he's much older, if he has even one ounce of goodness in him, he will realize the mistake he's made. He'll discover he sacrificed his relationship with you in pursuit of the wrong things. But that day might be a long time coming or might never happen at all. You are going to have to learn to accept this and stop punishing yourself for his mistakes."

Nova began to cry. Tears washed down her dirty cheeks. Tessa reached out her hand and gently laid it on top of Nova's as her voice softened. "I'm not the enemy here. It's just you and me, kid, and that is going to have to be enough." Tessa waited for a reply and got none, so she continued. "If you keep heading down this self-destructive path, I will throw up as many obstacles as I can to stop you. I will chase you to the ends of the earth and through the fires of hell because you are precious to me."

Full sobs rushed out of Nova as they sat silently in their car in the parking lot. From a distance, there was a clap of thunder and then a flash of lightning as the wind picked up and bent the spindly new trees surrounding them. Then fat raindrops pummeled the windshield as the thunderstorm bared down around them. Tessa pulled her broken daughter into her arms awkwardly over the console and murmured soft, reassuring sounds into her hair. As the rain intensified outside, whipping the wind and dumping a deluge on the hood of the Jeep, Tessa felt the storm inside her daughter subside. After several long moments, a series of three soft hiccups came from Nova, and then she uttered a full exhale as she pulled away. Tessa turned back to start the ignition and clicked on the windshield wipers. Their rhythmic whoosh from side to side whisked the rest of the rain drops away.

"I'm so stupid," Nova said.

"Untrue. You're brilliant, you're talented, and you're beautiful. But you're also incredible at making terrible decisions." Tessa leaned in and bumped Nova's shoulder with hers to lighten the mood. "Can we just turn this bus around?" she begged. "Can we draw a line in the sand and be done with it?"

"Yeah." Nova's answer was almost too soft to hear. "Can you take me home now?"

"Sure." Tessa drove Nova home to rest and headed to work, grateful to get back to the logical world of spreadsheets and schedule Cs.

Chapter Six

Tessa was grateful to have lunch with Kristie a few days later. Kristie was seated across from Tessa at one of her favorite healthy lunch hangouts. Against her will, Tessa ordered the Strawberry Sunrise, and it sat untouched in front of her. Across the table, Kristie dipped a spoon into her Acai bowl. It was filled to the brim with vibrant blueberries and a tan protein powder porridge. She lifted it to her mouth eagerly and swallowed, waiting for Tessa to begin.

"Arrested! Can you believe it? I'm still in shock." Tessa's voice cracked. She hadn't had a good night's sleep since the night Nova snuck out of the house. She was bone tired and stifled a yawn with the back of her hand. It was March in Nebraska, and a rogue winter snow storm deposited four inches of fresh powder in the Omaha metro, forcing Tessa to wear a thick sweater. She pressed her fingers to her temples to relieve the tightness there as a dull headache formed.

"Oh, honey, I can't imagine. No wonder you've been MIA the last few days."

"You know me. When things go sideways, I hunker down and keep to myself."

"I get it," Kristie said. "You're a private person. I knew when you were ready to talk about it, you'd open up."

"I don't know what to do anymore. I've taken everything away and grounded her for months. Nothing seems to phase Nova." Tessa said, "And this recent development is mortifying. I'm so embarrassed I can't even talk to my dad about it."

"Ed is the kindest human I know," Kristie said, reaching out to squeeze her hand. "He knows firsthand how hard it is to raise a teenager alone."

Tessa nodded. It had only been the two of them after her mother died.

"I've tried to make him proud my whole life, but I'm so ashamed at what a piss poor mother I've turned out to be."

"Never say that again," Kristie chastised her friend. "You are an amazing mother raising a challenging child. Luckily, mine were all rule followers. I don't know what I would have done if they weren't! Every child is different. Some of them have to learn the hard way."

Tessa felt herself relax for the first time. "That's the truth." She was already feeling better thanks to Kristie's unwavering support.

"So, what's next?"

"I have a couple of consultations set up with attorneys while we wait to see what her official charges are. Ugh!" Tessa let out a grunt of frustration. "Lawyers, and court, and restitution? Seriously, how did I get here?" She toyed with her spoon, dipping it into the blended mush, and letting it plop down into the bowl while she explained the next steps to Kristie. "Remind me. Why do we eat here?"

"Because you can't pound chips and drink margaritas every day. It's about *balance*," Kristie answered with a sweet smile.

"You're lucky I love you so much," Tessa groaned as she spooned an actual bite into her mouth and swallowed. Her face twisted in a scowl. Ingesting the ground-up spinach in her bowl was physically painful.

Kristie grinned at her reaction. "Come on, it's not that bad. Your heart will thank you."

"What am I supposed to do with this kid?" Tessa asked. "I feel like I'm failing her. Every single day."

"You love her, even when she makes it difficult," Kristie advised.

"Well, she's *definitely* making it difficult." Tessa ground her teeth together, talking out of one side of her mouth in dismay. "I forgot to tell you. She told me yesterday she doesn't want to be an art teacher anymore."

"Really? She's been talking about becoming a teacher for a year."

"I know! I was so excited for her to find a career in the arts she could enjoy that came with a solid paycheck and health insurance."

"Then what does she want to be?"

"An artist, specifically a *tattoo* artist."

Kristie's eyebrows shot up, and she smiled.

"What am I supposed to say to that?"

"This is going to be hard to hear. Brace yourself."

Tessa's eyes widened in surprise as Kristie reached out to squeeze her hand reassuringly. "Out with it, woman!

53

I'm on to you!" Tessa wagged her index finger at her friend. "You're trying to soften the psychological blow with physical contact."

Kristie laughed. "Busted." Her sparkling eyes met Tessa's blue ones. "Are you ready?"

"You're scaring me." Nervous laughter bubbled out of Tessa.

"You're supposed to say…" She paused for emphasis, then declared, "go for it!"

"What?" Tessa's forehead crinkled up in concern, and she shook her head no. "No way, she needs to be able to support herself. Nova needs to find a career that offers security and build a life for herself. You can't pay a mortgage when you're a tattoo artist. Heck, you can't even qualify for a loan."

"You mean, build a nice secure and stress-free life for herself like you have?" Kristie sucked her lips back, sealing them to prevent any more blunt truths from escaping. Her eyebrows danced with mirth at her forehead line. She knew exactly when to quit and was so lovable Tessa couldn't even get angry.

"Ouch, girl, you have to warn me before you decimate me with one of your truth bombs."

"I did, silly." She took another bite of her bowl as she let her words sink in. "Your biggest challenge is going to be supporting Nova's decisions when she's living a life you don't agree with."

Tessa gulped. The advice Kristie was giving was almost as difficult to swallow as the strawberry spinach bowl sitting in front of her.

"The best time for her to follow her heart is right now. When she isn't tied down with children or relationships.

She needs the space to explore who she is and what she's been put here to do. Don't ruin it or taint her decisions with your control because you're afraid to face your own fears."

Tessa balled up a fist, struck her chest with it, and laughed nervously. "Sweet Jesus, woman. Seriously, you are killing me today."

Kristie's exuberant smile softened the blow of her harsh words. "I love you, girl. Life is short, and it is a waste of time striving for acceptance and worthiness. Don't chain Nova to that fate. Free her from it."

"And what if she crashes and burns?"

"Then be her soft place to fall. Be the one person she can always count on, no matter what."

"I'm trying," Tessa said as she felt warm tears gather at her lash line.

"I know, babe," Kristie murmured softly. "You've been entrusted to raise this little soul because you and you alone have all the tools necessary to do it. Believe in yourself and your decisions."

Tessa let out a long sigh. "I don't know if I remember how."

Kristie reached out again and squeezed her forearm. "You do," she offered. "You just need to quiet the noise. Raising teenagers is hard, even in the best of circumstances."

"Nova's almost an adult. I feel like I'm running out of time."

"She's always going to need her mom. Honestly, it becomes easier once they are on their own for a while," Kristie offered, talking from experience since her own children were currently attending college. "They have to experience life outside the warm cocoon of their family. Go through a few hardships before they really understand all the sacrifices you've made for them. Just in the last year, Bryant called and told me I was right." She laughed. "I promise, your call is coming."

Tessa laughed. "Keeping hope alive. That is your superpower."

Kristie nodded with an engaging grin. "I'll take it!"

"I don't know what to do. It's been so frustrating. Ever since Nova became a teenager, there's been this disconnect," Tessa continued, focused on finding a solution. Kristie was so level-headed and gave the best advice.

"What if you did something to shake it up?"

"Like what?"

"Well, you are stuck in this dynamic right now, butting heads, but what if you went somewhere new? Maybe went on a journey together or had an adventure?"

Tessa pursed her lips and bit the inside of her cheek, thinking it over. The suggestion had seemingly come out of left field, but it had the distinct twinge of truth she couldn't deny. "I don't know." She pondered it. "I don't want to reward a child who is behaving badly."

"It's not a *reward*. It's a *reconnection*," she corrected. "A chance to press pause on all the drama, get away from the phone, the job, and the ten thousand other obligations that are weighing down your life right now, and build a bridge back to your daughter."

"But I am so close to making partner at the firm. I haven't taken so much as a sick day in the ten years I've been there, and my performance review is next week. I have a feeling it will come with a big announcement."

"Really?"

"When I was hired, they created a partnership track that explicitly spelled out becoming a named partner in the firm on my tenth anniversary," Tessa offered. "I've paid my dues, and now it is time to collect my reward."

Kristie added, "That's even *more* of a reason to take the time off. Seriously, this place is running you into the ground. If you don't take a beat to replenish, you're going to spontaneously combust."

Tessa chewed on the side of her cheek, contemplating Kristie's words. "Dad and I *were* kicking around the idea of taking Nova to the Grand Canyon this fall."

"Stop talking about it and DO IT!" Kristie's voice deepened into a commanding tone Tessa rarely heard from her friend.

"After my evaluation, I will think about it."

Kristie sighed and leaned back into the blue vinyl booth. "You're killing me, smalls! If, God forbid, you had a heart attack and died tomorrow, would the firm give one actual shit?" she asked, then answered her own question, "Hell no! They'd post your job description before your body was even cold and hire their next workhorse." She paused, then added, "But you know who *would* be inconsolable?"

"Nova," Tessa answered softly. Kristie was a tiny drill sergeant. She dug her heels in and continued.

"Yes! Nova! Nothing is an accident. You said it yourself: time is running out. When do you think you will get another opportunity to travel with your daughter?"

"I don't know." Tessa turned over the idea in her mind, finally coming to a realization. "You might be right. I used to be the kind of woman who would jump at an adventure like the one you're recommending! When did I become so boring?"

"Life has a way of dulling our blades. You aren't alone."

Tessa spooned another fruity glop into her mouth and swallowed it with a wincing frown at the sour note from an unripe kiwi.

"Is it that good?" Kristie teased.

"You know what? You're right! I'm gonna do it," Tessa enthused, making a snap decision, and the act reclaimed her power. Her own boldness unfurled like a fresh sprout from the dry earth, and she marveled at the simple joy of discovering she wasn't dead inside after all. "Now I just need to figure out the logistics."

"That's my girl!" Kristie exclaimed.

"Now, for the love of God, can we please walk over to the bakery and get a cupcake to cleanse our palettes? I think I've earned it."

Chapter Seven

The morning of her review, Tessa was a bottle of nervous energy. The professional carrot she'd been chasing for a decade was finally within her grasp, and she couldn't wait to bite into it. Last year, she'd witnessed Tim advance into partnership status, complete with an office with a view and an interior decorating allowance. For the last ten years, Tessa sacrificed so much to achieve this goal, long hours and inconvenient phone calls, keeping her head down and her eye on the prize. Knowing it was finally her moment to shine made her body thrum with excitement.

Her power suit hung on a hanger, getting refreshed by the steam from her long shower. It was the lucky charm she'd worn to land the Three Rivers account four years ago —a six-figure national corporate account that had been a monster to work on. Four years later, it was the most profitable account in the entire practice and had led to more referral business that kept Tessa's schedule completely packed. She didn't have to scramble to woo clients anymore to build her book of business. Instead, her time was better spent building on the successful relationships she was a natural at fostering. Tessa intimately understood, much more than her male counterparts, that business was about trust and building relationships. Over the years, she'd built a vast network around her that grew and grew.

Now, she was on the cusp of the promotion that would change her life, and she couldn't wait. She was going to take that trip with Nova, and she'd have the financial freedom to let the chips with Jason fall where they may. She hated being so reliant on him and wanted to stand on her own two feet. With the promotion, she could take over the lease and stop cashing the checks Jason sent that made her feel worthless.

Freshly showered, she wiped the foggy steam from the mirror with her damp towel. She combed her wet hair as she practiced her talking points, mumbling them to herself out loud. She pulled out the blow dryer and the flat iron and went to work straightening her long locks to a shiny shoulder-length curtain. Then she carefully applied her makeup, taking great pains to make sure it struck the balance between feminine and professional. Being a woman in a male-dominated career path had its challenges, and over the years, she'd learned to navigate them. She would be the first female named partner in the firm, and it filled her with a sense of pride.

Finally, happy with the results she saw in the mirror, she walked to the kitchen to make a protein shake where Nova was spooning Fruity Pebbles into her mouth, watching videos on her phone. Nova pulled her headphones from her ears and gave her a once-over.

"Why are you so dressed up?"

"It's a big day! I have my annual evaluation. I've been on a track to become partner, and today, your mom is going to be the first female named partner in the firm's history."

"Wow." Nova was taken aback, a welcome change from the usual apathetic disillusionment that was her normal expression. "Does it come with a huge raise?"

"Yep! And a killer office with my name on the door."

"That's awesome," Nova said, picking up the bowl from the counter to bring it to her lips, drinking the pink milk that remained from her cereal. "I hope you get it."

"Thanks, honey." Tessa pulled her into a hug, feeling her heart flutter with warmth in the presence of her daughter's approval. It was a welcome shift away from the lingering chaos of the last few months. "I've worked hard to get here, and we've both had to make sacrifices. Maybe we can do something big to celebrate."

"Ooh!" Nova loved a celebration. "Like what?"

"I don't know yet," Tessa answered. "Let me get through today and we'll decide together."

Nova groaned, "That's what you always say."

"But, this time, I mean it."

"Sure, you do."

"You'll see," Tessa rebutted, then glanced at her watch. "We have to leave in three minutes." She swallowed the rest of her protein shake and rinsed out the glass.

In a daze, she drove Nova to school, walking through her nine a.m. meeting in her mind with the partners at Sheffield, Bachoven, and Schmidt. She'd pulled all the reports to back up her successes at the firm and ran over the talking points again, mentally preparing to combat any objections with data and facts.

As she drove closer to work, her confidence grew. She felt a switch in her brain move from anxious to bold. Parking the car, she grabbed her bag and headed into the office. A self-assured thrill unfurled in her belly as she stepped quicker down the hall. Each step made her fizzy and effervescent on the wings of the impending acknowledgment of her accomplishments. Dropping her purse at her desk, she paused to calm her breathing before she walked to the conference room at the end of the hall.

Seated at the table already were three men dressed in suits: Simon Bachoven, Chuck Schmidt, and the newest named partner, Tim Sheffield.

"Tessa," Chuck greeted, standing to acknowledge her arrival. She reached over to shake his outstretched hand and offered him a confident smile. She beamed up at the face of the man who was going to double her salary in mere minutes. He'd been the one to hire her ten years ago and was her favorite of the named partners.

"Shall we begin?" Tim asked, and Tessa turned to offer him a smile that he didn't return and pulled out the chair to sit down. She glanced over at the men seated in front of her one by one, none of them making eye contact. The slight nicked at her power, but she shook it off and recentered, running over the bullet points in her head.

"We've been auditing your accounts and appreciate the work you have done for Sheffield, Bachoven, and Schmidt since you've been with us," Simon began. "At first glance, you have an impressive book of business, but upon further investigation, we uncovered some opportunities for additional billable services that you have not successfully offered your clients. Audit protection insurance has become a lucrative stream of income for all of our associates since we started offering it four years ago, but for some reason, your rate of sales of this service is twenty-two percent lower than that of your colleagues. Can you explain the discrepancy?" Simon asked, his snake eyes sliding up from the documents in front of him to meet hers.

Tessa felt the smile dissolving from her face and her mouth dried up. She stood and reached for the pitcher of water in the center of the table to pour herself a glass, taking a moment to process this unexpected downward turn. Her heart clamored in her chest and thumped through her ears. She took a long sip and then said, "I offer audit protection to every client, but when they ask me if I think it is worthwhile coverage, I tell them the truth. That only point-zero-six percent of all returns end in an audit. With those odds in mind, many have chosen to forgo the coverage."

The elder partner cleared his throat. "Perhaps presenting the option in a different light might encourage your clients to invest in the service."

"It's unethical to manipulate my clients into paying for a service they will most likely never need to utilize," Tessa tried to explain, standing her ground. "I've taken time to build relationships with all of my clients, and they trust me."

"Which is exactly why your closing rate on the audit insurance program should be higher," Tim interjected.

"Tim, here, has a ninety-seven percent close rate on audit protection. Good work," Simon shared as he clapped the younger accountant on the back with one thick, meaty hand.

"Thank you," Tim gushed as he sat taller in his leather seat. The interaction incensed Tessa, and she fought back.

"If an accountant does their job correctly, most companies won't face an audit in the first place."

"That is beside the point," Tim answered drily. "We are a business first and foremost. Revenue generation is of the utmost importance for all senior partners. We need to be united in our goals to reach the benchmarks set by the board of directors."

Chuck chimed in, "This kind of teamwork is essential to the success of Sheffield, Bachoven, and Schmidt. When we work together, we all win," he offered weakly, then tugged at the knot in his tie.

"But I brought in the Three Rivers account. It has the largest billable hours of any account in the entire firm. That should count for something."

"With audit protection, their billings would have increased another ten percent," Simon offered. "It looks to me like you've missed a lucrative opportunity here. Over the four years since we began the program, that's a significant sum of unclaimed revenue."

Tessa tasted acid, and her stomach clenched tight.

"And then there is also the matter of your social media profiles," Simon said, then he clicked on screenshots of pro-choice posts Tessa made shortly after Roe vs Wade was overturned. They filled the screen at the end of the room. Each one made them murmur in agreement. Tessa was outraged and would not be silenced.

"What *I* post on my *personal* social media profiles outside of my office hours should be of no concern to this firm."

"It is a reflection of your values and *our* values by association," Simon explained.

Tessa scrambled to defend herself. "What about the pro-firearm memes that Tim freely posted not too long after the Robb Elementary School shooting? Those were blatantly insensitive and polarizing."

"He's a veteran," Chuck explained it away. "He fought for our freedoms in Iraq, and out of respect for his service, I ask that you please tread lightly here."

"You've got to be kidding me." Tessa got to her feet. "This is a double standard." She shook with rage. "Your tone is dismissive and hostile. I have worked hard during my tenure here. All of my performance reviews have been exemplary. My book of business is thriving with a ninety-two percent retention rate. I'd wager it's higher than any other person in this room, including our heroic veteran, Tim."

She was awash in a sea of adrenaline. "You cannot belittle my accomplishments with a change to the metrics with which success and advancement are measured." Her body was taut with tension, tight like a drum. Thrumming inside, she was shaking with rage. "Chuck?" she asked, looking over at him. The older man refused to meet her eyes and shrunk in his chair. "You laid out the path to named partner when you hired me and gave me every assurance along the way that I was hitting all the necessary benchmarks. Now, at the eleventh hour, you are ripping it all away?" His silence spoke volumes. "Chuck? You have nothing to say?"

He continued to stare down at the papers in front of him. "The vote wasn't unanimous," he offered in explanation.

"Is that supposed to make me feel better?" Tessa couldn't stop herself from asking.

"You're just not partnership material." Simon continued, "I'm afraid we've decided to go a different direction."

Now, she was hopping mad. "A different direction?" Her voice was tighter than she wanted it to be, and she forced herself to take a long breath before continuing. "It's been a good ole boys club here from day one, and I was never given a genuine opportunity to succeed." She paused for a moment, gathering her thoughts. "You *can* absolutely decide to go a different direction, but so can I."

"That is true," Tim answered.

"Then I am tendering my resignation immediately." She made a snap decision that was equal parts terrifying and empowering.

Without hesitation, Tim made a quick call down to the security desk.

"You're calling security on me?" Tessa laughed in outraged shock.

"Please gather your things from your desk and leave the premises. Place your name badge and key fob in your top drawer," Simon advised and stood, signaling the end of the meeting. The security guard appeared at the door, and seeing Tessa's face, his head dropped.

"You're having Carl escort me out? This is offensive. What? Are you worried I'll steal bags of chips and K-cups from the break room?" Tessa shook her head, filled with disbelief. Their actions had utterly blindsided her. Never, not for one moment, did she think she'd be walking in front of the firing squad this morning. "Carl?" She laughed again at the absurdity. "I am the only person in this room who took the time to ask how your mother was doing after her heart attack. I gave you Christmas and birthday presents every year and treated you like an actual human being."

His face pinked up in shame. "Please, Ms. Donahue. I have to do my job."

Tessa huffed and strode out of the conference room, her head held high. "This is not right." She was led back to her desk where, in an act of pure defiance, she climbed on top of her desk chair in the middle of the large room packed with cubicles. "Can I have your attention, everyone?" she shouted out, her voice carrying to every nook and cranny of the packed office building. "If you are a woman employed by Sheffield, Bachoven, and Schmidt, do yourself a favor and begin your job search today. After *ten* years and an *unblemished* execution record, I should have become the first female named partner in this firm's history, but after what transpired a few moments ago in the conference room, I can assure you that the glass ceiling at Sheffield, Bachoven, and Schmidt is very much intact. A woman will never succeed here. Instead of wasting a decade of your life being spoon-fed promises they will eventually refute, cut your losses now and find a firm that values their female employees and rewards their contributions." She caught Kristie's wide eyes, who gave her a nod of support. You could hear a pin drop in the silence that followed.

Carl stood next to her, waiting for her diatribe to end, shifting from one foot to the other, clearly uncomfortable. Tessa stepped down and cleaned out her desk drawers, quickly shoving the contents into a box Carl handed her.

"I'm sorry, Ms. Donahue. I need this job," Carl

mumbled under his breath, out of earshot of the partners. "My wife is pregnant."

"It's not your fault, Carl." She finally cooled enough to address him. "You're just carrying out the orders of my misogynistic superiors."

"For the record, I agree with you. This is wrong," Carl said. "I can't believe they're doing you dirty like this."

"On that, we can agree," Tessa mumbled as she shoved her plant and the family photo into a cardboard box. She made quick work of the rest of it, itching to get out of the office. The air was so thin and toxic, it was making her sick. She left her key card and computer on her otherwise empty desk and walked out into the sunshine. Terrified yet free. Tumbling into a new reality with a teenage mouth to feed. She didn't let the tears come until she was locked safely in her house. She wouldn't allow them to have even one glimpse into her uncertainty and weakness. Tessa would keep that to herself.

Later that night, after Nova had gone to sleep, Tessa found herself in bed doing what any self-respecting middle-aged woman does when they are restless—cruising Pinterest. The algorithm nailed her wanderlust nature, filling her feed with photogenic travel destinations and tips. Distracted by pristine blue ocean water, she tapped and saved gorgeous photos of Bali and the Maldives in her "Places I Want to Go" board.

"Someday," she told herself and filed them away for reference later. Someday, when her life was more settled and secure. A train of wayward thoughts rushed through her mind on repeat.

No. Not someday, now.

What's stopping you?

Trying to recenter her thoughts, she scrolled down the page. Further and further down, thumbnails of gorgeous photographs of coastlines and umbrella drinks whizzed by in her home feed. Then one pin stopped her scroll and captivated her attention. It was a photograph of a modern treehouse taken at sunset, featuring a long, wooden gang-plank lit with fairy lights. The surrounding forest engulfed the diminutive structure, and the perceived solitude was what first captured Tessa's imagination. She tapped to enlarge the picture and take a closer look, enthralled by the idea of isolation in nature. Another tap on the photograph rerouted her to an Airbnb listing for the rental.

"Where is this?" she wondered out loud as she absent-mindedly opened a bag of wasabi almonds and munched on them. Sucking the spicy flavoring off before crunching them between her molars, she scrolled down the website. Tennessee. The Smoky Mountains. She'd never been there, and although it was on her bucket list of National Parks to visit, the Grand Canyon and Yosemite had always eclipsed it. Under the first listing, there were seven more treehouses all within sixty miles of The Great Smoky Mountains National Park. Each one was unique. One was the epitome of luxury and came with a nearly seven hundred dollars per night rental fee. At the other end of the spectrum was an elevated tree tent overlooking a beautiful river view. She was enchanted by them all, and the sweet euphoria of nostalgia inundated her as she recalled the moments she'd spent in the treehouse her father had built at her childhood home.

The treehouses spoke to her soul, beckoning from the depths of her happy childhood. Her father, Ed, was nimble. Even now in his seventies, he was building chicken coops and garden trellises and showed no signs of slowing down. When she was growing up, Ed was often at work, but there was a swath of time when she was seven when she remembered him being home for months. He'd been laid off, and he'd used the time to scour the swap sheet to acquire used building supplies. During the days, they would work together building the treehouse while he took classes at a community college at night to better his employment opportunities. That summer, Tessa learned how to swing a hammer, how to pre-drill for a screw, and the old adage: Measure twice and cut once. Working on a shoestring budget, they constructed a ladder built from rounded logs that over the years became satiny under Tessa and her friends' grubby hands.

She'd even gotten grounded once when she climbed on top of the roof and fell twelve feet into the bushes below, ending up with a broken elbow that never healed properly and an aversion to heights.

Now facing a similar employment break herself, she had a fresh appreciation for the fear and anxiety that must have reigned supreme during that time in her childhood, and a deep respect that he never succumbed to it. She glanced at the clock. Ed was a night owl, and she knew he'd still be awake watching *Late Night with Jimmy Fallon*. She picked up the phone and dialed his number.

"Hey, sweetheart," he answered. "I was just thinking about you." The tenderness in his voice broke her heart, and she started to cry. "Whoa, now, what is happening?" he asked gently, his words filled with genuine concern.

"I didn't make partner at the firm, Dad."

"Oh, honey, I know how hard you've worked to earn the promotion, and I am sorry you were disappointed." He then asked, "But the million-dollar question is, what are you going to do about it?"

She hesitated, then revealed, "I quit. And then was promptly escorted out by security, but not before climbing on my chair and giving everyone in the office an earful. I rallied against the misogynistic regime and the lack of professional opportunities at the firm for women."

On the other end of the line was a soft chuckle. "That's my girl. You've always been one to challenge the status quo."

The sentiment melted Tessa's heart. "I was just thinking about the treehouse we built when you were laid off when I was seven." She mentioned as her voice softened. "How did you do it?" Tessa asked. "You didn't find a decent job for almost two years, but you never let that ruin my childhood. Truthfully, I'm terrified. Inside, I am an emotional wreck. Not to mention, Nova's been acting out at school, and now I have this crisis to deal with on top of it."

"You just have to keep going. Put one foot in front of the other," he offered. "You have to build something to replace all that was destroyed. I built the treehouse because I needed a project, something creative to focus on so I could work through the fear. I felt like I'd failed you and your mother, and as a man, there is no worse feeling in the world."

"You didn't fail us, Dad." Tessa sighed. "But I understand the feeling. I'm stuck in a pit of failure myself."

"Tessa, you've always been resourceful and a hard worker. I'm certain you will discover your next step soon. In life, there are lots of forks in the road, and it looks like you've stumbled onto your next one. There are two paths in front of you now." He paused, then continued, "I know it doesn't feel like it, but it has given you the luxury of choice."

"It doesn't feel like a luxury. It feels like I set my life on fire only to watch it burn."

"Sometimes you have to burn everything to the ground so you can build back better. Why do you think wildfires level the national Parks every few years? Remember that time we went to Yellowstone right after the fires?"

She nodded, even though he couldn't see her. "I do. The air still smelled scorched, even though the fires had been out for months. The trees were gone and black soot was everywhere."

"Exactly."

"But I remember you pointing out neon green leaves emerging from the ashes. You told me to trust in the power of new beginnings."

"Even when you are surrounded by destruction, you can choose to see the new. This is an opportunity for you to really think about the direction your life is headed and to course correct."

"Like you did?"

"Yep." His voice was warm.

"I had a crazy idea."

"Now, I like the sound of that." His voice was playful, even at seventy-two.

"I haven't taken a real vacation in four years. Nova is almost an adult, and now I have nothing holding me here. I need to shake things up and think it's time for a grand adventure."

"Tell me more," he encouraged.

"I'm thinking about taking Nova on a treehouse tour in Tennessee. Near Sevierville, there is a cluster of them."

"Sevierville is also the gateway to the Great Smoky Mountains," he mentioned.

"Exactly!" she enthused. "We could go hiking and get out into the fresh air and spend some quality time together. I'm panicking, Dad. All those fond childhood memories I wanted to give Nova, we haven't made enough of them and I'm running out of time."

"Sweetheart, you are too hard on yourself. Mothering is a full-contact sport. I wish your mother was still here to help teach you the ropes."

"Me too," Tessa whispered. She'd passed away from pancreatic cancer when Tessa was ten. "But I don't think she'd be very proud of the mother I've become."

"I better never hear you say that again!" Ed scolded. "I know I'm not your mother, but I have learned a few things about mothering if you'd like to hear them."

"Of course."

"Follow your heart, Tessa. Slow down and listen to yourself. You've been so busy striving and ticking boxes on some imaginary list for as long as I can remember. Your work ethic is admirable, but honey, you're headed for burnout."

"I think I'm already there."

"Then this is a grand idea. I'd advise you to approach it differently, though. If I know my daughter, you're going to write a long list of mountains to conquer and activities to do. What if you decided to go with the flow and see what develops?"

"I don't know. I like to have a plan," she answered as she considered his suggestion.

"There's nothing wrong with that," he offered, then continued with caution, "until it consumes your life."

Tessa laughed. "I can never argue with you because you're always right."

"I don't know about that." He was humble. Ed was a great father because he was a great man. "I know your heart, honey, but does Nova?"

His words cut her to the core, and a choked sob sliced through the silence.

"Shush now," he murmured. "I didn't say that to hurt you. I've learned a lot in this long life I've lived, and if I could give you one piece of advice, it would be to humanize yourself with Nova. Let her see who you are. Even the playing field and remove the discipline dynamic. She is going to be eighteen next year anyway, and then whatever choices she makes will be her own. You're waging an unwinnable battle that is already over. It's time to stop the fighting."

Tessa exhaled through her pursed lips. "But what if she destroys her life?"

"Then she'll have to learn to rebuild. As a parent, it's difficult and sometimes downright painful to sit on the sidelines and watch them struggle. But the struggle is where all the growth happens." He paused. "You're fighting for control, but it's a false sense of control. Let go and see what transpires. Nova might surprise you."

They talked for a few more minutes, and then Tessa hung up the phone feeling lighter. Talking to her dad always had that effect on her. Finally, her thoughts stilled, and she was relaxed enough to fall into a deep sleep.

Chapter Eight

During the next week, Tessa coordinated and booked four treehouses for the second week of June back to back. It was a tricky scheduling nightmare that gave her a thrill of accomplishment when she'd completed all the reservations successfully. Out of habit, she made a detailed hour-by-hour itinerary for the trip, then tore it up and threw it in the garbage, replacing it with a looser one. She researched unique activities in the area and booked two interesting options, leaving the rest of the time open and unstructured as her dad suggested. Leaving all that precious time unplanned and unaccounted for made her twitchy, but she forced herself to leave it alone and vowed she'd go with the flow, even if it killed her.

She also took the opportunity to do some damage control with her clients. Tessa called them one by one to fill them in on her departure from the firm and outlined her next steps. She shared that she planned to take a vacation to spend time with her daughter, but in July, she would begin to interview at new firms and asked if they would be open to making a change.

All of her small business clients were in total support, but her meal ticket, the Three Rivers account, was not as easy to win over. They appreciated her hard work and would welcome a call when the dust settled, but continuity was paramount and they would remain at Sheffield, Bachoven, and Schmidt for the time being. Making the calls was a slog, as it forced her to explain the demoralizing situation over and over, but after call number ten, it got easier. She developed a professional-sounding, whitewashed version of the events that included cringeworthy buzzwords like synergy, pivot, and think outside the box. She was grateful when she hung up the phone after the last call and could look forward to their trip, which was now only six weeks away.

Jason's flow of financial aid continued, and every time Tessa paid the rent, she felt a little dirty. When she called to thank him, he was quiet and reserved and the usual warmth in his voice was absent.

"I'm taking Nova to Tennessee on vacation next month," she'd said after they exchanged pleasantries.

He scoffed at the idea. "You know she's not going to appreciate it."

"Maybe not," Tessa answered. "But I think I need this as much as she does." She hesitated then added, "When I get back, we need to talk about our future." It took everything in her to be bold enough to frankly address the growing chasm she felt between them. She was through waffling and being unwilling to address the elephant in the room. Tessa was counting on the forest and the mountains to fortify her resolve and give her clarity. She cleared her throat. "If there's even a future for us at all," she admitted, her voice barely above a whisper.

His silence on the other end was sobering. When he finally spoke, he agreed. The next month passed in a complete blur. Tessa kept up appearances for Nova the week after she quit. She dressed like she was headed to work, but then spent her time in the library or sitting in a coffee shop until it was time to pick Nova up after school. But running late one morning in late May, still dressed in yoga pants and tennis shoes, Nova became suspicious and asked, "Aren't you dressed a little casual for work?"

"Not anymore. I quit," Tessa admitted, unwilling to outright lie to her daughter.

"What? Why? What happened?" Nova's anxiety filled the interior of the car at such a rapid clip it stunned Tessa. "How are we going to pay our bills?"

"Whoa! Slow down, Nova. I've got it all handled," she lied, as much for herself as her daughter. When she walked out of the firm, she'd cut their safety net out from under them. Tessa knew she would eventually land on her feet, but she didn't want to share the gory details with Nova, who was often a whisper away from a downward spiral. "That's why I'm always telling you to live within your means. I have resources in savings that I can tap into." She wanted to add the words 'in an emergency,' but she left them out, knowing the word "emergency" would set Nova off. She offered her daughter a calm smile. "Besides, keeping you alive has always been *my* job. *Your* job is to stay in school and not get arrested." She meant it to be a joke, but the second the words left her lips, she wanted to take them back.

"Then it looks like we're both miserable failures," Nova responded.

"You're only a failure if you let yourself be," Tessa countered.

"Mom, sometimes your positivity is toxic."

"What do you mean?" Tessa was confused, her cheeks pinking up.

"You invalidate my human experience when you are always lecturing me to look on the bright side. It's like the only emotions I ever get to express are happy ones."

Tessa was taken aback. "But mindset is everything, honey. Your most important asset is the space between your ears."

Nova rewarded the mindset conversation in her usual way—with an eye roll.

"Honestly, I think you would have been proud of me," Tessa added. "I stood up on my chair and blew the whistle on the firm fostering a toxic masculinity culture for years. *And* I exposed the lack of advancement opportunities for women at the firm."

"You did?" Nova questioned, her eyes widening. In her mind, it was impossible to reconcile this shocking example of progressive feministic views with the woman who would not shut up about the danger of leaving wet towels on her floor.

"I did," Tessa confirmed, proud of herself. "What they did to me was wrong. I worked hard, and I deserved that promotion, but sometimes not getting what you want is the answer to a prayer."

"How can that be true?" Nova's brows knit up in disbelief.

"Sometimes what is out there waiting for you is something bigger, grander, and better than you could have ever imagined. The trick is being patient enough to let it unfold."

"But all your plans..." Nova was well versed in her mother's affinity for goal setting and itineraries.

"Plans are just that, plans. Life has its own agenda," Tessa offered. Knowing her words of wisdom always had a short shelf life with Nova, she changed gears and asked, "How did gym class go yesterday?" She knew Nova loathed gym, often opting to cut the class and hide out in the library. Her ability to offer school staff and teachers a litany of plausible excuses was legendary.

"Fine. I ran laps and made fun of people." Nova fussed with the crimson corset that cinched her waist into a tight circle layered atop a floor-length, black vintage dress. It was an updated Morticia Adams ensemble that was over the top for any high schooler.

"Good. You're going to need to get your buns in shape." Tessa dropped the first hint of their upcoming adventure, her tone playful.

"Why?"

"For an event I scheduled this summer," Tessa shared. She'd just made the final Airbnb payments and cringed when they all hit her credit card concurrently, but now that it was concrete, she was eager to share her excitement with Nova.

"What kind of event?" Nova was wary.

"We're going on a treehouse tour," Tessa revealed with a huge smile, hoping her joy would be infectious.

"A what?"

"A treehouse tour," Tessa repeated. Her enthusiasm

was deflating like a leaky balloon in the presence of Nova's disinterest.

She wanted Nova to be as pumped about the trip as she was, so she continued to explain. "You're graduating from high school next year, and we have this one final summer to make memories together. It's going to be the last grand adventure of your childhood."

"That's a little morbid, don't you think?" Nova asked. "Dark and twisty is usually my wheelhouse."

"I prefer to call it sentimental."

"Whatever helps you sleep at night," Nova remarked, but the thought of her impending adulthood and the responsibility it was cloaked in sobered her up. "I don't want to grow up. Adulthood does not sound fun."

Tessa laughed. "I'll be honest. For the most part, it isn't, but there will always be bright spots to look forward to. Just think, some of the best days of your life haven't even happened yet!"

Nova considered her statement. "Hmm. I like that. Gives me hope."

"Sometimes, a little hope is all you need." Tessa pulled into a parking spot in front of Nova's high school. She reached into her bag and pulled out her iPad. "See?" She tapped on photos of the treehouses and scrolled through a couple of the listings she booked on Airbnb.

"That could be cool," Nova said, showing a tiny speck of interest in the idea as she scrolled through the photos.

"It *will* be. We're going to hike and see the Great Smoky Mountains."

"What's so great about the Smoky Mountains?"

Tessa's jaw dropped. "Everything! Hiking in the forest is healing. There's this ancient Japanese practice called forest bathing. Have you heard of it? It's being hailed as one of the most cost-effective ways to increase well-being and health. Did you know Japan has spent about four million dollars researching its effects since 2004, and they have forty-eight dedicated therapy trails?"

"That's the mom I know and love. Hitting me with statistics and cold hard facts."

Tessa laughed. Nova was right, but it didn't stop her from continuing her sermon. "Forest bathing is so effective that other countries are hopping on board. Even in South Korea, the government has invested millions to create a National Forest Therapy Center."

"Yeah, I'm sure after Kim Jong-un spends a few hours bathing in the forest, he'll come away from the experience so centered and filled with inner peace, light, and love, he might rethink all the nukes," Nova joked, her inflection deadpan.

"You may think your sarcasm is a sick burn, but all *I* hear is you've been paying attention in World History class and can speak intelligently about world events." Tessa smiled, taking joy in her daughter's bright mind. She was rewarded with another eye roll.

"It's especially good for people who are fighting anxiety and depression. It will be a reset for both of us."

"Maybe," Nova mused quietly, then opened the door and gathered her black messenger bag from the floor. Tessa knew her daughter well enough to let it simmer. She needed a little extra time to get used to an idea.

"Love you."

"Love you, too," Nova parroted back, and Tessa watched her trudge toward the school, her black combat boots carrying her to first period.

Chapter Nine

S he met Kristie for happy hour a few days later.

"Hey, you!" Kristie said, reaching in for a hug before she sat down on the stool across from her. "I miss seeing you around the office." Kristie was wearing a bright yellow maxi dress that touched the ground.

"You're an absolute ray of sunshine in that dress," Tessa said, giving the menu a once over before setting it down and meeting Kristie's gaze. "I miss you, too," Tessa said softly. "It's strange not having to race around in the mornings. I was so used to running Nova to school and then right to work. Some days, I'd leave when it was dark and didn't come home until it was dark again. I've never had free time before. It's been a blessing *and* a curse."

"I bet." Kristie nodded. "It will take some getting used to. How're things?"

"Well, my lack of gainful employment is making Nova anxious," Tessa said.

"Kids don't do well with change," Kristie offered.

"Adults don't do well with it, either," Tessa admitted with a pained smile.

Kristie leaned in and lowered her voice. "Just between you and me, I've been looking for a new job, too."

Tessa's heart swelled with love for her compassionate friend. "You are so sweet to support me, but I don't expect you to leave just because I did."

"The only thing holding me there is the health insurance. The PET scans are brutal to the deductible, and our HSA has taken a big hit, but the second I line up another full-time position, I am jumping ship. I promise. How could I stay at a firm that screwed over my best friend?"

"I appreciate the sentiment." Tessa smiled. "You are a wonderful, loyal friend, but promise me you'll only leave if it makes sense for you and your family."

"Agreed." She flashed Tessa a quick smile. "Your dramatic exit was the stuff of legends. People are still talking about it." She grinned, recalling the moment. "Standing on your chair and condemning the patriarchy? That was badass. I've never been more proud."

"I surprised myself," Tessa admitted with a laugh. "I just couldn't swallow their lies anymore."

Kristie nodded then took a sip of her chocolate martini. The rim was dipped in chocolate shavings and sea salt. "So, what's next?"

Tessa glanced away. "What do you mean?"

"Where is this new life taking you, Ms. Donahue?"

"I'm still figuring it out, but I have decided to take your advice and create something new. I booked a week-long adventure for Nova and me in Tennessee. We're going to stay in four different treehouses near the Smoky Mountains."

"That sounds incredible!"

Tessa pulled up the Airbnb bookings on her phone and slid it over to Kristie. "The first one is a super primitive set-up. We start off in an elevated tree tent that features off-grid living and compostable toilets. They gradually get more bougie every time until we get to the last night. It's the grandest treehouse of them all, and at almost seven hundred a night, it should be." She scrolled through the listings, listening to Kristie ooh and ahh over the photos.

"Wow. Amazing!" Kristie enthused, her excitement contagious. "What about your fear of heights?"

"Um… I've decided to look at it as exposure therapy." Tessa brushed the phobia off and forged forward, recounting her plans. "I've been doing a ton of research. We're going to cook all our own meals over the campfire and go kayaking and hiking and see waterfalls in the Smokies."

"That sounds like the trip of a lifetime," Kristie said. "But can I encourage you to do one thing?"

"What?"

"Go with the flow? Be open to what can happen when you change your surroundings. I know you're a type A overachiever, but maybe think about approaching this from a place of softness. It is a vacation for *both* of you, and you might *both* benefit from some unscheduled downtime."

"You sound just like my dad!" Tessa laughed.

"Ed *is* a brilliant man." A huge grin bloomed on Kristie's face. He'd driven Kristie to a few of her chemo appointments when she was in a bind and sat with her while she received them. They had a special bond.

Tessa pursed her lips and nodded, gazing far away as she mulled it over. It was true. She thought back to the itinerary she'd torn up that was now deep in the bowels of the landfill. "You might have a point."

"Go there with zero expectations and see what happens. Loosen the reins, relax the desire to control the outcome, and just be together in the moment. Let this adventure *change* you." It was brilliant advice given from a place of love, even if it felt like she was asking the impossible.

"Can I agree to really think about it?" Tessa asked. "Or are you going to be like a dog with a bone until you convince me you're right?" She laughed. "You know, for someone so tiny, you sure can be a ruthless dictator."

"It's part of my charm," Kristie said with a grin.

"Okay, fine," Tessa agreed. "I guess, if I want things to change, then I need to change myself. It's not all on Nova. I'm going to abandon all my urges to over-schedule. You've worn me down. I surrender." She held up both her hands, and they laughed.

Chapter Ten

The next few weeks passed, and Tessa received a thick white envelope from the Omaha District Attorney's office. Dread filled her belly as she knew Nova's fate rested inside. She tore it open and flattened the papers with her palms to read it, and a white business card fluttered to the floor. Glancing down at the official documents, she learned Nova's court date was set up at the end of July. Grateful it wouldn't interfere with their plans, yet dreading the very idea of appearing in court, she set it aside.

She'd interviewed two lawyers with Nova present. It was an eye-opening exercise requiring a huge retainer that left them both shell-shocked. When they left the office carrying a thick stack of papers outlining the engagement agreement, Tessa chose tough love.

"When we get back from Tennessee, you are going to get a job and help pay some of these legal expenses."

"Okay," Nova said, her voice dull. The visit to the law firm killed the fight in her. She left the long meeting quieter and more reserved. Tessa narrowed the options to one attorney a few days later. For weeks, the engagement agreement and check for the retainer sat inside a stamped envelope ready to be mailed. Two days before she was required to mail it, Tessa received a call from an unknown number. Nova was accounted for, seated at the table eating breakfast, so instantly, she worried it was her dad.

"Hello?" she said breathlessly.

"Can I speak to Tessa Donahue?"

"Speaking."

"This is Officer Nemmers. I'm an investigator with the Omaha Police Department who has been assigned to your case. Do you have a moment?"

She glanced over at Nova, who was watching videos on her phone.

"Of course." She sat down on the stool next to Nova and waited.

"I wanted to talk to you about our Juvenile Diversion program. It's for first offenders, and if it's successfully completed, the charges can be removed from Nova's permanent record."

"Really?" The thrill of hope welled up in Tessa. She sat up, intimately understanding how pivotal of a moment this could be in Nova's life.

"Nova is right here. Do you mind if I put this call on speakerphone so she can hear about it?"

"Not at all."

Tessa covered the phone with her hand and bumped Nova's arm to get her attention. "You need to listen to this call."

Reluctantly, Nova pulled the headphones out of her ears and turned her attention to her mother's phone. Tessa switched to speakerphone mode. "Nova, this is Officer Nemmers."

"Hi, Nova. We'd like to offer you an opportunity to enter the diversion program. It takes six months to complete, requires weekly check-ins with the program supervisor at your high school, therapy sessions with your therapist, and…"

"But school's already out for the summer," Nova blurted, interrupting the officer.

She shot Nova a glare and made a zipping motion across her lips. "Please go on, Officer Nemmers."

"Your time in the program will begin when school starts back in the fall. In addition to the meetings, you must complete fifty hours of community service and attend school every day it is in session unless you have an illness. You cannot skip a class, be marked tardy, or get suspended from school." He paused and Tessa saw Nova lean closer, her eyes glued to the phone. "You also cannot be arrested or acquire any new charges, and you have to pass random drugs checks, *but* if you abide by all the program rules, your charges will be dropped."

"Will they be sealed or show up in a background check?' Tessa asked.

"No, actually, it puts them into a locked anonymous state where they cannot even be accessed by the system. It's like it never happened."

Tessa locked her eyes on Nova, who was hanging on every word. She *did* care.

"I will caution you that if any of the above criteria are unmet, you will be dropped from the program and the file that is sitting on my desk right now will be handed over to the court and you will need to appear in front of a judge."

"Does this mean we wouldn't need to engage an attorney? I mean, provided she completes the program?"

"Yes. The case would close with her successful completion of the program."

"That's an incredible offer! What do you think, Nova?" Tessa was nodding up and down enthusiastically, encouraging her to respond.

"For sure. I want to do it," Nova answered quickly, and relief washed in.

Tessa mouthed the words 'Thank him'.

"Thank you," Nova added, and Tessa wildly gesticulated to encourage her to elaborate.

"…for this… chance." Nova's nervousness dumbed down her extensive vocabulary.

"Fantastic! We will get the paperwork drawn up, and you will meet with Mrs. Clifton to get enrolled. Once you've completed the program, she'll file the paperwork with me, and the charges will be officially dropped."

"Thank you, Officer Nemmers. This is an amazing second chance, and I know Nova won't take it lightly."

"That's what we hope. Having a record makes life really difficult, and with the diversion program, we can give students who have made a mistake a second chance."

Tessa hung up the phone. "Isn't that awesome?"

"It is," Nova agreed.

"You understand this is a once-in-a-lifetime opportunity to clear your record, right?"

"I do," Nova answered.

"You should use the time off this summer to get the community service knocked out. You won't be able to half-ass it and skip classes anymore."

"Jesus, Mom, I know." Nova's voice tightened, and the storm clouds started to gather in her eyes.

"Okay." Tessa plucked the stamped envelope from its resting place by the dish with her keys. "We don't have to send this then."

Tessa was thrilled about Nova's second chance. She hoped Nova saw what a pivotal moment this was in her life. She could take a right and work the program and earn her freedom, or she could go left and dig a bigger hole, making every opportunity as an adult dry up. The scariest part was it was up to Nova. Tessa couldn't force her through the hoops. Nova would have to choose to jump through them on her own.

Chapter Eleven

The day before they left for Tennessee was spent running errands and paying bills. Late in the afternoon, Tessa dragged Nova to the grocery store. As she parked the car, wanting to get Nova on board, she enthused, "We're going to cook most of our meals over the campfire. Won't that be fun?"

"For who?" Nova asked with her usual snarky smirk.

"For *both* of us." Tessa grinned. She was hopeful and ready to take on the challenge. Nova wasn't as thrilled. "I researched some campfire recipes, and I know Papa taught you how to build a fire during your campouts together. If you don't practice those survival skills, you'll forget them. Use it or lose it, sister." Tessa chuckled at her own joke.

"Step into the twenty-first century with me, Mom," Nova teased, her eyes twinkling with sarcastic glee. She held out her palms and waved her fingers in the air. "It's a *magical* place where you can make fire appear with the simple turn of a knob."

Well-versed in her daughter's sarcasm, Tessa let it go

in one ear and out the other, determined not to let Nova's cynicism spoil her excitement. She was looking forward to getting back to nature. Life, when left to its own devices, seemed to spin faster and faster toward burnout. The only way to combat the sensation of constant overwhelm was to take a deliberate step back, to slow down and get back to the basics, and Tessa couldn't wait.

"Come on. Shake a leg," Tessa cajoled, leading the way into the brightly lit grocery store. Nova raced ahead, her dirty shoelaces tethered to red Vans dragging on the ground. She was wearing black cutoffs and a gray vintage Eagles concert t-shirt that she'd customized. Carefully, she'd cut down the back of the shirt vertically and removed six inches of material, and then created a makeshift corset out of safety pins. The result was a form-fitting, edgy garment that had the potential to scar you.

"Your shoes are untied," Tessa pointed out the obvious.

Nova waved her off and dawdled behind, enthralled by the Lofthouse cookies in pastel lavender and yellow that sat just beyond the nested shopping carts. Tessa stopped to yank a cart free and then wheeled it down the linoleum floors. She strolled down the produce aisle and added chopped pineapple, strawberries, and two oranges to her cart. Armed with a very thorough grocery list, she'd accounted for every item necessary to cook all of their meals for the first half of the trip. Tessa loved a list, and more than the list, she relished the feeling of checking something *off* the list. She'd read once that completing minor tasks gave your body a brief surge of dopamine, and she was addicted.

After watching an episode of the *Oprah Winfrey Show* where one of the low-carb evangelists advised staying out of the middle aisles to avoid processed food, Tessa adopted the habit of cruising the perimeter of the grocery store when she shopped. She wheeled the squeaky cart to the meat counter that sat on the back wall of the store where a pimply teenager with an apron and a paper hat asked, "Have you been helped, ma'am?"

"Not yet." She gave him a big smile. "Can I get a nice size sirloin?" She pointed at the one in the front of the case. "Maybe that one?" Tessa preferred to choose her own meat instead of subjecting her family to whatever was closest to the clerk. She did the same with bagged salad and dairy products, digging to the back of the display case in pursuit of perceived freshness.

"You got it." With a gloved hand, he pulled it out, weighed it on the scale, printed the label, and wrapped it in white butcher's paper before sliding it over the glass counter to Tessa.

"We're having steak?" Nova asked, sidling up to Tessa after her brief love affair with the donuts at the bakery concluded. She was wearing the first glimmer of an actual smile. Steak was one of her favorite meals that a frugal Tessa considered a splurge. The penny-pinching ways she'd adopted to make ends meet when she was newly divorced stuck. Being fiscally responsible came with the territory when you were an accountant, and even though she made more money working at the firm, she couldn't shake the habit. The years of self-control had accumulated the nest egg she was currently living on and gave her the luxury of waiting to find the perfect fit in her next firm when they returned from Tennessee.

"It's been a while. I figured we'd cut it into chunks and then let it marinate in the cooler on the drive down so it's ready to grill at the first treehouse," Tessa explained. "I was also thinking we should do a S'mores cook-off."

"What do you mean?"

"Apparently, traditional S'mores are a bore. Bloggers are creating all kinds of crazy combinations now—candied bacon, Snickers bars, or Samoa cookies instead of graham crackers. The sky's the limit! I say we try a different kind every night, and at the end of the trip, we can rank them."

Nova's eyes widened. "Who are you?"

"What do you mean? I know how to have fun, too." Tessa laughed. "Besides, it's a vacation. We're going to eat what we want, when we want. Since we're hiking, we'll be burning it off anyway most days."

Nova nodded, considering this new version of her mother. "What are the oranges for?"

"I found an orange brownie soufflé recipe online where you hollow out an orange, fill it with brownie batter, and roast it over the campfire."

"That seems pretty ambitious," Nova mused. "Can't we just swing by a bakery?"

"Where's the fun in that?' Tessa asked. "Imagine how much better a warm brownie will taste when you've cooked it with your hot little hands."

"You need to find better hobbies," Nova joked.

"Maybe." Tessa shrugged.

Witnessing this dramatic shift in Tessa's thinking, Nova pressed her luck. "Can we get snacks for the car ride down?"

"What kind of snacks?" Tessa asked looking down at the contents of the cart. "I've already got some fruit here and a box of granola."

"I'm talking junk, stuff with high fructose corn syrup

and xanthan gum. Ingredients you can't pronounce." Nova's lips quirked up at the corners. "You just said we're going to eat what we want, when we want."

Leave it to a teenager to take you literally and quote you back to yourself, she thought, but at least she was listening. Tessa heard Kristie's voice in her head. "Loosen the reins." She bit the inside of her cheek and made a concession.

"Okay, but let's get all our snacks here. When you buy crap at convenience stores, you pay a premium for it."

"Deal." Nova raced off to the middle aisles to search for junk food before Tessa changed her mind. Turning down a different aisle, Tessa added more items to the cart. Bread and buns, a few tin foil containers to grill in, and graham crackers. Then she added a carton of eggs, a package of cheese, a sweet Vidalia onion, and bite-size yellow fingerling potatoes. Crossing the last item off her list, she pushed the cart down the snack aisle, looking for Nova. Two aisles over, she found her and rolled the cart closer, where Nova deposited a family-size bag of Flaming Hot Cheetos and Sweet Tart Ropes, a red straw-like candy that was filled with bright blue goo.

"Whoa. Aren't you getting a little carried away?" Tessa asked after she watched Nova also add a bag of Munchos and a box of Hostess cupcakes.

"I might never get this chance again. I have to capitalize on it."

Tessa simpered at her daughter's accurate assessment. She wasn't wrong. "So, let's talk about our Great Smoky Mountains S'mores Bake-Off. I have a recipe for candied bacon S'mores, one where you use a peanut butter cup instead of the Hershey bar, and one using fudge stripe cookies instead of graham crackers. What do you think?"

"I'm down." Nova grinned as more heaps of sugar were stacked inside the cart. It was a new record. Tessa's usual sensible eating plan was toast in the sea of complex carbohydrates and artificial dyes that covered the bottom of the cart. Seeing Nova finally start to warm up to their trip, Tessa left the usual lectures about childhood obesity and diabetes at the door.

She'd had the same double standard most parents did when it came to what *she* ate and what she wanted Nova to consume. The kind of beliefs that had you binge eating ding dongs in the car on the way home or ice cream in the late night hours after your child went to bed. It was a 'do as I say, not as I do' philosophy Tessa employed, trying to be a good example in front of Nova. Surely, letting Nova eat junk to her heart's content for one week wouldn't undo all the hours she'd spent teaching healthy habits. Kristie was right; life *was* about balance.

They checked out their groceries and then drove home. Tessa scanned the front stoop with disappointment as she pulled into the garage. The Amazon packages she'd been stalking for days still hadn't arrived and, knowing her luck, wouldn't make it until after they'd left.

"Pack a swimming suit," Tessa advised as she went through the plastic bags of groceries on the countertop. "We have a twelve-hour drive tomorrow to get to our hotel in Clarksville, so make sure you pack some entertainment. I figured we could alternate driving."

Nova's eyebrows raised at the prospect. "Not sure that's a good idea," she mumbled. "No offense, Mom, but you're a control freak."

"It will be fine," Tessa insisted.

"We'll see," Nova responded with Tessa's favorite parental procrastination catchphrase then disappeared up into her bedroom. A few minutes later, Tessa heard music faintly drifting down the stairs.

Getting back to her list, Tessa rejoiced when she heard the doorbell ring. She ran to the door on stocking-clad feet and let out a whoop of glee, seeing two cardboard boxes that had been delayed for days now resting on the stoop.

Inside one box was a Pudgy Pie maker, a nostalgic surprise she'd ordered for Nova. It was a rectangular cast-iron box that was held together by two long handles that screwed into the base. The pie maker was a throwback to when Nova was five and had gone camping with her grandfather in the woods and made campfire pies for the first time.

Little Nova was so enamored with the process of buttering the bread, adding her toppings, and then placing the black box into the red coals while it sizzled away. Late one night scrolling Pinterest, several pins for campfire pie iron recipes appeared, and Tessa couldn't resist buying the maker, hoping to reenact a fond memory from Nova's childhood.

In the past two weeks, Tessa had become an authority on pie iron flavors and options. Pizza flavored, eggs and bacon, even Boston cream pies made with flaky crescent roll dough were possible. She couldn't wait to try it out.

Reading the directions, she realized the cast iron had to be seasoned before they could use it.

"Shoot." Quickly, she spread a thin layer of vegetable oil onto the cast iron with a paper towel and preheated the oven. Then she slipped it inside on a cookie sheet and set the timer for one hour.

The other box had a teal deck of cards in it. It was another impulse purchase she hoped would help bridge the gap between them. It was a game called *The AND*.

Frustrated and desperate to connect with Nova during this trip, she'd Googled, "How to have meaningful conversations with your teenager." Embarrassed that she'd had to turn to Google for answers that she was certain every other mother already innately knew, she fell down rabbit holes of well-meaning but unrelatable homeschool blogs. Eventually, she clicked on The Skin Deep website and learned *The AND* card game promised to provide a unique experience that allowed people to enjoy the power of human connection from anywhere in the world.

With a bit of trepidation, she clicked 'add to cart'. Now holding the deck in her hands, she felt foolish, and she hid the pack of cards deep in her suitcase. She hoped the right moment would present itself where she could pull it out and Nova would be open-minded enough to play.

The next few hours were a flurry of activity for both Tessa and Nova. Tessa consulted her checklists and even went so far as to pour salt, pepper, and pizza seasoning into small Ziploc bags to use when she cooked. Tessa planned meticulously for all contingencies and thought through every meal they would cook together, making sure each ingredient was accounted for on her list.

"Nova, bring your suitcase to the door," she called out, and a few minutes later, Nova appeared, dragging a suitcase on wheels behind her.

"What's with all the coolers?" Nova asked. "Isn't it overkill?"

"No, my dear, let me present to you our patent pending three cooler system." Tessa waved one arm over to the blue cooler on the floor, Vanna White style. "One for our dry items, to keep the critters at bay so we don't wake up to raccoons three slices deep in our bread." She whipped her left arm to the white cooler on rollers. "One for our cold items we'll load in the morning," Then she picked up the soft-sided cooler bag and shot Nova a winning smile. "And one for sandwiches to eat on the way down and when we go on hikes."

"What an exciting food storage breakthrough!" Nova teased.

"Okay, smarty pants, next week when you're devouring a delicious ham and cheese sandwich and don't have to wring out waterlogged cheese slices before you take a bite, I'll expect to hear your undying gratitude."

"Oh, you'll hear it," Nova deadpanned.

Knowing when to let it drop, Tessa asked, "Did you pack everything you're going to need? Let me look inside your suitcase."

"Jesus, Mom, I'm almost an adult. Chill."

"I just want to make sure you didn't forget anything."

"If I forget something important, then I will live with the consequences." Nova dug in.

Tessa wanted to say, "But if I look *now,* you can avoid those consequences altogether," but she stopped herself. When Nova got an idea in her head, she was stubborn. There was no changing her mind. Tessa had been proud of this trait when it first reared its head in kindergarten. She'd said to herself, "My girl has a backbone. She will not be weak and bend to peer pressure." Now into her teenage years, the hard-headedness backfired, and the trait had morphed into challenging authority. It took everything in Tessa to let it go.

"Okay, but if you're missing something we could have brought from home and we have to buy a replacement, I am going to take the money out of your savings."

"Fine," Nova answered, her shoulders set.

"Okay. That's a wrap. One more sleep before we hit the open road," Tessa said. "Are you ready?"

"As ready as I'll ever be."

Part 2

Chapter Twelve

Tessa rose the next morning when it was still dark. She brewed a cup of coffee and went over the myriad of checklists that covered the countertops while she sipped at it. A sleepy Nova joined her in the kitchen when she was making sandwiches for the drive down.

"Ham and cheese or turkey?" she asked.

"Ham," Nova answered, pouring a bowl of cereal.

An hour later, they packed up the Jeep and were ready to hit the open road. After running through her mental checklist one more time, she pulled away from the townhouse and, as it grew smaller in her rearview mirror, felt her mood lift. The townhouse held so many broken promises and had become a monument to her failing relationship with Jason and the strained one with her daughter. To drive away from it and put proper distance between her failures and her heart energized Tessa. She reached over and turned on her playlist, and Nova groaned. It was filled with late 80s and early 90s hits.

"Driver's choice. You can play yours when you drive," Tessa offered.

"Fine." Nova reclined her seat back in the Jeep and put her feet up on the dash.

"Don't do that, honey," she cautioned. "If we get in an accident, you could be paralyzed for life."

"You worry too much."

"Probably, but let's not tempt fate, huh?"

"Okay. Whatever makes you feel better." Nova pulled her pillow out from the pile in the back and snuggled up to the window, closing her eyes to drift to sleep. The miles spooled out as Tessa drove the Jeep down highways, led by her navigation app, with the cruise control set at a habitual nine miles over the speed limit. The phrase "nine you're fine, ten you're mine" was deeply ingrained from her own driving lessons with her father over twenty years ago.

At noon, they stopped for gas and a bathroom break when Tessa was close to bursting from her morning coffee. Nova went inside while she pumped gas. Once Tessa used the facilities, thankful they were mostly clean, she walked back out to see Nova leaning against the driver's side of the Jeep.

"Can I drive?"

"Ah…" Tessa hesitated.

"Come on, Mom, you promised." It was true, she did. Keeping promises to her daughter was important to Tessa because Donny never did. With a heavy sigh, she agreed and reluctantly handed over the keys.

Tessa walked to the passenger side of the Jeep and got settled in while Nova adjusted the mirrors. She crossed the seatbelt across her chest and slowly eased her way from the pump and onto the road leading back to the highway.

"Get in the other lane," Tessa advised as Nova turned on her turn signal.

Another car was in her blind spot, making Tessa's heartbeat accelerate.

"Look out."

"Mom. I *know*. I see it." Nova hit the gas and darted around the car, then made a right-hand turn and sped up to highway speed on the ramp. She shot past the speed limit as she merged into traffic.

"Slow down," Tessa urged. "You're still on a conditional license."

"I know," Nova muttered as she veered into traffic, pressing the gas pedal down. A few seconds later, she made a lane change without checking the blind spot and was rewarded with the powerful blast of a horn from a car that zoomed by and made them both anxious.

"Nova! You must check your blind spot *every* time. You could have caused an accident."

Nova refused to respond and focused on the road straight ahead, and Tessa could feel the tension building. Her daughter gripped the steering wheel with white knuckles and her lips were set in a hard line. For the next several miles, Tessa was hyper-attentive to every turn and lane change Nova made, glancing back and forth over her shoulders and leaning closer to see the traffic behind them blocking Nova's view of the mirror. Her body was actively engaged in the physical actions of driving, without actually doing it.

They sped down the highway while Tessa barked out a litany of corrections, "Hit the gas!"

"Slow down!"

"You gotta go!"

Every suggestion increased the apprehension in the car until Nova finally had enough and turned on the right turn signal and started to brake.

"What are you doing?" Tessa's voice was edged with frustration. "You can't slow down on the interstate! Most accidents happen when cars are going *too* slow."

Nova's expression was stony as she continued to decelerate before finally pulling the car off on the shoulder. She shifted the Jeep into park and crossed her arms in an angsty huff.

"Why did you stop?" Tessa asked. "We need to keep moving so we can make good time."

"I can't drive when you're micromanaging me."

"Well, someone has to make sure we arrive alive." Tessa leaned on the sarcasm that Nova preferred, hoping it would make her smile. It didn't, and she continued trying to make jokes that didn't land. "Have you learned nothing from Alanis Morrisette? We can't die on the way to our vacation. It's too ironic." She forced a laugh, and Nova shot her a glare.

"Seriously, stop. You can't control everything or every outcome. You have to learn to trust me."

"I *do* trust you," Tessa lied.

Nova's eye roll was epic. "You and I both know that's not the truth. I knew this was a bad idea."

She yanked the keys from the ignition and dropped them in her mother's hand. Then she swung open the door and exited the vehicle, refusing to make eye contact when she crossed paths with Tessa, who reclaimed the driver's seat. Guilt settled in as Tessa readjusted the mirrors and then merged smoothly back out into traffic. Nova reclined her seat again and turned away, then put in her ear buds and zoned out.

Tessa was filled with remorse, stealing glances at her daughter's back. She exhaled the frustration she felt with herself. Nova was right. She couldn't relax and let go of control. Tessa had spent the lion's share of Nova's childhood strictly supervising every aspect of her child's life. Now that she had almost completed her mission and the finish line was in sight, she was paralyzed with fear at the idea of relinquishing control.

Tessa spent her life consumed with planning and preparing for the worst-case scenario. It was a coping mechanism she'd developed early after losing her mom, but now she could see it was getting in her way with Nova. Driving down the highway, she wondered, what if all her micromanaging was time and energy wasted? Did one ounce of her planning really save anyone from danger in the long run? Or would they have still landed right where they were, regardless? The answer was shrouded in a sense of profound loss she wasn't ready to accept yet, so she pushed it away.

Tessa listened to music for the remainder of the drive while Nova slept in the seat next to her. Nearing dinner time, she pulled off the interstate and drove the two-lane road that led toward Clarksville, Tennessee. She felt relief rush in when the day's twelve-hour drive was finally coming to an end.

The constant stop-and-go traffic woke Nova, and she pulled the lever to pop the seat upright and looked around with a yawn and a stretch. There was a formidable brown concrete wall on their right that enclosed the Fort Campbell Army Base. The street they drove down followed along the wall as the acres of the Army base stretched out for miles.

"Jason was stationed here," Tessa said to make conversation as they continued to drive down the road further into Clarksville. Traffic lights stopped them at every intersection and made the last few miles drag on forever. On the left-hand side of the road, for the next several miles, there was a tattoo parlor, strip club, and Army surplus store on every block. The shops were so repetitive that even Nova sat up and took notice.

"What's with all the strip clubs around here?" she asked.

"Well, Fort Campbell is filled with soldiers who are away from their wives and loved ones. I guess they want to see boobs when they get a little leisure time," Tessa answered truthfully, the way she always preferred to answer, even if it was uncomfortable.

Nova considered the comment and, knowing Jason had spent eight years in the Army, she asked, "Does Jason have any tattoos?"

"No," Tessa answered. "But he was stationed here in the nineties for almost two years."

"Well, I guess we both know where he spent his free time," Nova joked, her eyebrows waggling with glee at the alleged salacious infractions of an authority figure.

"Maybe. I guess I can't really blame the guy," Tessa tossed back with a shrug. "But Jason said he worked constantly at Fort Campbell. The Army didn't give him much R&R when he was stationed here."

"Yeah, he worked on seeing those boobies!" Nova snorted and punched an imaginary speed bag with her tightened fist, an over-the-top comedy routine that made Tessa laugh.

They passed a huge military cemetery. Right before they crossed the plane of it, she heard Nova suck in a huge inhale and then hold her breath.

"Some things never change," Tessa remarked, remembering the first time she'd witnessed Nova's superstitious act. When Tessa asked for an explanation, a kindergarten Nova replied, "If you don't hold your breath, then the ghosts will get jealous." They were still coasting by the cemetery. It went on for almost three city blocks, making Nova's cheeks pink up from lack of oxygen.

"Hey, Nova," Tessa began, pointing over at the cemetery. "Did you know? Everyone is dying to get in there."

Nova sputtered as her breath exhaled, then groaned. "That sounds like something Papa would say, and now thanks to you, I'm going to be haunted forever by jealous ghosts."

"You'll be fine." Tessa laughed. "You know, when I was in my twenties, I worked at Papa's office, and across the street was a cemetery. Any time a funeral procession would pull up, he'd say, "Looks like they are gonna go plant one today."

Nova burst out laughing.

"I know, right? Totally inappropriate." Tessa smiled at the memory. "Sarcasm *is* the language of our people, but at least you come by it honestly."

Getting close to dinner time, Tessa asked, "Are you hungry?"

"I could eat."

Tessa pulled her phone from the console and handed it over to Nova. "Open the TripAdvisor app and find us a good place to try. One rule—no chains and no restaurants we have back home."

Nova settled in to scroll for a long while before saying, "Liberty Park Grill has a great patio overlooking a pond and a pier."

"That sounds promising. Look at their menu and read a couple of reviews."

A few minutes later, Nova said, "It has a pretty decent strawberry salad for you, but I have my eye on the mac and cheeseburger."

"Works for me. Can you add it to the navigation?" Nova changed the route, then placed the phone back on the console. A few minutes later, Tessa was grateful to pull into the parking lot at the Liberty Park Grill. After a long day of driving with only two stops to fuel up, her joints creaked from disuse when she got out of the Jeep. She stretched her back, pulling her shoulder blades together and lacing her fingers behind her hips. Her toes were tingling from driving too long and being too cramped in the tight confines of the Jeep.

At the hostess stand, Tessa gave a sweet teenager her phone number to text when their table was ready, and she pulled Nova in for a forced side hug. "Let's go stretch our legs a bit while we wait."

Liberty Park Grill overlooked a marina that was filled with slips for luxury boats. It was nestled into a beautiful hilly park with a stone walking bridge and trails that connected the park to the marina. The sun felt warm on her shoulders as Tessa walked with Nova in companionable silence, noticing it was the first time they'd walked together in a while. She was grateful that even after their driving spat hours earlier, Nova set aside her normal desire for isolation and indulged Tessa's request without whining.

"What have you been watching lately?" Tessa asked, keeping the topics light.

"I'm kind of obsessed with Bailey Sarian right now. She's got a Murder, Mystery, and Makeup Monday Show on YouTube."

"That's an odd combination."

"You'd think so, but it works. She's got almost seven million subscribers," Nova stated as evidence of her massive success.

"I weep for this generation," Tessa quipped, then asked, "What's it about?" She was always curious about Nova's interests, searching for clues to understand her daughter better. When Nova became a teenager, the task turned much more difficult. She felt like she'd been given half of a map written in a foreign language.

"She tells you the gory details of a true crime case while you watch her create a dramatic makeup look."

"Seven million people want to watch that?"

"Yep," Nova declared and continued walking.

"Why are you so attracted to the strange and unusual?" Tessa asked, wanting to understand what piqued Nova's curiosity.

"Because I, myself, *am* strange and unusual," Nova enthused with a dramatic voice, giving Tessa a twinge of déjà vu. The answer was just outside her reach but then came rushing back.

"Beetlejuice! Beetlejuice! Beetlejuice!" Tessa sang out. "Good one!"

"You are correct!" Nova confirmed. It was a game they'd played since Nova was little, singing song lyrics and quoting movie lines to each other as answers to questions in the middle of their everyday life. She couldn't remember the last time the mood had been light enough for them to play it.

They walked past the covered patio, whose twinkling lights had just come on as the sun dipped below the horizon line and cast pinks and oranges into the clouds that dotted the sky. Nova skipped ahead down a long staircase to the water where boats sat in slips. The dock was new but covered in spiderwebs, and the water spilling out underneath it was a murky brown, obscuring the view. Nova leaned over the dock, scanning the depths of the water below when a huge carp spawned up and flopped back down, eliciting a scared yelp from her. She ran back and grabbed her mother's arm.

"Don't worry, honey, I'll save you from the big, bad fish." Tessa laughed.

"That was terrifying," Nova said. "Did you see the size of his lips?"

Tessa laughed at the melodramatic words teenagers preferred, knowing she'd been just as guilty of using them herself. Life had a way of numbing you down and mellowing you out. By the time you were forty, you were jaded and apathetic, and the size of fish lips was the least of your concerns.

At her hip, the phone vibrated.

"Looks like our table is ready."

They climbed back up the steps and entered the restaurant, asking to be seated on the large patio to enjoy the evening sky. On wooden chairs, flocks of birds that swooped in and out entertained them, dive bombing for wayward French fries toddlers flung to the ground. A server walked by, a tall teenage boy with long wavy hair and shirt cuffs that were rolled to the elbows that revealed his tattooed forearms.

"I think I love that man," Nova blurted and Tessa laughed.

"You fall in love a million times a day."

"I'm a teenager. That's what we're supposed to do."

Nova had a point. Tessa remembered what it was like being a teenager when going to a new place meant the possibility of finding a new crush. That thrill in your belly at the mere hint of attraction. The last time she'd felt those butterflies was when she met Jason.

Jason. A dart to her heart. She'd been trying to give him the space he asked for but also needed to listen to her own heart that craved clarity. She was looking forward to the time and space to really evaluate what she wanted without taking into consideration all the other factors that made her head spin. Tessa was resolved to leave Tennessee with a decision made.

"Can I get a root beer?" Nova interrupted her side-tracked mind.

Tessa wasn't a fan of soft drinks in general, and her first instinct was to say no, but she fought it.

"Why not?" she relented, and Nova let out a little whoop of joy.

As foretold by her daughter, Tessa ordered the straw-berry and spinach salad, and Nova, who'd never met a carb she didn't adore, went all in on a decadent cheeseburger with a macaroni and cheese bun and a side of French fries.

When their food was brought to the table, she swiped a few of Nova's fries and dug into her salad. "We'll get some rest and then get up in the morning and head to our first treehouse."

"Can't wait," Nova deadpanned, and Tessa wished she really meant it.

Chapter Thirteen

"How about a podcast?" Nova asked. After a greasy but delicious Waffle House breakfast and a pit stop at a county park to kill time, they were now only ninety minutes from their destination. In an effort to build a bridge and soften the hurt feelings from yesterday, she let Nova put on her playlist for the last leg of their journey. It was an eclectic blend of show tunes, grunge bands, and classic rock.

"Sure," Tessa agreed. She couldn't bear another rousing rendition of "Look Down" from Les Misérables. The first time, Nova performed it hysterically, lowering the register of her voice to the basement, her usual soprano becoming an out-of-range low bass that made Tessa chuckle. And then she went on to play it six... more... times.

"If I have to hear *Look Down* one more time today, I might drive us straight into oncoming traffic to end the suffering," Tessa admitted with a smirk. Nova couldn't help herself and started singing it again as Tessa groaned and covered her ears with her free hand and a shoulder, contorting her body to protect it from the assault of the now-offensive Broadway hit. "Find a podcast now, dealer's choice," Tessa ordered.

Nova scrolled through the options while Tessa drove them deeper into the woods. The Airbnb host had given Tessa coordinates instead of an address.

"Look at that!" she'd exclaimed. "They gave us longitude and latitude instead of a street address. How's that for adventurous?"

"Yeah, Mom, we're practically Robin Crusoes," Nova offered, as she continued to scroll through the podcast selections.

"Uh, it's Robin-*son* Crusoes," Tessa corrected. "Though I hope there aren't any cannibals on this island." She looked down at her long, thick legs. Not the powerhouse they once were, but respectable. "You're the one who needs to worry, Nove. You're the human equivalent of veal. Since you spend so much time lying around all day on your phone, your flesh would be far more tender than mine," she explained with a wink.

Nova's eyebrows shot up and her lips pulled tight. "Hey!"

"I'm kidding," Tessa admitted. "Just getting your goat."

"You and the farm animal references. It's so tragic," Nova replied as she scrolled and scrolled.

"Just pick one!" Tessa cried as she reached over and turned down the volume on the first few notes of "Look Down" that were cueing up again from the show tune that was on repeat. "My ears are bleeding."

"It's got to be the *right* one. I feel like I only have one chance to introduce you properly to the true crime movement," Nova said. As she pondered the choice, it overjoyed Tessa to finally hear, "Found it." She connected her phone to Bluetooth and turned up the volume as the buttery vocal stylings of Keith Morrison spooled out the teaser of Dateline's *"The Thing About Pam."*

Tessa focused on the story of deceit, lies, and murder as she followed the GPS's instructions. She turned off the interstate onto a curvy single-lane road thirty minutes from their final destination. Her fingers gripped the steering wheel and her foot hit the gas, trying to keep up with the 45 MPH posted speed limit that made anxiety flutter in her belly. She wasn't used to driving on roads that had no shoulders and where you couldn't see the path over ten yards ahead. The drive was a roller coaster that cued up a combination of panic and anticipated fear in her gut. She glanced in the rear-view mirror, noticing a pick-up truck closing in on her and eventually tailgating behind them.

"Is that a confederate flag?" Nova asked, glancing behind her out the rear window where a red flag on a pole was jammed into the tailgate of the truck and flitting in the breeze.

"I'm afraid so," Tessa confirmed, and she pressed harder on the gas pedal, desperate to put distance between her Jeep and the truck, but it wasn't working. The faster she went, the closer they followed. "I hope they turn off at the intersection coming up," Tessa admitted as she continued to snatch glances at them, rearing closer, the podcast increasing her uneasiness. She considered pulling over to let them pass, but there was no shoulder.

"This is how we die. They follow us to the end of a gravel road where there are no witnesses and then bury us in shallow graves." Nova's overactive imagination cranked up and spooled out the horrific tale of their eminent demise as Tessa continued to swerve deeper into the backwoods of Tennessee.

The sight of a second confederate flag flying proudly on a house silenced Nova's further description of the more lurid details. Tessa reached over and locked the door, the reassuring metallic *thunk* of the lock not giving her the peace of mind she hoped it would.

"Don't worry about it. We're driving in broad daylight, and besides, I think we're almost there," Tessa said, not sure if she was trying to calm herself down or Nova. After a tense twenty minutes, she was relieved when the truck made a left-hand turn and disappeared. She let the breath she'd been holding for miles escape in one long, hot exhale.

Stopped at a stop sign, Tessa looked down at the GPS, directing her to make a right turn. When she glanced at the road she'd be turning on, trepidation seized her belly. It was a narrow gravel road that was a straight shot up. The kind of road her Jeep had never traveled on back home, in the pancake-flat plains of Nebraska. She bit the inside of her lip and said a little prayer that her Jeep could make the journey up. It wasn't a 4x4 and was useless in the winters as slick roads seemed to be its Kryptonite. Not having a choice and motivated to get to the end of this long journey, she pressed the gas pedal to the floor to start up the road. Almost instantly, the wheels started to spin out on the gravel.

"We are not getting stuck here," Tessa said out loud and reached forward to turn off the podcast.

"Hey!" Nova protested.

"I need to concentrate," she barked back with enough roughness that Nova let it go. "We're almost there, but this part is nerve-racking." The road narrowed down to one lane that traveled up the side of a mountain in a tunnel of trees. The branches hit the top of the Jeep as she barreled up it, afraid to go too slowly and get stuck.

"We have no choice but to keep going forward," Tessa said. "I need you to be my eyes. I can't take them off the road." Nova picked up the phone and started calling out the turns. Going deeper into the woods of the rural forest that swallowed them, Tessa briefly wondered what would happen if the GPS was wrong.

"Google, don't fail us now," she muttered under her breath. "Let me see the screen."

Nova turned the phone and Tessa was relieved to see the little flag getting closer with each passing minute. The last miles seemed to drag on endlessly because she couldn't drive faster than twenty miles an hour. When the hand-carved sign appeared on a split-rail fence that said, "GlampVentures," she rejoiced.

With a deep sigh to release the built-up tension, Tessa got out of the Jeep, grateful for a respite from the curvy hills as their hosts walked out of their home to welcome them with huge smiles.

"You made it," Kristin said, her voice dripping with the sweet tang of southern hospitality.

"Barely." Tessa laughed as she opened the trunk to fish out their suitcases and coolers.

"We have to take you up to the campsite in this," Anthony said. Tessa glanced over at a windowless, black, off-road 4x4 Jeep and the road next to it that started out with such a steep incline she doubted any other vehicle could handle it. Anthony grabbed the heavy bags, and they made quick work of settling all their luggage and supplies into the back of the 4x4.

Using the bar, Tessa hoisted herself into the passenger seat, and Anthony backed up and began to traverse up the steepest gravel road she'd ever been on. Only going five miles an hour, it lurched and jockeyed them up the hilly terrain while hot bursts of air and the occasional bug hit their faces.

"It's like riding a rollercoaster," Tessa mused. "I've never gone off-roading like this before." She was in awe as Anthony shifted into deeper gears, navigating the one-way road up to their campsite.

"We actually had to put these roads in ourselves," he offered, and Tessa believed him, looking down into the tree-covered ravine that was a steep drop-off just inches from the narrow road they were on as the vehicle rocked and rolled up the hill.

"My dad is totally off the grid," Anthony said with pride. "He has one bill under $400 for propane for the year, and that is it."

"Wow. That's incredible," Tessa said. Off the grid, a lifestyle she'd always thought was fascinating and a total departure from the fast-paced life they were living. She got a peek of the gorgeous sky through the trees as the Jeep climbed up higher. "The view!" she exclaimed, astonished.

"Oh, just wait," Kristin said with a secret smile.

They climbed the final hill on the seventeen-acre property, and then he rolled the Jeep down to a stop in front of a thick strap that spanned the clearing and parked. Tessa and Nova climbed out of the Jeep and took their first few steps out onto the land. The view was absolutely spectacular.

"You don't call this campsite Hellavue for nothing!" Tessa said, taking it all in. Off the ground about five feet, a suspended tree tent overlooked a thirty-foot opening flanked by old-growth trees and forest. Below was a calm river and beyond were the faint gradient blue hues of seven different mountain ranges in the distance. Directly across from the campsite was a stunning pastoral view of a farm, where little bales of hay, appearing barely a quarter of an inch in size, dotted the hills. A train blasted its horn twice across the way, the only evidence of civilization. It was breathtaking.

The tent was floating off the ground, tethered to a triangular patch of trees with bright orange ratchet straps.

"How do you get in it?' Tessa asked, anxiously avoiding getting too close to the steep drop-off. Next to her, Nova was quiet as she often was in front of strangers.

Kristin ducked under the tent and, at the center, unzipped three zippers and said, "You can climb up using the picnic table." She demonstrated by climbing on the table, and her head disappeared inside the tent. A minute later, she popped back down to the ground with a grin.

Anthony unpacked the rest of their bags and the coolers. He pulled out a lighter and showed Tessa how to light the propane camp stove. "You can make coffee on this or cook on it." At one end of the picnic table was a five-gallon container of water with a battery-operated spout. "Just wave your hands in front." He demonstrated, and a trickle of water came out of the spigot and the overflow was caught in a galvanized metal tub.

"Everything you need is right here," Kristin said as she patted several see-through tubs. She pulled out two hand-made satchels of coffee and handed them to Tessa. "It's fresh Starbucks I ground this morning."

"You're a lifesaver," Tessa said, tucking them into one of the tubs.

Facing the view was a comfortable outdoor loveseat with a soft cushion. To the right and nestled into the side of the mountain sat the fire ring with a cooking rack and a pair of Adirondack chairs. For a little extra money, they had provided firewood and kindling and had it all laid out and ready to use.

"If you need more firewood, you just let us know," Anthony offered, then led them a few feet further to the right where a small cabin was nestled into the trees with a pad of gray gravel underneath it.

"If it rains, there's a futon you can sleep on in here," Kristin mentioned as she opened the wooden door to the little cabin. "It will keep you dry." Tessa and Nova followed her inside. The cabin was about eight feet wide by ten feet long and housed a composting toilet and another five-gallon pitcher of water and a collection bin. In more tubs, fluffy white towels were rolled into a neat pile and another container held bug spray, soaps, shampoo, and conditioner.

"Have y'all ever used a composting toilet before?" Anthony asked.

Nova, who hadn't been paying close attention, was now all ears.

"After you do your business, you're going to want to pull the little door out slowly to flush, or you might have unexpected results." He delivered the advice with a knowing smile.

Tessa glanced over and noticed Nova's eyes were wide and her nose was wrinkled in disgust. "Duly noted," Tessa said, suppressing a smile. Glancing around, she was amazed. "You've truly thought of everything!" They walked back outside, and Nova pointed to a big black bag tethered high to the side of the cabin.

"What's that?"

"It's a solar shower," Anthony explained. He stood under it and whipped the shower curtain around a half-moon track, disappearing behind it.

"Outside?" Nova was in shock, her jaw almost hitting the gravel underneath them.

"You have total privacy up here," Anthony assured to set her mind at ease as he tugged the curtain back in place. "Besides you two, there are only two other couples on the property. But the sites are so far away from each other you're not going to even know they're here." It was supposed to put Nova at ease, but Tessa realized it had the opposite effect when she thrust her fingernails into her mouth and chewed.

"There are solar lights all around the tent that will come on automatically at dusk," Kristin explained and then pulled out a small battery-operated lantern and showed Nova how to turn it on.

"Before I forget, we'd like to go kayaking tomorrow," Tessa mentioned.

"Great, just send us a text when you're ready to go and we'll take you out."

Anthony handed her a DeWalt USB speaker. "Just so you can keep your phones charged. It should last the entire stay, but if not, just send us a text and we'll bring you a fresh battery."

It was a relief. After the nail-biting journey it took to get up the mountain to the campsite, Tessa knew they could not easily navigate the road back down in the event of an emergency. Even Nova seemed to relax more fully in its presence.

"Okay, I think that is everything. If you run into trouble or need anything at all, just send a text," Kristin said. "Hope y'all have a great time." They climbed back into the Jeep and started the descent back to their home at the bottom of the mountain.

Not sure what to do, Tessa noticed underfoot was powdered sawdust, which was a surprisingly soft, natural carpet. She pulled her sandals off as Nova disappeared into the little house, emerging triumphantly with a hammock that she strung between two stumps. Facing the view, Nova nestled her body inside and wrapped the black neoprene around herself while Tessa pulled out a coloring book and pencils and claimed the end of the loveseat after dragging it several feet back from the edge of the cliff that went straight down.

Friendly squirrels darted up trees and watched them from their perch higher in the branches. All the sounds of modern life, the traffic, and the people were gone.

"It feels like we're the only two people left in the world," Tessa mused, appreciating the silence. A few leisurely hours passed as Tessa colored and Nova took a nap in the hammock. Unplugging felt foreign at first; the awkwardness of not having a rigorous schedule to adhere to took an adjustment. The only item on their agenda that evening was dinner, and the luxury of wallowing in nothingness was decadent.

"Want to help me start the fire so we can make dinner?" she asked when Nova finally stirred. With a nod, she crawled out of the hammock and moved over to the fire ring. Tessa struggled to build a teepee of wood that kept collapsing on itself. Finally successful, she used the fire starter and kindling to light it. On three separate occasions, the flame smoldered and then went out.

"You're not very good at this," Nova remarked with a smirk.

"It's been a while," Tessa admitted, refusing to give up on the tiny flame that was fighting to grow into something more substantial. She peeled apart another loose twig, feeding the fire dry bark to build on, and blew air gently to fan the flame. After several minutes of coaxing, the orange flame grew and licked at the logs impatiently.

Finding success, Tessa stood in front of the fire and shouted out in a loud, low, theatrical voice, waving her hands up in the air, "Look at what I have created! I have made fire!"

Across from her, Nova concentrated, "That Tom Hanks movie with the face on the volleyball you made me watch." She snapped her fingers together, and her forehead knit while she concentrated harder. "I can't think of the name of it."

"Castaway!" Tessa answered. "Close enough."

They watched the fire strengthen and added another log.

"Are you hungry?"

"Starved," Nova admitted.

Tessa walked over to the cold cooler resting on the

ground by the picnic table and pulled out the steak bites. Using tin foil, she assembled a packet of potatoes, adding knobs of pale yellow butter and sprinkles of salt and pepper. Being just superstitious enough, she tossed a pinch over her shoulder for luck, then carried the food back to the fire. Using the tongs provided, she swiveled the grill rack that was attached to the fire pit closer to the flame.

"Want to listen to more of my boy, Keith?" Nova asked. They were deep into the podcast about Pam Hupp's outrageous plan to murder her best friend and frame her husband.

"How about a compromise? We'll listen to the podcast while we're cooking, but I want us to have some quiet time, too," Tessa reasoned while she placed the foil packet on the grilling rack. The butter sputtered and sizzled inside it as her stomach growled again.

"Fine," Nova agreed and brought over the speaker. Twenty minutes later, Tessa added a couple more logs and added the steak bites to the grill. The instant sear was satisfying, and the caramelized soy and Worcestershire sauce made her stomach rumble. The steak bites cooked quickly in the scorching heat and, using the tongs, she pulled them off and deposited the fire roasted meat on plates. She picked up a chunk with her fingers and popped it into her mouth.

"This is so good," Tessa groaned.

Even Nova had to agree. They devoured the rest of the steak bites and the piping hot potatoes while Keith Morrison led them deeper into the pit of Pam's insanity.

"Let's try the candied bacon S'mores tonight," Tessa decided and walked back to the cooler to gather the ingredients. She pulled apart four slices of raw bacon, laid them on another sheet of foil, and then sprinkled on the brown sugar and cayenne mixture she'd had the foresight to pack in the cooler before they left.

Four pieces of candied bacon sizzled away on the fire as Nova roasted marshmallows and Tessa assembled chocolate squares and graham crackers.

With the ambient temperature in the eighties and the proximity to the fire, the chocolate squares softened quickly. Combining the ingredients together, the hot bacon made the chocolate melt into a shiny pool, and the toasted marshmallow became glue, holding it all together. Tessa took a big bite and groaned in delight.

"Oh my gosh. This is amazing," she gushed with her cheeks stuffed like the squirrel that darted up the tree earlier. "Sweet and savory is my jam." She took another bite, and the soft chocolate and bacon married together in her mouth, earning another moan of pleasure.

"Jeez, Mom, do you need to be alone with that?"

"Maybe." Tessa smiled. "It's that good. What do *you* think?"

"I like the classic version better."

"You're dead to me." Tessa waved off her opinion with a grin, then settled back into the chair, her muscles sore from driving, totally content. A few hours later, the sun began to set. The clouds looked like cotton candy, close enough to almost touch. Pink-tinged light washed the trunks of trees in the forest surrounding them. Across the river, golden light outlined every object, illuminating worn barns and fuzzy hay bales. It covered the landscape with the hazy romantic filter photographers called 'golden hour'. To enjoy it more fully, Tessa folded herself into the empty hammock. It cradled her as it rocked side to side, and she watched a spider feverishly spinning while the last few precious minutes before sunset sped by.

"Look at that, Nova," she exclaimed. "Talk about work ethic."

Nova rolled her eyes. "You and your work ethic. We're on vacation. Besides, she's working her little spidery legs to the bone when we both know tomorrow morning all her work will be destroyed."

Tessa laughed at her pragmatic view of the world. Nova oscillated between cutting cynicism and dramatics, as most teenagers do.

"Just because it's going to be destroyed tomorrow doesn't mean it wasn't worth the effort," Tessa said.

"I know what you're doing," Nova accused as she sat on the picnic table and colored with her pencil set.

"What?"

"You're trying to brainwash me with inspirational life lessons."

Tessa chuckled. She was busted. "Maybe," she admitted, "but is it working?"

"No," Nova answered.

Darkness fell, and they finally climbed into the tree tent. Inside it, all the bedding was rolled up in a pile in a corner. They spread out the egg crate mats, blankets, and pillows and folded themselves into the mat like a taco, as Kristen suggested. Lying on her side, Tessa peeked out through the mesh window of the tent, and a bird flew so close, she felt the whisper of its wings brush her cheek. She closed her eyes, listening to the soundtrack of the forest. There were birds chirping and some splashes from the lake below. The tree tent was more comfortable than she'd ever imagined. It was like sleeping in a flattened hammock as the wind gently rocked them to dreamland.

As the night shift began, she could hear rambunctious critters scurrying on the ground underneath them. A few minutes later, exhausted from the physicality of the day, she drifted off to sleep as the waxing moon rose on the other side of the lake.

Chapter Fourteen

Tessa's eyes fluttered open as the first peach-colored streaks shot up over the horizon. The air was chilly, and she shivered, then stretched her long legs out in the tent, plotting her next move. The tent gently swayed as she glanced over at Nova, still asleep. Her daughter's face was softened in slumber and was more relaxed than she'd seen it in ages.

When Nova was an infant, Tessa would slip back into the nursery long after she was passed out—milk drunk from a late-night feeding—and just marvel at her daughter. Tessa would reach down and brush the baby-soft hairs from her velvety forehead, and the tenderness of the moment would crush her with its intensity. Memorizing the curve of her ear and the swell of her tiny chin, knowing she would never feel love this perfect and pure again, and it was true. She'd never felt its equal.

Rocking in the gentle wind, Tessa watched Nova sleep for a bit as the rising sun revealed more and more of her daughter's face. The smattering of freckles across her cheeks and nose. Her long, strawberry blonde eyelashes were free from their usual gothic assault from a coal black mascara wand. She felt the same tug on her heartstrings that she'd felt in the nursery so many years ago, but now, the passage of time made the moment more poignant. She hadn't known how fast those years would speed by, or the full tilt-a-whirl sensation that would accompany them.

Before Nova could awaken and declare her creepy for watching her sleep, Tessa tore herself away, quietly unzipped the tent, and shimmied out of it, landing on the picnic table below. In the cool breeze, the tent swayed, and she watched for movement, but Nova didn't stir. In the distance, a woodpecker was already hard at work drilling on a tree, its mechanical *tat-tat-tat* punching through the quiet of the morning. Higher in the trees that surrounded the tree tent, birds were engaging in a song battle. Notes would ring out in the forest, and then a few seconds later, a sing-song response would begin to trill.

Quietly, Tessa filled a tin coffee pitcher with water and then pulled the propane stove off the table and into the center of the open area on top of the gravel. With Nova inside, the tent was hanging so low it would have burst into flames if she'd tried to heat it on the picnic table.

She plunked the homemade sachet of coffee grounds wrapped in a filter in the pot and lit the pilot on the stove, pleased when it crackled right to life. Twenty minutes later, she coaxed weak but drinkable coffee into a mug, sipped on it, and savored the sounds of the forest awakening. Unaware and still groggy, she sat down on the soft loveseat facing the lake, jumping back up quickly when the damp chill hit the back of her thighs. It was covered in morning dew, so she went into the outhouse and brought a towel out to sit on. The sky brightened into a clear blue morning as the sun rose over the hills and began its ascent into the sky.

Being away from home, she didn't feel the need to be productive, to fill the nooks and crannies of her day with tasks to check off. An undercurrent of anticipation hummed through her limbs. The day was rife with possibilities instead of obligations. She couldn't remember when she'd had an entire day where she wasn't rushing to work, providing a taxi service to appointments, or responding to a crisis with Nova. Acknowledging the space for the first time, she felt deep gratitude begin to seep into every corner of her being.

What a gift it was to have the luxury of time away with Nova. Anything could happen on this trip, and there would be moments she was sure would be used as fodder for stories to tell her future grandchildren. "Let me tell you about the time I took your mom to the Smokies…"

A scurry of movement on the forest floor caught her eye, and she scanned the leaves before she located the creature. A tiny brown toad, no bigger than the tip of her pinkie, hopped away. Delicate and precious, it was definitely a sight she hadn't slowed down to see in years. She felt a sense of wonder wash over her in tune with the heartbeat of nature. There were so few places in the world that were naturally beautiful and remained untouched by man's desire for profit and to stand in one was awe-inspiring.

She glanced around the campsite, understanding that they were back to the basics. They would fill their days with simpler tasks, becoming human beings again instead of human doings. She felt the urge to breathe more deeply and slow down as her constricted heart began to gently unwind. It was the respite her frazzled soul desperately craved.

Filled with light and joy, she decided to take a walk up the gravel road they'd come in on. The birds indulged her in an echoing symphony of forest sounds, then she felt the tickle of a silken spider web across her face. Terrified, she let out a yelp and then feverishly brushed the offensive web from her cheeks, praying the spider wasn't already finding its new home on her shoulder. She took a few more steps and encountered more gossamer spider webs streaking across her skin, launching her immediately into Kung Fu mode, karate chopping the surrounding air.

From the tent, she heard Nova's laughter ring out. "Get 'em, Mama!" Tessa turned around briskly and headed back to Nova. "I hope those spiders didn't crawl inside your ears and lay eggs."

The idea made Tessa shake like a wet dog and jiggle a finger in both ears just in case. "Yeah, I wanted to be immersed in nature, but that was a little *too* immersed." She rubbed her hands down her limbs and, finally satisfied the spiders were not taking shelter on her, switched gears to make breakfast.

Grateful to have a simple task to focus on, Tessa set the propane stove up on the picnic table and pulled out four slices of bacon, cooking them over the vibrant blue flame of the camp stove. She sliced up onions and caramelized them, and then added the leftover grilled potatoes and a couple of eggs. She scooped the scramble out onto two plates, and they ate quietly as the sun crept higher in the sky.

"Food tastes better when you eat it outside," Tessa said. "Don't you think?"

Nova shot her a jaded response. "It tastes the same to me."

Around eleven, she sent a message to their hosts to let them know they were ready to go kayaking. Ten minutes later, she could hear the Jeep traveling up the mountain. She packed a cooler with fruit and bottled water.

"Come here." She waved Nova over. "Let me spray you with sunscreen."

"I can do it," Nova said, pulling the bottle from Tessa's hand.

"But you can't get your back," Tessa reasoned, trying to be helpful.

"I got it, Mom." Annoyed, Nova sprayed half the bottle of it into the air around her body and handed it back as Kristin and Anthony pulled up in the Jeep.

"Try the front seat," Tessa encouraged Nova as she hopped in the back with Kristin. The Jeep descended into the woods. It jostled and jockeyed down the steep terrain, meandering down the gravel roads Anthony and his family built by hand. They skidded to a stop near the bottom and followed their hosts out to the waterline. Tessa's feet sunk deep into the mud the closer she got to the shore. Her sandals made a sucking noise as she pulled them out of the black mud and then stepped down again, worried she might lose one. The grainy mud squished between her toes, and a swarm of mosquitos zinged around her blackened feet. Tessa was grateful to immerse them in the water and rinse off.

After a quick lesson from Kristin and Anthony on how to attach the paddles to the kayaks if they just wanted to float, they pushed Tessa and Nova off from the shore.

The oars sliced through the water, and in the distance,

a fish spawned up out of the cloudy depths and belly-flopped back into the lake like a chubby middle schooler on the high dive. Water bugs skittered across the surface of the lake, walking on water like modern-day Jesuses. With the dam open this time of year, water flowed into the Rankin Bottoms Wildlife Refuge. Tessa hummed as she paddled out to the island as tufts of grass waved in the wind. The sky was overcast, and the air was pregnant with the kind of humidity Tennessee is famous for.

Known for its bird-watching, the refuge didn't disappoint. A gray egret pumped its powerful wings, then landed on a patch of land fifty feet ahead of Tessa. A white crane joined him after it looped in wide, graceful circles, its mile-high legs gracefully holding up its delicate feathered body. Tessa paddled further and then glanced behind her, noticing Nova had already given up on the exercise portion of their day. She floated in her kayak as Tessa continued to close in on the birds. The lake was filled with fluffy seed pods floating on the smooth surface. Startling her, a crash echoed from the woods, and Tessa darted her eyes closer to the source of the noise, surprised to see a fawn bounding up and down like a carousel horse through the dense foliage on the island.

Tessa was always most at home on the water. She rowed back to Nova, and they kayaked together, rocking hard when a boat passed and the waves were higher in their wake.

"Isn't this awesome?" Tessa asked.

"Yeah. It's great," Nova deadpanned, reaching down to swat a mosquito away. Tessa always knew it would be harder to convince Nova that nature deserved more attention than her phone did, but she would never stop trying.

They paddled for a few more hours, tied themselves together to eat the pineapple she'd brought, and then paddled back to the dock. Anthony helped them beach the kayaks and then drove them back to the campsite.

Once there, Tessa asked Nova, "How about a shower?"

"No freaking way," she blurted, fully understanding it would require her to be naked as a jaybird outside.

"Come on," Tessa cajoled. "You have to try. It's part of the experience. It's an *adventure*."

"Absolutely not," she replied, heading back to the hammock. "I'll sleep in my filth tonight, but knock yourself out."

"Fine." Tessa grabbed a towel and the body wash, stripped off her sweaty clothing and shoes, and then gingerly stepped onto the gravel base under the shower. The sharp stones dug into her tender feet as she yanked the shower curtain in a circle around her and popped up the spigot to release the water. Though the water was warm, it only came out as a trickle. A burst of cool wind caught the shower curtain, and it stuck to Tessa's wet legs. She shut the spigot and scrubbed her body, battling the clammy shower curtain, finally giving up totally and yanking it open to shower boldly in the nude.

"Nova, whatever you do, don't look over here. You'll be scarred for life," she bellowed out as she rinsed off as quickly as possible. She dried off and dressed in fresh clothing, grateful the camp shower experience was over.

"I would give that three stars," Tessa offered as she walked closer to Nova. "It works in a pinch, but I've become soft and dependent on luxuries like plentiful warm water, good pressure, and the ability to stand comfortably in the stream of it."

She pulled out hotdogs from the cooler. "How about some lips and assholes?" Tessa joked.

"What?" Nova was confused.

"From *The Great Outdoors*. Dan Aykroyd?" Still not registering, she muttered, "Man, I have failed you as a mother." She busied herself pulling out buns, condiments, and a bag of potato chips.

"Nova, grab the roasting sticks," she called over her shoulder as she carried supplies to the pit. They gathered around the campfire ring, this time practically pros at lighting it and getting the twigs and kindling assembled into the teepee form. Minutes later, they grilled hotdogs until they were charred and then slathered them in mustard.

"I hate hot dogs," Tessa admitted, "but when you grill one on an open flame, they hit differently."

Nova nodded. "Not too bad."

The fire began to dwindle as she got out the fixings for the new S'mores flavor trial.

"Want to try the peanut butter cups version?" Tessa asked.

"Sure," Nova said, spearing a marshmallow on a roasting stick.

"Did you know that there is a tiny percentage of rodent filth and hair inside every peanut butter cup?"

"No way," Nova said, refusing to believe her favorite candy was tainted.

"Think about it. They have to store massive amounts of peanuts in a warehouse to produce them, and rats love peanuts. I don't know if it's true, but I heard that statistic once in biology class in high school and I never forgot it."

"I'll take my chances." Nova smirked, diving in

anyway. She turned on "The Thing About Pam" podcast, and they listened in horror as Pam lied to the police and swindled her best friend's children out of life insurance money for years.

"It's always about life insurance," Tessa mumbled. "Listen, Nova, if you're ever in a relationship and they bring out the papers to increase your death benefit, you need to run."

"Let me guess, another one of your ingenious life lessons?" Nova smirked.

"Yep." She bit into the S'more. The warmth from the marshmallow and the proximity to the fire melted the peanut butter cup. It was gooey and oozing out between the graham crackers and down Tessa's wrist, but she didn't care. It was delicious.

"This is a solid number two," Tessa remarked, enjoying Nova's snicker. "What do you think?"

"Your girl likes to stick to the classics," Nova countered, and Tessa rolled her eyes as she roasted another marshmallow and put together the classic S'more with extra chocolate. It became a melted, dripping mess that dribbled chocolate and strings of marshmallow goo down Nova's chin.

"If you never try new things, you'll never know what's out there," Tessa reasoned. It was more advice that fell on deaf ears.

A few moments later, Nova cried out, "My legs!" Tessa glanced over to see her doughy thighs scissored by a deep red slash of sunburn.

Biting back the "I told you so" that hovered on the tip of her tongue, she threw up her hands and asked, "Seriously, child, how do you miss the *front* of your legs?"

"Practice."

"There's some after-burn lotion in my bag in the cabin," she offered as she leaned back in the chair, listening to Pam Hupp's outrageous crime spree winding down.

"Lotion is for wimps." Nova refused the offer for relief and stubbornly stayed glued to her chair, riveted by Keith Morrison's hypnotic voice or wallowing in typical teenager laziness. Tessa wasn't sure which.

That evening was another spectacular sunset that Tessa claimed in the hammock while Nova continued to color at the picnic table. She took photos as the basic blue was transformed to lavender and peach by the setting sun. The sun lowered and then tucked behind the hills, intensifying the pastel glow. High on the hill, swaying in the hammock, she watched the sky darken and the solar lights turn on at dusk.

Hours later, zipped into the tent, the deep night edged closer to a full moon. Tessa heard the critters become more lively. Below them, she heard the cup she left on the table bounce against the wood and then clatter to the ground.

"What was that?" Nova asked, fear painting her features.

"Sounds like the trash pandas are throwing a wicked rager," Tessa answered. "You know how teenagers can be."

Twenty feet away, they heard the clang of the garbage can hit the dirt. From the trees, it sounded like squirrels were engaged in a game of tag that left the loser squealing and winded.

"Goodnight, sweetheart," Tessa said and rolled over to look out the mesh window, feeling the breeze tickle her face. "Goodnight, moon," she whispered as she relaxed, the two words transporting her back to the little dinosaur lamp on Nova's bedside table when she was two years old. *Goodnight Moon* was Nova's favorite board book for the better part of two years, and the edges of it had become ragged and worn with frequent use. Every night, she'd beg Tessa to read it to her, and when she'd get to the end, Nova would sing out, "Again! Mommy! Again!" And even though Tessa was often exhausted, she'd start over and read it again until Nova's eyes finally fluttered closed and sleep stilled her tiny body that was constantly in motion.

How could that have been over fifteen years ago? Tessa wondered with a yawn, and a few minutes later she heard Nova's breathing deepen and slow. Up in the middle of nowhere, while the sounds of the night serenaded her, the tree tent rocked them to sleep in the gentle breeze. A few minutes later, Tessa dozed off, grateful for the off-grid adventure they'd had at Hellavue.

Chapter Fifteen

T he next morning, they ate an early breakfast, packed up their bags, and called Kristin and Anthony for a ride back down to their Jeep. Nova claimed the front seat again, enjoying the roller coaster ride down the mountain.

"Thank you so much for your hospitality. We had a great time, and the view was just outstanding!" Tessa gushed while Nova started to load their backpacks into the Jeep and Anthony and Kristin helped them repack the coolers.

"Could you take our photo in front of your sign?" Tessa asked, handing her phone over to Kristin. She glanced over at Nova, who tamped down her displeasure at the photo request and hooked her elbow on the sign.

"Be sure to leave us a review on social media," Kristin called out.

"You got it," Tessa agreed, and with a wave, they were back in the Jeep. Tessa set the GPS to Laurel Falls in the Great Smokey Mountain National Park and started the trek back to the highway. It wasn't as scary this time. Instead of narrowing, the roads widened. They made a brief pit stop for gas and ice to refill the coolers that were getting dangerously close to food poisoning temperatures and continued their journey.

From the edge of Newport, Tennessee, a small town that was just a speck on the map, she drove closer to the national park. The roads were still winding and curvy, but she was getting acclimated to them.

"Did you know the Smokey Mountains are the only national park that has never charged an entrance fee?" Tessa rattled off the random fact, making small talk. "They tried to change the law, but the people of Tennessee rebelled. Isn't that cool?"

A bored Nova didn't reply, just continued to gaze out the window.

"*And* the Smokies are by far the most visited national park, with over fourteen million visitors each year."

"That's great, Mom." Nova's tone was blasé.

"That's over *double* the visitors to the Grand Canyon!" Tessa exclaimed. Seeing it was going to take a lot more tantalizing conversation to get a rise out of Nova this early in the morning, she gave up. Traffic slowed to a crawl outside the park entrance, and as they got closer to Laurel Falls, traffic reduced to a bumper-to-bumper trickle.

"Looks like all fourteen million decided to come to Laurel Falls today," Nova mused as Tessa crept through the small parking lots at the trailhead, looking for a spot. Four-wheel-drive Gator off-road vehicles shot by them and popped up over the curb to park on the grassy areas in front of the parking lots.

"Lucky," Nova remarked.

Behind their Jeep, a pack of retired motorcyclists

pulled up, their exhaust pipes roaring like thunder. Frustrated, Tessa circled three more times before she gave up finding decent parking and turned around to go back the way they came. She eventually settled for a pull-out at the bottom of a steep hill almost a mile away from the trailhead. Even then, she had to park illegally.

Forcing on a smile, the first wall of heat hit her square in the jaw when she opened the door. At ten am in June, the air was already oppressive, and the blanket of humidity made the hairs around her face twist and fray. Sweat prickled at her hairline and broke out in beads that tracked down her face. She reached into her bag and pulled out hiking liners and a pair of wool socks and handed them to Nova.

"Put these on. I ordered us special hiking socks so you don't get blisters."

"Nah, I'm good."

"Suit yourself." Tessa sat on the curb and pulled on both pairs of socks and then her well-worn hiking boots. They were the pair she'd owned since college and refused to send to the landfill. The boots were her lucky charm, her wanderlust talisman, and one of her most prized possessions. Trapped in the soles of those boots was organic matter from every adventure she'd ever undertaken. Yellowstone when she graduated from college. Pike's Peak before Nova was born. But her crowning achievement had been scaling Aconcagua in the Andes Mountain Range in Chile when she was nineteen. The years they'd spent in the punishing elements had faded the boots down to a muted gray.

A small part of her longed to be the young woman again who'd purchased them over twenty years ago. The woman who was hungry for adventure and never backed down from a challenge. Time faded the boots, and it had also dampened down her own colors over time. She yearned to reclaim that part of herself. To get back in touch with the woman she was before life intervened. She put her foot inside the boot and it felt like home. Having been broken in for years, molded to fit her feet, they were a comfort.

Finally geared up, she stood and packed two bottles of water and a few cereal bars into her backpack for the journey.

"Ready?" Tessa asked.

"As I'll ever be."

They trudged up the hill to the trailhead in ninety-three-degree heat. Sweat broke out at her neckline and dripped down her back as she followed a long line of people who'd suffered the same parking fate. They followed closely behind a multi-generational family pushing a baby carriage up the gravely and uneven path. It was a straight uphill climb. Tessa's calves burned as the incline was unforgiving and relentless. She was winded, sucking in gulps of air in the scorching sun, relieved when they finally reached the trailhead drenched in sweat from the effort.

"Thank God!" Tessa exclaimed as cooler temperatures prevailed now that they were away from the black asphalt jungle of the main road. She pulled the backpack off her back, pulled out two sweating bottles of water, and offered one to Nova. She chugged half of hers, then put it back, rationing the water. Mentally, she calculated how much they would need to complete the hike to Laurel Falls and back to the car. The climb was all uphill and a challenge to navigate. She glanced over at Nova, who was silent. Neither of them had the energy to speak, breathe, and climb all at the same time.

Something had to give, and it was the delightful banter that took the hit. It was a short hike, only two-point-six miles round trip. Tessa thought it would be a cakewalk and a good one to cut their teeth on, but the first half was the hardest part of the journey.

Laurel Falls was a mecca, drawing enormous crowds of diverse people walking in a single-file line up the mountain. Gasping for air as they continued to climb, Tessa moved to the side to allow the accumulating group of people behind her to pass. It was an elderly couple navigating the climb with ease. Behind them was a woman in an upper body cast, complete with the prop to hold her arm away from her body, and then a pair of young parents with toddlers strapped into massive backpacks.

"If *they* can do it, *we* can do it," Tessa remarked.

Breathing heavily, she stopped to take breaks often, which irritated Nova.

"We'll never be done with this if we have to stop every five minutes."

"The point isn't to be done," Tessa said. "It's always about the journey, not the destination."

"Here we go again, spouting platitudes from motivational posters framed in every therapist's office."

"Could you tone down the attitude a little?" Tessa glanced over at a family who quickly skirted around them, and her cheeks pinked up in embarrassment, knowing they'd overheard the exchange. She pulled off the backpack and passed the water to Nova before taking a long drink herself. "Can you carry it for a while? The heat is getting to me."

"You're the one who brought it."

"Because it's almost a hundred degrees, Nova! We had to pack water or we could both get heatstroke."

"Well, at least this trip would be over then!"

Frustrated, the heat was making them both cranky, and Nova was fraying the last strings of her patience. Tessa strapped it back on but cautioned, "You can't have anything inside it if you don't help carry it." It was an empty threat she'd never enforce, brought on by the oppressive heat and coupled with her irritation.

Nova shrugged, just as stubborn as her mother. "That's fine. I don't want anything in there."

Tessa bit back the rest of her annoyance, and they continued to climb higher into the woods. They navigated over shiny tree roots smoothed by millions of feet that brushed across them on their journey to Laurel Falls. There were whole families making pilgrimages up to the waterfall, and a stroller could navigate the first half of the route, but midway there, the path deteriorated. The asphalt was fragmented and cracked from water damage creating trip hazards. Tessa briefly wondered if the family they'd followed on the road would be forced to turn back.

They kept going, in the beeline of people hiking up the mountain as Tessa led the way, circling higher and higher on a mission to the waterfall. She rounded one final corner and heard the rushing water, then a wall of much cooler air hit her face and she closed her eyes to savor the welcome respite.

"Doesn't that feel good?" she asked Nova, letting the cooler air wash over her body. A few steps further and she got her first glimpse of Laurel Falls. A deluge of water dumped from forty feet above down to a basin smoothed by the friction of rushing water. Whole families stood in front of the waterfall. Upon seeing a mother stretch her arm out unsuccessfully to take a group selfie of six people, Tessa walked over and said, "Here, let me help you."

"Thank you." The mom beamed at her. Tessa took three quick photos and then handed the phone back with a smile. A group of children splashed in the rock basin where the rushing water from the upper section of Laurel Falls first collected, laughing as the ice-cold water rained down on them. It formed a mist that cooled the air, then trickled to the second basin before it rushed down another rock face. Tessa and Nova were gathered among a hundred other hikers enjoying the much cooler temperatures and the break from the punishing humidity.

"Want to put your feet in the water?" Tessa asked Nova. "It's nice and cool."

"But then I'll have to walk back to the car with wet feet."

"Suit yourself." Tessa sat down on the rock, not letting her daughter's disinterest ruin her enthusiasm. She peeled off her shoes and both layers of hiking socks and submerged her feet in the cold water. The chill was a shock to the system, and the flat rock bed was incredibly slippery. Enjoying the contrast from the blistering heat on the journey there, she closed her eyes for a few minutes. Hearing a gasp and a loud commotion behind her, her eyes popped open. She whipped her head around to discover Nova had face-planted into the slippery base of the rock.

"Oh, honey!" Tessa jumped up to help Nova find her feet. "Are you hurt?"

146

Red-faced and with a huge, embarrassed smile, she muttered under her breath, "Just my pride."

Tessa led her back to where she had been seated. About thirty feet below them, adventurous hikers climbed down the rocky edges of the waterfall to the second clearing below. A family of Mennonites clad in full prairie dresses, long pants, and straw hats walked across downed logs and played in the small pools of water that gathered at the base of the waterfall. The treacherous descent required to get to this basin was outside Tessa's usual comfort level.

"Want to try to climb down there?" Tessa asked, waggling her eyebrows in excitement.

"Ah, I don't know." Nova looked around for a path and, seeing it was straight down, chewed on her fingernail. "Conquering fears is more your thing."

"You have to get outside your comfort zone. That's where all the real growth happens," Tessa explained, then pointed to a small child, barely five years old, that was boldly walking across a log at the bottom of the falls. "It can't be that bad. If that little guy can do it, so can we!"

Knowing her mom wasn't going to give up, Nova gave in. With a nervous smile, Tessa tucked her hiking boots and socks into the backpack and picked her way down the massive staircase of boulders barefoot. The first few feet were easy and gave her a false sense of confidence, but then there was a seven-foot span of straight down, smooth rock to slide down. Tessa sat on the rock, scooting down it, inch by inch. Her toes sought out subtle ridges on the face of the stone to slow her descent. When she landed at the bottom, she beamed and waited for Nova, who was petrified. Frozen on the ledge above her, she let two other hikers pass.

"You can do this," Tessa encouraged from the bottom. "Scoot to the right, then use those two ridges to slow yourself down."

Nova closed her eyes and took a deep breath, then followed her mother's instructions. She missed the first ledge and began to pick up speed as she slid down the face of the slippery rock. Fear filled her eyes, and she went white. Tessa sprang into action and used her upper body strength to slow her roll enough to provide a softer landing.

"See? I've got you." Tessa balled her hands at her hips and looked around. "Wasn't it worth it?" Finally at the bottom, Nova was relieved and rendered speechless, unable to utter even a snarky comment.

The air was even cooler now that they had lowered themselves another thirty feet. The rushing water from above hit the first basin where they started, then the overflow rushed down to the lower level they were currently standing on. In its entirety, Laurel Falls was a stunning eighty feet of raw hydro power.

"I'm going to walk across that tree," Tessa said. "You can join me if you like."

"I think getting down here was enough time spent outside my comfort zone for today. You go. I'm going to save my energy for the trip back."

Tessa hugged the smooth log with all ten toes and outstretched her arms for balance. She navigated the twenty feet to the other side and then back again, watching two children fishing for minnows with nets below. Nova was waiting, sitting on a rock, her shorts gray with a swoosh of mud racing down her hip and leg from sliding down the face of the rock.

"It might be easier to climb up barefoot," Tessa offered.

"Nope," Nova said. She stood and dusted her hands off before climbing up the first section of the boulder. Nova was halfway past the most treacherous part when she misjudged the foothold and came sliding back down to meet Tessa at the bottom. Covered in dirt and leaves, and muttering curse words under her breath, she sat down and yanked off her shoes and socks and jammed them into Tessa's opened backpack.

"Start over there. I'll give you a boost to get to the first foothold," Tessa offered. "The rock is more textured on the far right side. You should be able to get enough leverage to push yourself higher with your toes. See that little ledge about halfway up? You get there, and you're scot-free."

Nova nodded and followed the instructions, and Tessa bent down and locked her fingers together, creating a flat span for Nova's foot. Using all her upper body strength, Tessa tugged her laced fingers up as high as she could, and Nova was able to scramble up the rock face to the first foothold.

"You got it now!" Tessa encouraged.

Nova's limbs were shaking with effort. She froze and clung to the wall. "I can't do it," she cried.

"You can," Tessa commended. "Listen to me. Reach up and to the left, and grab the ridge there with your left hand." Nova obeyed. "Now the leg. You're doing great, honey."

Nova's entire body was trembling, her face buried in the stone. "Now, on the count of three, you push your weight up with your legs. One. Two."

On the second count, Nova forced her leg up and into

149

the foothold, and then, with a burst of adrenaline, she scampered up the remaining three footholds to finally land at the top to thunderous applause. Nova's cheeks pinked up, and Tessa whistled a loud wolf whistle, grateful for the encouragement from the other bystanders.

"Nice job, Nove!" she shouted up at her with a grin. "My turn."

Tessa inched her way up the face of the boulder, using only three-quarters of an inch for the handholds. Her fingers and toes were sore and trembling as she scaled the face of the rock inch by inch. With her heart pounding and her calves on fire, she was grateful when she finally landed on the rock next to Nova.

"I'm really proud of you, honey," she praised with an exhausted grin. The corners of Nova's mouth quirked up in response. "Ready to head back?" Tessa asked, already knowing the answer. She unzipped the backpack and dispersed their shoes and socks. When she lifted the backpack to rest it on her shoulders to begin the hike back to the car, it surprised her when Nova tugged it away and put it on her own instead.

"There might be hope for you after all," Tessa teased, ruffling Nova's hair and pulling her sheepish daughter in for a hug.

Lighter, they walked back the way they came, dodging groups and small families. The path down the mountain was much easier, and they chatted about mundane things.

"How about some ice cream?" Tessa asked as they descended, the ninety-degree heat making pools of sweat trickle down their backs. Their t-shirts were soaked with a pungent mixture of water and sweat and clung to their bellies.

"I'm down," Nova said with a small smile.

"Considering I turned our two-mile hike into over four miles, I think we've earned it. We'll find an ice cream shop in Sevierville and then head to the next treehouse."

Nova was relieved, and a genuine smile spread across her face when she realized her forced time in nature was over and there was ice cream on the way.

Tessa followed the GPS instructions to *TripAdvisor's* top local ice cream parlor, Cruz Farm Ice Cream. Driving the Jeep out of the pristine natural setting of the Great Smoky Mountains was a sharp contrast to the town of Sevierville, Tennessee. It was only two miles outside the national park, but the second biggest tourist trap she'd ever laid eyes on.

"This is the Vegas of the south." Tessa was in awe as she drove down the strip where both sides were covered in arcades and go-kart establishments. They drove by the curious upside-down building that housed WonderWorks. Further down, Nova pointed out a massive King Kong statue standing on top of the Hollywood sign that housed a wax museum. The town was a mecca of overdeveloped family entertainment. Bright, eye-popping colors screamed up and down every surface, clamoring for visitors' attention and dollars. It was a land of over-exaggeration and make-believe, and the kind of commercialized travel destination Tessa usually avoided at all costs.

At several stop lights, she shivered at the sight of zipline towers where riders dangled precariously over the concrete jungle.

She pointed to one platform, the highest on the strip, and said, "That's my worst nightmare."

"How's that any different from climbing the rocks at Laurel Falls?"

"It's night and day different! For one, if you fall off that contraption, you're dead."

"They wear safety harnesses, Mom," Nova explained and held up her arm where a plum colored bruise was developing amid several scrapes and scratches as evidence to the contrary. "As you can see, it wasn't exactly a soft landing at the falls." She leaned forward and glanced up at the platform intrigued. "Looks like such a rush! I'd totally take my chances."

The light turned green, and Tessa hit the gas, happy to put the platforms in the rearview mirror. She finally pulled into the packed parking lot at Cruz Farm Ice Cream, noticing a line of customers reaching outside the door.

"Ugh." Nova was annoyed seeing all the people waiting.

"Trust me, a line is a good thing. Come on, I bet it moves fast."

It did and within ten minutes, they made it to the register where the largest menu of soft-serve flavors awaited them. Delicious combinations like sweet cream and strawberry sorbet and stranger ones like sweet potato. The shop was like stepping back in time. Red and white checkered decor dominated the space, with red vinyl swiveling stools perched on one end of a long Formica table. The girls working the shop were dressed in red and white checkered aprons with their hair in fifties-style sweeping ponytails. Nova ordered her go-to chocolate soft serve with gummy butterflies, and Tessa ordered a Salty Cow in a dish. She savored her salted caramel and creamy chocolate ice cream with a smile on her face, listening to

Nova's munching sounds as she enjoyed her cone. When they finished, she pulled up the address of the next treehouse on her GPS.

"Ready?" she asked, happy to see that Nova's energy was restored, and she was in better spirits due to the influx of sugar. "The next treehouse is only fifteen minutes from here at a place called Treetopia."

They got back into the Jeep and followed GPS's directions. Nova was quiet in the seat next to her, and the route was winding and filled with lots of turns, forcing Tessa to concentrate. Reaching the final turn into the driveway at Treetopia, Tessa hesitated. It was a hairpin turn on a gravel road with such a steep incline she briefly wondered if her Jeep could climb it. Saying a little Hail Mary, she pressed the pedal down, giving the car enough gas to pop up the steep driveway and then higher up the mountain where the treehouse awaited. The Jeep climbed straight up, finally reaching a small parking pull-out where the copper-colored tin roof of the Bark Treehouse was visible from the road. Tessa parked the Jeep with an exhausted grimace, noting the considerable walking distance from the Jeep to the treehouse.

"Looks like we're going to have to walk a ways," she said. "Let's grab what we can, and when it cools down, we'll come back for the rest."

Too worn out to argue after the events of the day, Nova grabbed two backpacks and dragged a cooler behind her. They wandered down a long path until the trees opened up, and they got their first proper look at the Bark Treehouse.

"Wow." Tessa stopped, looking at it for the first time. The exterior was an octagon shape and covered in dark brown bark siding that mimicked the trees surrounding it. Huge windows let in light on four of the eight sides, and a tin roof circled a living tree that shot out of the top like a cowlick. Surrounding the treehouse was a wraparound deck that housed glider rockers and a charcoal grill.

"It's like a Hobbit house," Nova remarked, and Tessa didn't disagree. Beyond the treehouse, the mountains of Sevierville were a stunning green backdrop where plumes of bluish smoke were visible in the mountain ranges underneath a bright blue sky.

"See that?" Tessa pointed out, "The blue smoke is a visual phenomenon created by the combination of high humidity and organic compounds emitted on summer days. It's how the Smokies got their name."

"That's great, Mom, but please tell me this house has air conditioning."

The heat index was over a hundred and ten, and they were both drenched in sweat and smelling pretty ripe by the time they landed at the front door.

"It does."

"Praise Jesus!" Nova joked, raising her hands to the sky like a television evangelist.

Tessa unlocked the handmade wooden door. It was constructed of logs and shaped like a gothic church window. She pushed it open with her forearm and was shocked when there were only a few centimeters of clear-ance between it and the kitchen countertop. Stepping inside, her feet hit the astroturf that carpeted the entire first floor.

"That's an odd choice," Tessa remarked, feeling the scratch of it tickle the tips of her sandal-encased toes.

In the center of the treehouse, a living tree was covered

in rough-hewn cedar and grew up through the center of the ceiling between two skylights.

Tessa followed Nova up a very steep set of narrow stairs that led to a loft with a queen-size bed. The rest of the loft contained a lounging area around the tree that was made of a web of bungee cords fastened to the perimeter.

"Cool!" Nova enthused as she stepped out onto the bungee surface and then lay down. Tessa followed her out onto it, feeling jittery as the cords sank with her additional weight. The treehouse was drenched in natural light from the huge windows that ringed it and the skylights that exposed the cerulean blue sky.

"We'll get a taste of tiny house living here," Tessa exclaimed. "I've always wanted to try it!"

Nova smirked. "You want to try everything."

"Guilty." Tessa shrugged. "At only a hundred and ten square feet, this is the smallest treehouse we'll stay in. I booked them in a sequence, so each one gets better as the trip goes on." Nova pulled out a yoga mat and unrolled it on the suspended bungee floor to lie on. "It's pretty neat, though, huh?"

"Yeah, not bad."

Eager to get settled into their tiny space, Tessa walked down the stairs and around the tree to the kitchen to check out the amenities. It was tucked into the inside of the curved wall and was a pie-shaped minuscule nine square feet. The bathroom was around the tree on the bottom floor, complete with a rounded shower and toilet, with a tacky romantic heart design carved into the faux wood toilet seat. There were two narrow reclining chairs and a wall-mounted TV that Nova turned on immediately while Tessa tried to figure out how to turn on the air conditioner.

Already logged into someone's Netflix account, Nova said, "Let's see what Adam's taste is like." She flipped through his previously watched list before landing on *Schitt's Creek*. After long showers with plentiful hot water, Tessa and Nova binged half of the first season before calling it an early night and climbing back up the steep stairs to the bed.

She hadn't shared a bed with Nova since she was little, when Nova would take up residence in the cozy space between her legs and rest her head on Tessa's belly as a pillow while they watched *SpongeBob SquarePants*. "Mommy's wegs!" she'd declare before plopping down with a sippy cup filled with milk and her favorite blanket. It was a sweet memory that hadn't surfaced in years, and the rediscovery of it made her surge with warmth.

Nova fell asleep almost instantly. The moonlight flooded in from the skylight above them and traced her daughter's features. Tessa reached out and tucked a stray hair behind her cheek, and an exhausted Nova didn't even move. Tessa felt joy bloom in her heart as she drifted off to sleep, grateful for this precious time with her daughter.

Chapter Sixteen

The next morning, Tessa was thrilled to see a real single-cup coffee maker nestled into the triangle-shaped alcove of the kitchen. She brewed a cup in the dark and then took it out onto the deck outside, where the sky was just beginning to lighten with the imminent sunrise. An almost full moon disappeared, and the stars dissolved into the clear light of day. She sipped the coffee slowly, savoring the sound of rushing water that could be seen from her perch in the trees. Knowing that Nova was going to sleep in, she made another cup and stood outside. Her mug said, "Adventure is Calling." She hoisted it up and took a photo of her hand holding the cup with the Smokies in their full glory behind it and texted it to Kristie.

Kristie: *Gorgeous! Super jelly. How's it going?*
Tessa: *Pretty decent, actually. We're both still alive.*
Kristie: *I would consider that a win. Can't wait to hear all about it.*

She studied the photo and thought about sending it to Jason, a habit she'd developed during their two years together. The time away was both good and bad because it gave her time to reflect and decide. It was always harder to be objective and understand her own feelings in his presence. With a heavy sigh, she tucked the phone back into her pocket and kept the photo to herself. She didn't want to pull their issues into this experience and distract her from her purpose. It had been a two-steps-forward, three-steps-back start, but she felt they'd made some progress yesterday. Even baby steps were steps forward.

She took another sip of coffee as a sweet little hummingbird zinged by, its wings flapping so fast they were a blur. It was covered in lime green feathers, and shimmering iridescent markings ran up its back. The bird darted over to the trumpet flower vine clinging to the gigantic tree closest to the treehouse as Tessa watched.

Tessa did some stretches and yoga poses on the deck while waiting for Nova to make an appearance and then attempted twenty minutes of meditation. It was a futile exercise where her busy mind darted from topic to topic like the hummingbird she'd just seen buzzing from bloom to bloom. A few hours later, Nova finally appeared, her face creased with sleep and her eyes half opened.

"Breakfast?" she asked, and Nova nodded. In the tiny kitchen on a hot plate, she scrambled four eggs and cooked thick slices of peppery bacon.

"I thought we'd go find the river," Tessa mentioned. "I can see it from the deck." If Nova was annoyed, she hid it well. Nova rubbed her feet back and forth on the astroturf.

"There's one thing this stuff is good for…" She sighed in pleasure as she continued to brush her ankles faster against the rough green surface, looking blissed out, the way a dog does when you scratch under its chin. "Itching my bug bites."

"You know, you've been delicious to biting insects since you were tiny," Tessa remembered, never one to pass up a quick jaunt down memory lane. "Your skin would swell up with pink welts as big as my fist."

"Lucky me." She itched faster. "I've got bug bites on top of bug bites." Tessa walked over to inspect and noticed a growing network of insect bites crawling up Nova's legs. "I've got just the thing." From her backpack, she pulled out an after-bite stick. "Rub this on them."

"I don't need it," Nova replied. "I'm tough."

"Oh? Like you didn't need sunscreen the other day?" Tessa shot back, pointing to the still-red upper thighs and calves that were now also covered in pink splotches. Her own ankles were riddled, too, so she bent down to rub the stick on them, relishing a comforting, warming sensation that quickly tamed the itching. "It helps." She waved the white stick in the air. "Last chance."

"Okay." Even Nova's teenage stubbornness had its limits. She pulled the tube from Tessa's hand and began to rub it in.

"Wow, that bruise doubled overnight." Tessa pointed at Nova's forearm where a dark purple bruise covered a six-inch span. It was the first point of contact with the ground when she'd face-planted yesterday.

"At least I didn't hurt the pretty." Nova smirked, circling her hand to indicate her face and then following it up with a couple of dramatic eyelash flutters that made Tessa chuckle.

After breakfast and before Nova could turn on the TV,

she said, "Let's go!" and Nova groaned. Tessa gathered up a backpack and some drinks and walked out into the thick humidity, climbing down the steep drive to find an entrance to the river below. After walking around aimlessly and finding nothing but dead ends, Tessa had to admit defeat.

Vacation rentals chewed up the edges of the river, and it was all private property. Nova was mortified by her suggestion to cross someone's yard to access the river. "I guess it's not meant to be," Tessa mused as she shielded Nova's thin body from an oncoming semi-truck. The road was winding and dangerous with no shoulder. One curve was especially treacherous, forcing them to walk into the blind spot of oncoming traffic. If a morning commuter was glancing down at their phone at the wrong time, Tessa was sure they'd become roadkill. It was a relief when they finally reached the less-trafficked lane that led back up to the treehouse.

"Can I have a free day today?" Nova asked. Their calves were burning from the climb, and they were both soaked in sweat and exhausted from the effort of the slow but intense walk back.

Tessa mulled her request over. She didn't want this trip to be pure torture for Nova, so she compromised. "It's your vacation, too, and the first one we've taken in a long time." Nova's eyes bloomed with hope. Tessa decided instead of making every moment a meaningful interaction, she would try to carve out pockets of them, allowing Nova some down time to decompress. "Okay," Tessa agreed.

Nova let out a whoop and disappeared inside to watch more episodes of *Schitt's Creek* and gobble down fistfuls of fluorescent orange Flaming Hot Cheetos.

Up in the loft, Tessa rolled out the yoga mat on the bungee platform and brought out her kindle to read. About an hour into her book, the episode of *Schitt's Creek* Nova was watching below got her full attention. In it, Johnny and Moira were lamenting the fact that even though they'd lived with their grown children, Alexis and David, they didn't really know them. Tessa bolted upright on the mat and became engrossed in the show and smiled. This was the exact reason she'd wanted to take this trip with Nova. The episode felt like a serendipitous Easter egg the universe planted for her to discover. Seeing it as a sign, she resolved to get the card game out that night.

Nova was noticeably less irritated that evening after a long day of lounging in front of the TV. "Let's build the fire," Tessa suggested, and Nova helped her build a decent teepee from the firewood. She crumpled a piece of newspaper into a ball with her fist before lighting it, and minutes later, the fire roared to life. In the tiny kitchen, Tessa formed patties from ground beef and added buns, cheese, sliced onion, and ruby red tomatoes she'd purchased from a roadside stand. The meat sizzled on the grates, and a few minutes later, the hamburgers were ready.

"What kind of S'mores should we make tonight?" she asked after the burgers were eaten.

"Samoa?" Nova suggested.

"I like your style, kid. Can you go inside and get the marshmallows and the box of cookies? If we're feeling really crazy, we can add a few Hershey Nibs to the mix."

"Wow!" Nova waved her hands in the air side-to-side, jazz hands style. "Look who's living on the edge now!"

Tessa laughed. They ate quietly as the sun dropped behind the mountain. Its last rays needled through the trees tinting every branch with shimmering golden light. "Isn't it pretty?" she asked Nova.

"Yeah," she agreed as she speared the first marshmallow to make a S'more and handed Tessa the other stick. Tessa poked the metal through a soft marshmallow center and began turning it patiently in the fire like it was a rotisserie. Across from her, Nova's instantly burst into flame.

"Agh! I ruined it. How do you do that?" Nova asked a few minutes later when a perfectly toasted marshmallow rested at the end of Tessa's stick.

"Patience."

"That's your answer to everything," Nova said.

"The older you get, the more you understand patience *is* the answer to almost any problem," Tessa explained as she pulled the warm marshmallow off the stick and smashed it between two Samoa cookies, then instead of eating it, handed it over to Nova.

"Aww." Nova was touched by the gesture, and her acknowledgment made Tessa's heart swell. She speared another marshmallow on the end of her stick and made herself a Samoa sandwich with another perfectly toasted marshmallow.

"So?" she asked Nova as she took her first bite.

"It's really good," Nova answered. "Better than the bacon."

"Lies!" she declared. "Bacon makes everything better."

They gazed into the fire as the solar lights came on

overhead. Strung across posts, the Edison bulbs emitted a sweet, soft glow. With a flutter of insecurity in her belly, she pulled the teal deck of cards from its hiding place in the pocket of her sweatshirt. She held them up so Nova could see.

"I want to play a game," she announced in a creepy Jigsaw impression.

"Saw!" Nova guessed correctly. They'd suffered through all ten together, each movie in the franchise worse than the last.

"Yep, it's like that, but no one is going to die tonight."

"What is it?" Nova was wary.

"A card game that is supposed to inspire authentic conversation between people."

"Don't you think, when you need a game to inspire authentic conversation, you've already lost the battle?" Nova asked, and Tessa was not surprised. She expected some push back, so she appealed to reason.

"You had a whole day to decompress, so I'd like you to have an open mind. I promise it won't take longer than thirty minutes, and when we're done, you can go right back to *Schitt's Creek*." Tessa was apprehensive and hoped Nova would actively participate. Nova remained silent, so Tessa kept talking and lowered her voice as she leaned closer to reveal a truth.

"That episode of *Schitt's Creek* really hit home for me. Just like Johnny and Moira, I realized I don't know who you truly are. It's the reason I bought this game and wanted to take this trip in the first place. I've been guilty of manipulating you into what I want you to be, and that is wrong." She held up the deck of cards and added, "This will give us a chance to get to know each other on a deeper level, woman to woman, and I want that more than anything, Nova."

"Okay." Nova was guarded in the presence of her mother's uncharacteristic vulnerability. Still wary, Nova wrapped her arms tightly across her chest. Not hearing her refuse, Tessa explained the rules.

"Our chairs have to be close together and facing each other," Tessa instructed, pushing two empty chairs at the fire pit close together and offering her a seat in one. "You can choose not to answer one question in your hand, but you will have to submit to sustained eye contact for thirty seconds."

Nova laughed uncomfortably. "Yeah. That's not happening."

"We each take a few cards and then alternate asking the questions." They arranged the cards in their hands. "You start," she encouraged.

"What's something you don't want me to ask you?" Nova said.

"Wow, that's a really tough one right out of the gate," Tessa mused. "There really isn't much that falls in that category." She struggled for a minute. Tessa was a pretty open book, but then an answer presented itself. "I don't want you to ask me how I really feel about your dad. I think that would open a whole Pandora's box that neither of us would survive."

"Agreed." Nova released a guarded chuckle.

"What do you think I want most from life?" Tessa asked, her gaze lingering on the card. The question was shockingly intimate and the type of conversation they avoided like the plague.

"For me to be happy."

The truth made Tessa gasp. Even though it looked like Nova wasn't paying attention, she clearly was. "You're right, but I never asked what happiness looks like for you."

Nova gulped and her eyes darted away from her mother's to the shadows.

"Tell me. I want to know," Tessa whispered.

Nova blew a hot breath between her lips. "I don't think I know *how* to be happy," she admitted truthfully, and it broke Tessa's heart.

"It's okay to be unsure. Happiness evolves over time. It is an ever-moving target. The things that made me happy in my twenties aren't even on my list now," Tessa admitted. "You'll figure it out, and when you do, I'd love for you to share it with me."

Nova chewed on her bottom lip, and a fat tear rolled down her cheek that she quickly swiped away. Tessa reached out to squeeze her hand, relieved when she didn't pull back. Nova let out a nervous laugh, and then, embarrassed by her emotions and eager to take the focus off herself, she asked the next question. "What's one lesson our family could learn together?"

"How to communicate with each other more effectively. You and Jason have been pitted against each other lately, and I'm stuck in the middle. It creates this whole destructive dynamic I hate."

Nova looked down at the cards in her lap with a guilty pout. "Yeah," she whispered. "I hate it, too."

"Time can change things. Maybe it will get better after this trip." Tessa's voice was filled with longing, and Nova's eyes met her mother's for one long moment before she tore them away and shuffled the cards in her hands.

"This is a weird one. You ready?" Tessa asked.

"Yeah."

"Look into my eyes and describe what you feel." Tessa leaned closer with a big, goofy smile. "Look into my eyes."

"I *feel* uncomfortable." Nova dissolved into a pile of giggles.

"Look into my eyes," Tessa ribbed, leaning even closer. "You have to do it."

"Feelings are gross." Nova continued to giggle.

"Describe what you feel." Tessa waggled her eyebrows. "About *me.*"

"No," Nova protested through another round of nervous laughter.

"I'm not on my deathbed, but someday I will be. So, look into my eyes now, while I'm still alive, and tell me what you *feel*," Tessa coaxed.

"That's a big nope." Nova twisted her body away with another giggle.

"Come on."

"Okay. I feel unwavering ambivalence," Nova blurted to stop the piercing eye contact.

"Oh, Sweet Jesus. You're terrible at this."

Nova quickly read the next card. "When do you come to me for help instead of others in the family?"

"I don't."

"True. I think you overcompensate. Since Dad has zero boundaries, you think you need super boundaries."

"Does it come with a cape?" Tessa asked with a wink while she considered Nova's response. "You might be right. I never thought it was acceptable to force children to carry adult baggage."

The revelation stung, and Nova's gaze dropped to her

lap. Tessa knew she was flying too close to the sun and moved on to the next question.

"What's a moment you will never forget from our time together?" After a pregnant pause that stung, she added, "Come on, Nove. We've had some good times together. It hasn't been *all* bad." After another painful pause, Tessa snapped her fingers and asked, "What about the day we went to the aquarium in Florida?" It was a memory from their last vacation together as a family before the divorce.

"That's because it was an *aquarium*," Nova explained. "I've been obsessed with aquariums since birth."

"Remember that day? You were little, probably only six or seven, and we had to walk there. It was almost a mile away. I wasn't sure you'd make it."

"Where was Dad?"

"He didn't want to go."

"Oh." Nova pressed her lips together and averted her eyes again. Tessa felt a surge of outrage, reliving the memory. Donny decided to stay back and visit a gallery instead, an activity that would have bored little Nova to tears. Tessa put her foot down and made plans without him that Nova would enjoy.

"It was the off-season, and you were the only little one in attendance, so you got picked every time they asked for a volunteer from the audience. Otto the sea lion gave you a kiss and clapped for you."

"Oh, Otto," Nova swooned dramatically. "You were the only man for me." She turned to Tessa. "You never forget your first kiss." The memory made her smile. "And I got to make the dolphins dance."

"It was the best day of your life," Tessa confirmed and leaned in to add, "It was one of the best days of mine, too."

The memory made them both grin. The embers in the fire were reduced to a soft orange glow, and the cicadas started to hum.

"Your turn," Tessa encouraged.

"When was the last time you were scared about a decision I made?"

"That's a loaded question," Tessa teased, trying to dissolve some of the tension it brought up but failed. She swallowed hard. "The vandalism and the suspension with Brendan," she finally admitted.

Nova's face crumpled, remembering the events, and she nodded.

"I don't want you to make an impulsive decision and screw up your life forever. I see you digging holes for yourself with your actions, and it sets you up for a struggle. Life is hard enough on its own."

The question sobered them both up, and the ensuing silence hung heavy. Tessa rushed to ask her final question on the card in her hand. "When do you think I feel most alive?"

"When you hike outside and get to a beautiful place like the waterfalls we saw today."

"Yep. It's restorative for me to be out in the woods. I know you hated our hike, but I loved it."

"I don't get it, but I respect it," Nova offered.

"It's good to re-center yourself on Mother Earth. She knows. She loves. I understand her intimately, mother to mother," Tessa explained as she gathered the discarded cards from Nova's hand and tucked them away.

"Well, that's the game. What did you think?"

"It was alright."

"We'll play it again," Tessa offered and was surprised

when Nova didn't argue. "Let's take a picture with the cards so we can remember this forever."

"Of course, who would ever want to forget this moment?" Nova's words were infused with her typical cynical wit, but she submitted to the photo and then went back inside. Tessa sat outside as the stars began to twinkle high in the navy sky. They had said more honest words to each other in the previous hour than they had in the entire last year. It was a gift.

Chapter Seventeen

The next day, Tessa navigated back to the Great Smoky Mountains and toward Grotto Falls, guided by the GPS. Tennessee's winding roads were drastically different from their Midwestern straightforward counterparts. They were curvy and seductive, smooth blacktop paths that unfurled like black ribbons up and down the mountains. Once inside the national park, she turned onto the one-way road headed toward Grotto Falls. It wove up the mountain between the trees, and about five miles from Grotto Falls, the traffic backed up to a standstill. Tessa was stuck in a long pilgrimage of cars from New York, Pennsylvania, South Dakota, and Michigan that inched along the narrowing one-way road, making the five-mile journey lengthen to an hour.

"We couldn't even turn around if we wanted to," Tessa remarked as the car rolled forward, stuck in a single-lane processional up the mountain. Every once in a while, there was a bump out on the trail for an emergency, but the cars were packed in tight on the narrow road like sardines. A mile from the trailhead, traffic stopped completely, and she ascertained that finding parking was going to be like finding a needle in a haystack. She briefly considered snagging a single pull-out half a mile from the trailhead, but then her calf muscles rebelled and she pressed down on the gas pedal, vividly remembering the straight-up mile they'd hiked to get to Laurel Falls two days ago.

"Nova, have you ever heard about the Law of Attraction?" Tessa asked.

"No."

"Basically, like attracts like, so in order for us to attract the perfect parking spot at the trailhead, we need to see it in our mind's eye. Simply envision it will be there when we need it, and it's ours."

Nova rolled her eyes. "Someone drank too much of the metaphysical Kool-Aid this morning."

"Ah. Everyone's a skeptic." Tessa waved away her cynicism and continued to fill her in on the concept, but it was met with resistance. To illustrate the point, she said, "Thank you, universe, for providing for us and helping us manifest the perfect parking spot." She turned toward Nova with a grin. "It's going to happen. I can feel it. You wait and see."

The timing of the universe would have to be impeccable since they'd followed no less than a hundred cars up to the trail entrance. She leaned forward in anticipation, saying a silent prayer in her head.

"You should have grabbed the one back there when we had a chance," Nova pointed out as they crawled forward.

"My calves are still sore from the last time we had to park a mile away. The universe will provide," Tessa replied, continuing to inch farther up as seeds of doubt took root in her belly. Around the corner, she got her first glimpse of the parking lot. It was even smaller than the one at Laurel Falls, with only fifteen spots in total. But low and behold, as they rounded the final bend, there was not only one but *two* open parking spots. She squealed with delight and eased the Jeep into the closest one.

"See!" Tessa said, thrilled and grinning ear to ear. "It worked. It was meant to be."

Nova didn't share in her joy and instead busied herself with getting a backpack together voluntarily, an act that Tessa considered a victory from their previous hike.

"You were probably hoping there wouldn't be one so you could convince me to drive by, weren't you?" Tessa guessed correctly by the way Nova pressed her lips together and gave a small, curt nod. Not letting Nova's ambivalence bother her, she packed up water bottles, handing one to Nova, some Nutri-grain bars, bug spray, and sunscreen, and they struck out to hike up the trail.

At the trailhead, they passed by a sweaty man who'd just completed the hike. He was perched on a rock in the already sweltering ninety-degree heat and exclaimed, "That wasn't a mile and a half! They must mean as the crow flies."

Ignoring him, Tessa pressed on in pursuit of natural beauty. Behind her, Nova picked up her pace and, when she was shoulder to shoulder with her mother, said, "Did you hear him? It's over two miles there. That means four round-trip!"

"I did, but I trust the sign we just passed that said Grotto Falls was one-point-four miles away, not the words of some stranger sitting outside the trailhead."

"He was just up there. He knows," Nova argued.

172

Dismissing Nova's pleas, Tessa kept picking her way up the trail. It was steep. The kind of climb that makes your calves burn and your lungs ache. They walked straight up in silence for almost an hour. The immense effort of climbing required all their resources. Tessa was gasping for air, her body so physically taxed she couldn't carry on a conversation.

Behind her, Tessa felt a palpable shift as Nova got more irritated the deeper they pressed into the forest. Nova fell behind, and angry teenage energy drifted in her wake, hovering like a black cloud. Refusing to let Nova's negativity bring her down, Tessa admired the beautiful downed trees covered in lime-green moss and gold fungi. The path had many manmade log staircases built by park rangers and long lengths of tree roots were exposed and glossy from the friction of millions of hiking boots. Tessa tripped on more than a few of them, reeling forward, expecting to hear Nova's chuckle behind her, but she was silent.

Unable to catch her breath, Tessa stopped on the side of the trail and looked down at her watch. Her heart rate was climbing into the high one-sixties, a number she hadn't seen in a long time. It was becoming evident she'd underestimated how difficult the climbs would be after a decade spent working a cushy desk job.

"I have to rest for a minute," she explained when Nova finally caught up. Her lungs were taxed and tested to their maximum capacity, breathing in the thinning air. Nova batted mosquitos around her, waving them away. Annoyance rolled off her in waves in the over ninety-degree heat. She swatted at her arm, and Tessa saw her exposed skin was becoming an ugly mass of conjoined insect bites.

"Do you want some bug spray?" Tessa offered.

"The bottle is broken."

"What? It's brand new! Let me see." An apathetic Nova fished it out of her backpack and handed it over. Tessa pressed hard on the nozzle several times to no avail, then screwed off the lid, seeing the little tube that should be there to feed it was missing. As a last resort, she held it upside down and pressed the dispenser, and was rewarded with a fine mist. "Try it this way."

"I don't want it."

Frustrated, Tessa continued, "Just put some on. It will help."

"Nope." She crossed her arms across her chest and dug in.

Her defiance frustrated Tessa. "What's wrong with you today? You're choosing to be miserable."

"I'm not a hiker, Mom. I hate this." Nova wiped a hand across her sweaty face and then continued to swat at the swarm of mosquitos in the air. Her t-shirt was soaked in sweat and serving as a beacon, drawing them in.

"Well, it's happening, so get on board." Tessa turned back, frustrated with her stubbornness, and trekked further up the trail. The hate in the air was a heavy cloud behind Tessa, but she refused to acknowledge it. Tessa continued to lead the way, glancing down at her watch from time to time, seeing her feet-of-climb rising with each step.

"We're almost there," Tessa cried over her shoulder to encourage Nova, relieved when her watch finally registered a mile. "We're close." She dropped back, waiting for Nova to join her. "One more little burst of energy and we'll be there." A woman, red-faced and obese, was hiking the bumpy terrain with a cane. She wove around them, refusing to give up. The sight inspired Tessa to continue.

Nova grunted her response, following obediently behind in silence. When she finally heard the sound of rushing water, Tessa let out a whoop of joy. Around a curve, enormous boulders climbed up the side of the mountain, where water crashed down from a twenty-five-foot waterfall onto the rocks below. There was a path to walk behind the waterfall and have your picture taken, but she knew she'd be pressing her luck to ask Nova to do any more hiking at that point. Instead, Tessa asked a kind lady in front of her, "Can you take a photo of us with the water-fall in the background?"

"Of course," she answered.

Tessa stood next to Nova and wrapped her arm around Nova's waist.

"Smile," the woman said before taking a quick snap.

Nova stood stiffly next to her, forcing a smile just to get it over with. The woman handed the phone back to Tessa.

"Thank you." Tessa started back down the makeshift staircase made of rocks and railroad ties that ran up the side of the stream. "Let's go find a good rock to sit on. I want to put my feet in the water." She peeled off the hiking socks and shoes and dipped her toes into the clear water. It was cool and refreshing, a welcome respite from the searing heat they endured to get there. She encouraged Nova to do the same.

"It feels great. You should try this. Being barefoot in the forest resets your hormones."

Nova was sullen and shook her head no, refusing to give in and enjoy it, so Tessa gave up trying to convince her to take part. Tessa moved away from the perch Nova claimed on a rock, her legs crisscrossed and her eyes downcast, seemingly in mourning, even amidst the cooler temperatures and spectacular beauty of Grotto Falls.

Sitting on her own boulder, Tessa watched families pick their way across the rocks to take photos. After about twenty minutes, Tessa conceded and gathered Nova up to begin the descent back to the car.

The trip back down the mountain was all downhill. On their journey up, they'd scaled almost five hundred feet of climb, but the way back was effortless. Every step closer to the car, Nova's icy frustration melted away bit by bit. By the time she got to the Jeep, Nova was speaking to her again, and they decided together to find a picnic spot, locate a grocery store, and drive over to the next treehouse.

As they drove out of the parking lot at Grotto Falls, Tessa was shocked to see the sheer number of vehicles haphazardly parked on the side of the road. Even two miles from Grotto falls on the single-lane one-way road, they still had to inch by them.

"We got so lucky!" Tessa exclaimed.

"You won't shut up about manifestation," Nova teased.

"We could have been one of these poor schmucks abandoning their car on the side of the road two miles from the trailhead." Tessa navigated through the park traffic, bumper to bumper again.

"Look, Mom. You manifested another one." Nova pointed to a single free parking spot in front of the entrance to the historical structures on Roaring Forks Parkway.

This time, Tessa rolled her eyes. "I'm just happy to see the stick has been removed."

"What stick?'

"The one that was jammed up your butt at Grotto Falls."

Nova shot her a sheepish glance. "Sorry," she mumbled as Tessa pulled in.

Getting back out into the scorching summer heat, they followed groups of people walking down a sidewalk that led to primitive structures straight out of the 1800s. The doorways were low, only about five feet high, and they both had to duck to enter.

"Wow. People must have been shorter in 1825," Tessa remarked. "I guess it makes sense. They didn't have access to food like we do. They had to go out and hunt for it and often went hungry."

"Nah, it's probably all the incest." Nova smirked.

Tessa chuckled, glad to see Nova's trademark sarcasm and snark had returned. If Tessa had to choose between sullen and sarcastic, snark was the clear winner.

There were a few bats hanging upside down in one of the structures where a crowd gathered. "Hell to the no. I just can't," Tessa admitted, backing up with a shiver, refusing to enter the dwelling. "Bats freak me out. Ever since your grandma told me they would burrow into my hair when I was five."

"That's an old superstition. Bats want nothing to do with your hair, Mom. They aren't nesting mammals," Nova informed Tessa and boldly walked closer. Fascinated, she closed in and studied them for several long minutes before rejoining Tessa outside.

"Did you know female bats can form strong bonds with each other?" Nova asked.

"I did *not*," Tessa answered. "Hmm. That's pretty cool."

"And they rub noses on each other to show affection."

"Like Eskimo kisses?" Tessa asked.

"Kinda." Nova nodded. "They've gotten a bad rap, what with Dracula and all."

"Maybe it's time to give them a second chance."

They continued to walk down the path where a much smaller structure stood with only one window.

"What do you think that was for?" Tessa asked.

"That's where they put the womenfolk when they got too uppity," Nova said sarcastically.

"Such rapist wit!" Tessa declared, and Nova snorted with a chuckle.

"What?"

"It's *rapier* wit, Mom. Named after a French sword used in duels."

"Oops." Tessa grimaced. Nova led the way down a trail. Tessa wasn't sure whether Nova was getting a second wind or wanting to make up for her bad attitude earlier, but either way, it was a welcome improvement. Nova darted ahead further into the woods, and Tessa quickened her pace. Twenty minutes later, Nova let out a blood-curdling scream. Panicked, Tessa ran toward her daughter. She was frozen on the trail, one skinny arm akimbo, pointed to a grassy area only a few feet away.

"What?" Tessa said, her eyes darting around the trail, searching for danger.

"It's a snake," Nova whispered like the reptile could hear. Her wide eyes filled with fear. Only three feet away from her daughter, she saw its tongue dart out toward Nova's bare shins, and panic raced through her. It was a four-foot snake slithering ever closer. Tessa looked for the distinct black chevron markings of a timber rattlesnake.

Identifying them, her heart quickened in her chest.

"Mom?" Nova's voice cracked as the snake slithered inches closer. Its head raised up, and Tessa heard a rattle. It was a loud buzz she knew was a warning before it would strike.

"Don't make any sudden moves," Tessa advised her. She forced her voice to remain calm and said, "Slowly back away and step toward me." Nova took one step back, her hands balled into fists and quivering in fear. The snake's head bobbed and weaved closer, its tail letting out another ominous rattle.

"Mom?" Nova cried.

"Don't be afraid, honey. Take another step toward me," Tessa directed. "A little faster now."

Nova took two more tentative back steps toward Tessa and then another.

"That's it." Tessa's eyes were locked on the serpent that was still within striking distance. Reaching her limit, Nova turned on her heel and ran away, screaming. The snake lurched toward her but fell short. Nova never looked back. Shrieking her way back toward the Jeep, she sprinted down the trail. Tessa backed away slowly, her eyes still locked on the rattler until it was safe enough to turn around and race toward her daughter.

She caught up to Nova a quarter mile away, who was doubled over and gasping for air. Tessa reached out her hand and pulled Nova toward her. Clinging to her mother, Nova's body trembled with the aftershocks of terror. Tessa murmured, "You're safe now. It's okay."

"Can we get the hell out of here?" Nova begged, her frightened eyes darting around the dense foliage on the forest floor surrounding them. Tessa nodded and pulled two long branches from the ground, stripped them down, and handed one to Nova. "Swipe the stick from side to side in front of you. It will save you from any more surprises on the trail. Stay close. I'll lead the way."

Ten minutes later, with the Jeep in sight, Nova abandoned her stick and sprinted to it. Dramatically, she wrapped her arms around the hood and hugged the vehicle. Tessa pulled the key fob from her pocket. The door chirped, the locks opened, and then Nova jumped at the chance to settle herself inside. A few minutes later, Tessa pulled the cooler out of the back and, after settling into the driver's seat, handed it to Nova.

"I think we've had enough excitement in the great outdoors for one day."

Nova nodded and pulled out an orange soda, an Arnold Palmer half and half, and two sandwiches. They ate in the car, made a pit stop at a grocery store, and then began the drive to Walland Forest.

"How about another podcast?" Tessa asked.

Nova released a creepy laugh. "Ah-ha! My brain-washing is complete. Welcome to the dark side," she teased as she scrolled through options on her phone.

"One more by my man, Keith," Nova declared with an infectious grin as she cranked up *Mommy Doomsday*. Tessa got sucked into the story as the calming voice spooled out the frightening tale. They wove out and around another mountain, entranced by the grim recounting of Lori Vallow's descent into religious extremism.

"Five husbands?" Tessa repeated.

"Fifth time's the charm, Mom," Nova offered. "Just wait, Keith's getting to the good part. Where her new husband convinces Lori her children are satanic zombies that need to be eliminated."

"What in the actual hell?" Tessa was stunned. "You can't make this stuff up."

The outrageous podcast made the drive in the Jeep zip along. Feeling reckless from time to time, they rocketed up and down the hills. The drive was filled with switchbacks and endless curves, and Tessa was relieved when it finally opened up beyond more than two skinny lanes. It took almost another hour to make it to the next treehouse, and when they finally pulled in, she was instantly enchanted.

"Wow!" Tessa exclaimed. "Let's get out and explore! I think this might be my favorite treehouse of all!"

Chapter Eighteen

T essa popped out of the Jeep and was giddy with excitement as she walked down the long wooden bridge that connected the treehouse to the gravel road. The treehouse was brand new, but so purposefully sighted into the landscape it looked like it had always been there. It was constructed around four enormous trees at least forty feet tall each whose branches practically touched the sky. The surrounding forest encircled it, cloaking the treehouse in privacy.

The treehouse itself was about eighteen feet by eighteen feet and featured a diagonal tin roof that sheltered it from the rain. Attached to the house was an enormous wraparound deck. Easily twice as big as the house, it extended the living space out underneath the canopy of emerald green trees. Holes had been cut through the deck to allow the trees to grow naturally and provide shade.

On the spacious deck were a canvas hammock, a gas fire table, and a dining table with an umbrella. Nova squealed with delight when she saw the canvas hammock and, in her haste to try it out, misjudged where she should sit. The hammock lurched up into the air and promptly dumped her on the deck.

"Easy there, killer," Tessa said with a giggle. Nova was laughing at herself, all legs and elbows in a ball on the ground. She awkwardly found her feet, then scampered down the back staircase. Under the main deck was a lower deck with a wrought-iron table and chairs tucked under an overhang. Tessa stood on the platform watching squirrels dart from one tree to the next while a faint trickle of water dribbled down a creek bed that wove through the property. Nova jogged across a little wooden bridge that led to a fire pit.

Her genuine excitement tugged on Tessa's heartstrings. It reminded her of the carefree summer days of Nova's childhood they'd spent searching for new playgrounds and the thrill on her daughter's face as she tested out the novel equipment in each one. In her mind's eye, she saw little Nova with her strawberry blonde hair carefully divided into equal pigtails that curled up at the ends. Grinning from ear to ear and missing her front teeth, she balanced on a beam and slid down a slide. Her exuberance for life and new experiences was contagious. Tessa loved those lazy childhood days most of all, when joy was just a Happy Meal and twenty minutes at the park away.

Tessa followed Nova's steps across the bridge, noticing the firewood stacked in a neat pile. A gentle wind rustled through the trees and kept the mosquitos away as Nova tossed pebbles in the creek, and the bird song forced Tessa to take a deeper breath.

"Should we check out the inside?" Tessa asked.

"Yeah!" Nova scampered back over the bridge and up

the stairs to the front door, where Tessa punched in the code and walked into a much cooler burst of air.

Inside, the cathedral ceiling made the tiny footprint feel spacious. "Oh my gosh! A real kitchen." Tessa was amazed. It was the first one they'd seen in such a small space. Curious, she opened up all the drawers and doors to see it fully stocked with dishes and pots and pans. On the countertop sat an air fryer and coffee maker. A tiny refrigerator with a freezer component was tucked under the countertop. Across from the kitchen was a tiny table for two made of logs with wooden folding chairs. Beyond the dining area was a king-size bed tucked into an alcove. The entire back wall was filled with windows and a glass patio door that drenched the treehouse with natural light.

Nova turned the corner from the kitchen to the bedroom and froze. Two deer heads and a pheasant in flight were mounted to the wall on either side of the bed. "Taxidermy as decor? How am I supposed to sleep when they're staring at me all night long with their big, dead eyes?" She flopped down dramatically on the bed with a sigh.

"Somehow, I think you'll manage," Tessa answered, unfettered by her plea. "Smell that?" Tessa asked Nova and closed her eyes, inhaling the deep cedar scent. Cedar planking covered the walls, and it reminded Tessa of her grandmother's cedar-lined hope chest.

"Smells like wood chips."

"It's cedar. Maybe it's an air freshener, but man, it sure sets the perfect tone!"

To the right of the front door was a large bathroom with a full-size shower and well-lit vanity with a wicker basket filled with spa-quality toiletries. Tessa pulled the remote control from the basket and cranked down the wall-mounted air conditioner. Then she unlocked and opened the patio door, where a top-of-the-line gas grill waited two steps away from air conditioning.

"They've thought of everything! I think I could live here forever!" Tessa enthused. It was always the little things that made life easier which she appreciated the most. "Let's unload, and then we can relax," Tessa suggested.

A few minutes later, they were unpacking the cooler when they heard a quick, jaunty rap at the door. Tessa crossed to open it to a smiling older gentleman.

"I've heard y'all need to do some laundry?" He was short-statured, wearing a faded ball cap and a huge smile. He stuck out his hand. "I'm John."

Tessa shook his hand. "I'm Tessa and this is Nova."

"You're in luck. The big house isn't rented until the weekend. I figure I'll take you over there right quick and you can use the washer and dryer. You can even stay there and watch TV while it runs if y'all want." Sweet southern twang clung to every word.

"That's really generous. Thank you!" Tessa said.

John led them down a short cobblestone path to a large cabin built for a family reunion. On a concrete pad sat a huge hot tub. "You can use this if you want," he offered, stopping to take the time to show her how to turn on the music and how to pull the cover on and off.

"Wow. That sounds wonderful." It was still oppressively hot. The heat index was a scorching one hundred and twelve degrees, but Tessa was grateful for the offer.

They followed him into the larger house. It too had a wraparound deck and the inside walls were hewn from logs. Glancing up, she saw a canoe suspended from the cathedral ceiling. In the living room, a cushy, overstuffed leather couch sat in front of a huge TV, and a thoughtful bookcase was tucked into an alcove under the steps of the loft. John walked them through the entire house, pointing out all the unique features while Tessa marveled at his craftsmanship. Both houses were solidly constructed and thoughtfully decorated, and he was bursting with pride, showing off his handiwork.

"You've done an amazing job," Tessa declared as Nova fell in step behind her, having been forced into the impromptu tour by an over-eager John. He never stopped talking, his obvious pride flowing out of his mouth in a torrent of syllables that made it impossible to get a word in edgewise. With a twinkle in his blue eyes, he was a fountain of useless information.

"My boss called up and asked for the highest speed internet. He went top of the line here and spared no expense. He said, 'John, people need to work and we need to make sure they can do it. I don't care what it costs. You get the fastest internet they got!'" He shrugged his shoulders, his face twisted up in a smile, laugh lines cut deep into his tanned cheeks. "I reckon people just don't know how to relax anymore. It's such a shame."

He led them into the bathroom where the floors were covered in dark natural slate. "You want to use the shower over here? I don't care! You want to cook a pizza in this oven? Knock yourself out! Between you and me, I wouldn't lie down on the beds or anything because we haven't cleaned it from the last tenants yet, but y'all make yourselves at home!"

Tessa stifled a giggle. His energy was off the charts.

He walked them into the laundry room off the master bedroom.

"Here's everything you need. The soap, the dryer sheets. All of it. Use it all. I don't care! Won't hurt nothin'."

They followed him back out to the deck. "Now, I'm just up the hill there." He pointed to a trail. "If you need anything, and I mean *anything*, you let me know. You can send a message and I'll take care of it. Y'all have a great stay here."

He left them on the deck and then disappeared into the trees, walking up the trail to what Tessa figured was probably his home. When he was out of earshot, Nova said, "What just happened? I've never heard someone talk so much yet say so little."

Tessa laughed. "He's just proud of his handiwork and trying to be welcoming."

"Yep. We'll go with that." Nova followed her back into their treehouse, and Tessa spent the next two hours doing laundry and reading a good book.

After dinner, Tessa was lying in the hammock on the deck, enjoying the light shifting into the darkness of night. The lights came on at sunset and washed the deck in a warm glow. She heard the sliding door open and Nova appeared barefoot, dressed in pajama pants with alligators and a faded navy blue hoodie.

"What's up, Buttercup?" Tessa asked, pushing her legs to the side and climbing out of the hammock.

Nova pulled the deck of cards from the pocket of her hoodie and waved them at Tessa.

"You want to play?" Tessa was shocked and touched but forced herself to play it cool. Teenagers were as skittish as baby fawns in the woods and just as unpredictable. Tessa walked over to the table and turned two chairs to face each other, patting one for Nova. A memory flashed through her mind. "When you were four years old, you always begged me to play Old Maid. Do you remember that?"

"Yes." Nova laughed. "I was obsessed!"

"Now that you are older, I can reveal my radical game winning strategy." Tessa's eyes twinkled with barely concealed mischief. "It was revolutionary. I'm not sure you're ready to learn my secrets."

"Spill it," Nova demanded.

"I always placed the Old Maid card higher than the rest of the cards in my hand and turned it closer to you." Tessa laughed hysterically while Nova feigned shock.

"Every single time, you'd select the tallest, closest card!" Tessa dissolved into more uncontrollable giggles.

"I feel manipulated." Nova shook her head in disappointment. "You should be ashamed."

"No shame in my game." Tessa grinned.

"You couldn't let me win?"

"Of course not, sweetheart. You have to earn your own victories. It means more. The world isn't going to let you win."

Tessa looked through the cards in her hands. "Do you want to go first?"

"Sure." She looked down to read from the card. "If you could have something of mine, what would it be and why?"

"I would love a book of your original poems. Remember the one you wrote for my birthday? You have such a gift with words, honey."

Nova pinked up and shrugged off the compliment.

"If I had half the talent you have, I would shout it from the rooftops! You're such a creative force. The poetry, the paintings. You have more talent in your pinky finger than I have in my entire body."

"But I'm an idiot when it comes to math and science."

"Well, first of all, you are *not* an idiot." Tessa explained, "The job of the public school system is to churn out well-rounded cogs that can plug into society's wheels. Worker bees keep the archaic system rolling, but true genius lies in finding your real talents and laser-sharpening them. If you look at all the great success stories in the world today, people at the top of their game focused on their one true thing. The one task they can do better than anyone else."

"How do you figure out what that is?"

"You have to play. Experiment."

"Is being an accountant your one true thing?" Nova asked.

"This probably sounds weird, but yes. I get a lot of personal satisfaction and joy in helping my clients reach their goals. I know numbers and spreadsheets can seem boring, but there is a sense of purpose I feel when I get everything to reconcile."

"Super nerd!" Nova curved one hand around her mouth and shouted out into the forest that surrounded them, and her voice echoed.

"Guilty as charged," Tessa admitted, raising her right hand. "I can lose myself in it and hours go by. That's how you know you're on the right track. When you get so immersed in what you're doing, the time flies."

189

"That's how I feel about drawing and designing tattoos."

"Then you owe it to yourself to explore it as a career."

"What? You're not going to lecture me on the importance of having fail-safe employment? Or how you can't eat sketches?"

Tessa sighed sheepishly. "I am going to stop doing that. The truth is I've been guilty of suffocating your dreams and your wild and wonderful spirit with my desire to keep you safe, and it's finally time to admit it isn't working. "

"What?!" Nova was shocked. "I'm going to need a second to process those statements."

Tessa shook her head. "It's your one life, honey, and it's time I let you start living it."

"Really?"

"It is. You are a capable young woman who will find her way. I am sure of it."

"You are?" Her eyes widened in shock.

"I am."

Nova gulped, feeling the weight of it settle on her heart. Tessa reached out to squeeze her leg. "Stop putting so much pressure on yourself! You're going to fail, but you're also going to succeed, and along the way, you'll learn tenacity and grit and how to overcome challenges. The time to throw caution to the wind and take big risks is when you are young. When you don't have a family to feed or a partner to placate. I want you to go out there and chase your dream, wherever it leads, and if you stumble and need a place to catch your breath, you always have me."

Nova's eyes filled with tears, and she blinked them

away, digesting her mother's words. "Too much emotion. Next card, please!"

"What was the experience that connected us the best, and why?" Tessa asked.

"Probably living in the little apartment across from the elementary school, when it was just us."

"Really?" Tessa was shocked. "What made you love it so much?" It was the smallest apartment they'd ever lived in, and Tessa's memories of it were cloaked in failure. She was struggling to afford childcare and put food on the table after the divorce left her with a mountain of debt. She'd had to cut back in every way to pay it off, and when she signed the lease, she sobbed. The feelings of shame and loss cut so deep.

"Because I had you all to myself." Nova's voice softened, and Tessa felt a deep pang in the recesses of her heart. The period of time she'd considered a blemish on her years of motherhood was quality time Nova cherished. The revelation was mind-blowing, proving again that two people who go through the same experience can have vastly different perspectives of it.

"If you could choose three people to share an intimate meal with, who would they be? And why?" Nova asked.

"Are we talking living or dead?"

"Any three people."

Tessa thought for a long moment, then answered, "These are in no particular order. I would love to share a meal with Betty White. She was a legend."

"That's a good one." Nova nodded.

"Number two would be my mom. She's been gone for almost forty years now, and I miss her so much." Tessa felt tears well up and she whispered, "I wish she'd met you."

191

Tears broke the surface and tracked down her cheeks, and she brushed them away with a sad smile.

The answer made Nova somber, and she blurted out a startling revelation. "I've been taking you for granted," she said, her voice barely a whisper.

"Oh, honey." Tessa sighed.

"No, I want you to hear me out," Nova continued. "I lash out at you because, most of the time, you're the only one there. I can see now, I was wrong. You're the only person who's always been in my corner."

Tessa melted. She reached out to Nova and squeezed her hand. "You do not know how much I needed to hear you say that. Thank you."

"So, who's the third?"

"Probably Tony Robbins because he's so inspiring and incredible at pumping me up." Seeing a blank look on Nova's face, Tessa explained, "He's a motivational speaker."

"Motivational speakers are just money-hungry narcissists who feed off the sad and depressed."

"I disagree."

"No!" Nova continued passionately. "I have so much resentment in my heart and soul for that sell-out answer."

"You need to learn to let go," Tessa said with a laugh. "I stand by my choices. Okay…" She pulled the next card out of her hand. "What change in myself could I make to improve my relationship with you?" Tessa asked, curious to hear Nova's answer.

"Let go a little. Let my actions be *my* actions and don't take so much responsibility for them."

Tessa was stunned by her insight. Even Nova understood her tendency to fix and take responsibility was unhealthy. It was time to stop doing it.

"How do you hope our relationship will change in the next ten years?" Nova asked.

"I want to release control and stop acting like your life is an extension of mine. And more than anything, I want to see you step out into the world and dazzle it with your gifts and build a life that is satisfying for yourself."

Nova swallowed hard. The answer left her speechless.

"Here's a good one." Tessa smiled. "If you could change one thing about me, what would it be? And why?"

"The micromanagement. You need to chill out."

She couldn't disagree.

"Last card," Nova said. "What would make you never speak to me again?"

"Wow. I don't think there's anything you could do that would make me cut off contact with you completely. Especially after I lost my mother so young."

"There's got to be something," Nova pushed. "I feel like if I murdered someone..." she interjected, her cynical brain looking for loopholes.

"I would still *love* you, but God, it would be hard to accept the decision you made." Tessa added, "Now, I hope it's not a limit you actively seek out, but I don't see it happening. I just don't."

Nova pursed her lips and bit the inside of her cheek. Tessa reached out to squeeze her forearm and quietly added, "You don't have to keep testing me. I see what you're doing, and I understand why you're doing it— you're testing my commitment to you. It makes sense for you to doubt my intentions when your father has walked away, time and time again, but I *never* will."

Nova's forehead knitted up, and hot tears filled the bottom of her lashes. With a sad laugh, she turned away and brushed them off with her fingertips where the nails were bitten down to the skin.

"I stick," Tessa added. "And that is why we fight. I will never sit idly by and watch your self-destruction. I will fight for your safety and happiness with every fiber of my being."

"Why don't you just give up on me like everyone else has?"

"That will never happen." Tessa vowed, "No matter what, I will always be the one person standing in between you and your desire to self-destruct."

Nova burst into tears then, and Tessa stood and took her trembling daughter into her arms. She cupped the back of her head into her embrace like she had when Nova was a toddler and inconsolable. Nova let out a choked sob that made a tear roll down Tessa's face. She took a step back and gathered her daughter's face in her hands, brushing Nova's warm tears away with her thumbs, and forcing her to make eye contact. The walls Nova had erected around herself were coming down brick by brick, and a swell of goodness filled Tessa's heart.

"I want you to hear this. You are the most important person in the entire world to me. There is nothing you could ever do to change my love for you. We are connected forever in a way that can never be severed."

Nova nodded, and she continued, "I hate seeing you hurting yourself the way you have been. The next time you look in the mirror, I want you to see what I see." Tessa brushed the stray hairs back from her daughter's face. "You are beautiful inside and out. Your heart is a treasure, and only people that treat you well deserve access to it. Your life is important. You have a purpose, and you will find it." She kissed her forehead and then pulled her in for one more hug. "And most of all, I love you."

Nova clung to her mother. "I love you, too," she said before pulling back with a sheepish smile and then disappearing back inside the treehouse.

Tessa walked back to the glider on the deck, watching the moonrise. Her heart swelled with love for Nova. High above the treetops, a huge strawberry full moon climbed into the sky. It was a magnificent sight, with a pale pink cast, and Tessa felt her heart shift in the presence of it. Soft moonlight illuminated the lines of each branch of the forest that shielded their treehouse. She stared into the pink orb, grateful for the breakthrough with Nova, one she never saw coming.

Chapter Nineteen

The next morning, Tessa finished her book on the deck, waiting for Nova to wake up. Around nine, Nova pulled open the slider and appeared next to her, her hair sticking up in adorable cowlicks, eyes swollen from sleep. Her lips were pale, and fresh freckles dotted her cheeks from all their time in the sun.

"Remember when I used to name all your freckles and call them angel kisses?"

Nova laughed, and the nostalgia earned Tessa an eye roll. "You're such a sap."

"True story," Tessa agreed as Nova sat down on the chair. "Since it's going to be so hot, I bought us tickets for a river float today. The outfitter is only about fifteen minutes from here."

"That sounds fun." Nova stood and stretched her arms high above her head, exposing a flash of skin at her navel.

"How do yogurt parfaits sound for breakfast?"

"Good." Nova was being especially agreeable.

Tessa went inside and whipped up yogurt and granola

parfaits with blueberries and strawberries, and they gobbled them down on the deck of the treehouse. The air was already humid and climbing to record-setting heat index temperatures.

"Get your suit on. We're leaving in ten minutes." Tessa busied herself with washing the few dishes breakfast created and then putting on her swimming shorts and a tankini, covering her exposed skin with sunscreen.

The pink on Nova's legs from the kayaking had finally calmed down into a tolerable blush color. She accepted the sunscreen willingly this time, lesson learned.

They got in the Jeep and headed toward Townsend, Tennessee.

"I've never done a river float before, and I've always wanted to try it," Tessa admitted as she pulled into a parking lot that was beginning to fill up at ten am. "I packed you an old pair of sandals you can wear in the water." She pulled on a different pair herself, grabbed a couple bottles of water, her keys, and the phone, and they got in a long line that snaked along a curved path to the cash registers. After they checked the car keys and got bracelets attached to their wrists, they followed the crowd that shuffled to tall racks filled with hundreds of life jackets.

"Ew." Nova cringed, paralyzed in front of the racks. Her nose crinkled in disgust.

"They're still moist," Tessa confirmed with a grimace.

"Never say that word to me ever again." Nova batted the offensive air in front of her nose. "Can you smell that?" There was an undeniable wave of body odor wafting from the rack of yellow jackets.

"Once it's wet, I bet you don't even notice," Tessa offered, hoping it was true because they reeked.

"These are the bowling shoes of Tennessee. Nothing like being forced to wear a flotation device soaked in the sweat of a stranger," Nova declared as Tessa walked her over to the farthest rack.

"These might be a little less offensive," she instructed and then strapped one on that was mostly dry to show Nova it was okay. She took a deep inhale. "After the first ten seconds, you don't smell a thing."

Nova jumped as high as she could, grabbed the farthest jacket, and put it on, not bothering to secure the buckles.

"Grab a tube," Tessa said as she pulled one from the towering pile and carried it by its blue handle. Nova fell in step with her, and they walked down a tunnel to the entrance where a guide offered instructions.

"You must stay in the water at all times. The land on either side is private property until you get to the area with our signs. There you can stop and swim as long as you like. There's even a ladder where you can get out and cliff dive. Have fun!"

The temperature was already one-oh-four with the heat index climbing, and Little River's cool water felt amazing on Tessa's feet as she watched Nova lay down her tube and float away quickly, getting pulled by the current. Tessa plopped down her own tube, then slipped on the algae-covered rocks, landing hard on it with an awkward laugh. She used her arms and legs to try to catch up with Nova before she disappeared from sight in the sea of humans on yellow tubes that dotted the intake point.

Much further down, Nova clung to the branch of an exposed log in the river and waited for Tessa. As she paddled over to Nova, rocks scraped along her body in the shallower parts. Tessa learned to sit up in the tube higher so she could float over them, feeling rocks scratch along her bottom and legs as she floated. The water was shallow in parts and covered with jagged stones that Tessa pushed her feet against to dislodge her tube and continued her float down the river. Getting stuck a few times in her rush to get to Nova, she attempted to stand on the slippery rocks, but navigating the lake bottom with the huge yellow tube became like watching a slapstick physical comedy routine. Every step was treacherous on algae-covered rocks and sent her tumbling down into the rushing water.

Finally, Nova was in sight. She reached out for the handle of Nova's tube and let the water carry them further down the river.

"This is so relaxing," Tessa said.

"I didn't know what to expect, but it is," Nova agreed. They floated for several long minutes, letting the current carry them deeper. Nova paddled them over to the faster-moving rapids, ever the thrill seeker.

Tessa remained on the tube, even when they got stuck on the rocks, and Nova would stand and drag her into deeper water. They drifted toward the current that was picking up in an area where water crashed over rocks and created a dip that was more like white water rafting. Then the river bottomed out, and they got stuck in a slippery rock bed. Tessa stood up to walk to a deeper spot when Nova burst out laughing.

"What?" Tessa asked, immediately understanding Nova was laughing *at* her, not *with* her.

"Your swim shorts." Nova dissolved into giggles again, barely able to spit out the words. It took a full minute before she regained enough composure to say, "You ripped your pants."

The chords of the SpongeBob song from Nova's childhood cued up in her brain. She cranked her head over her shoulder to look at her backside, which was challenging while holding on to the clumsy inner tube and attempting to walk through slippery rocks at the same time. Entire families on inner tubes drifted by her as she twisted at the waist to see what was so funny, and Nova's giggles turned into a full-on roaring spectacle.

Then she saw it. A flash of white skin that had never been kissed by the sun before, enjoying its very first rays. The rocks had torn away the entire seam of her swim shorts, revealing a ten-inch open gash of her right butt cheek. Laughing at herself and feeling her other cheeks flush scarlet, she quipped, "Could have been worse. This is only a half-moon. It could have been a full one, baby!"

"You better cover that up or you're going to have to go door to door when we get home to inform all our neighbors of your new sex offender status," Nova offered with sarcastic glee.

She had a point, so Tessa yanked the tube up her hip to hide the tear from the large family groups that were right behind them.

"I can't believe I didn't feel it happen."

"You mean you didn't recognize the cool rush of water to your no-no spots?" Nova asked, still sporting a huge grin on her face.

"I felt nothing. It's a good thing you noticed, or I'd be walking around for hours with half my ass hanging out unaware."

Freed from the rock bed, she lay back down on her

tube and they continued down the river, letting the current pull them where it wanted.

Seeing a sign on the shore that said "Snakes Crossing," Nova's eyes darted around nervously. "Do you think that's legit?'

"I doubt it," Tessa offered, seeing the fresh panic cue up on Nova's face.

Nova was cautious and pulled her feet out of the water, containing her arms and legs inside the tube. When they hit shallow patches, it was Tessa's turn to yank Nova's tube back and forth to free them from the rocks so they could drift further down the river.

They hit another patch of rapids and Tessa cried out, "I'm never letting go, Jack! I'm never letting go!"

"That's an easy one. *Titanic*," Nova answered with a huge grin.

Around the next bend, there were signs posted. Swimming allowed. There was a ladder on the bank and a huge rock formation that jutted out of the water and into the sky about twenty-five feet. They stopped and watched men scale it and jump off into the water below to the smattering of applause from their families floating on connected tubes.

"I kind of want to do it," Nova admitted as they watched a burly father hoist himself out of the lake. The weight of the water pulled down his swim trunks and exposed his crack several inches while Nova snickered.

"He reminds me of someone." Tessa snorted and felt an odd kinship with the man who found himself in the same predicament she was, exposed by nature during a family float. Thankfully, he reached back and tugged up the shorts, and they watched him cannonball into the water after jumping off the rock.

Happy to see him surface and understanding it was deep enough for him to jump safely, she encouraged Nova. "You should do it! You might not get another chance."

Seeing the pull-up bars were about thirty feet away, she said, "Nah."

"We aren't leaving until you do it at least once. Come on. Live a little."

It was the nudge she needed. "Okay, fine."

"Never dive into water you don't know," Tessa cautioned. "Go feet first."

"You suck the fun out of everything, Mom. Come on. Live a little," she mocked back.

"I'll hold on to the tubes," Tessa offered, and Nova swam away over to the bars. She escaped Tessa's view as she climbed up the cliff. At the top of the rock, she hesitated for one single second, then backed up and ran to launch herself into the water. She tucked her knees in tight, executing the perfect cannonball.

"Yay!" Tessa sang out, and next to her a few people clapped. Nova swam back to her with a huge smile of triumph on her face.

"It's good to do things that scare you from time to time. Makes you feel alive."

"That's never really been a problem for me." Nova's lips curled into a smirk.

"Good point."

Nova picked her way across the slippery rocks to knee-deep water and lay back down on the tube again. They floated between pockets of deep shade and then out into the blasting sun. When they hit another faster set of rapids,

Nova's legs dangled, bashing against the rocks. The water turned more violent, yanking her limbs at precarious angles and twisting her ankles when she tried to stand up and fight to free herself from the rocks.

"Ow!"

Tessa panicked, seeing Nova struggle, wondering how far they were away from the nearest Urgent Care Clinic.

"Careful, honey. Get back on the tube."

The water was just doing what it was designed to do, moving as fast as possible, going from serene to dangerous in a flash. Her heart accelerated, and she shouted out warnings to Nova, hoping neither of them would require medical assistance. She was relieved when the water slowed down and they gently floated again.

Trees flanked the banks, some of them covered in salmon-colored flowers. The flowering branches were heavy-laden with fuzzy seed pods the size of a palm that drifted down to float on the water.

Finally, at the outtake point, Tessa clenched her torn swim shorts together and accepted a hand from the guide to climb safely to shore.

"Wasn't that great?" she asked Nova.

"Yeah," Nova agreed. "It was super fun."

After they got out of the Little River, they jumped on the shuttle bus that took them back to the Jeep. Tessa's hand clenched the pieces of her ripped suit together. A woman glanced over at Tessa, and she explained, "I had a little wardrobe malfunction." She laughed. "A Janet Jackson at the Super Bowl moment."

At the car, they changed into dry clothes.

"You hungry?"

"Starving," Nova confirmed.

The closest restaurant was Peaceful Side Social Brewery + Craft Kitchen. It had a patio strung with festive lights, and when they walked in, the smell of cooking food was heavenly.

"My mouth is watering," Tessa said.

"I want a greasy burger," Nova stated, looking over the options.

There were dishes like fried pork belly, truffle fries, and smoked trout dip, but not a single burger on the menu.

"It's taking everything in me to walk away from this delicious smell," Tessa admitted with a disappointed smile. The next option was a hole-in-the-wall dive bar and diner called Townsend Pancake Shop. She sighed, pulled in, and walked inside a massive pole building with dark paneling and filled with open booths. They sat down at a table lacquered with advertisements and a vinyl booth sticky with syrup. A waitress in her late fifties, her hair pulled back into a long gray ponytail, came over with a sweet smile wearing an orange Tennessee Titans jersey. Tessa knew football was a religion in the south, second only to the Baptists that had a church on every corner. She also knew Tennesseans never missed an opportunity to show support for the home team.

The waitress took their order, and they waited. Tessa's stomach was growling and ready for a burger and fries after their long day on the river. The waitress reappeared with two baskets a few minutes later, and they dug in, chewing the first few bites in silence.

Munching on the fries doused in ketchup, Tessa mused aloud, "We've eaten all the eggs, and I don't want to have to buy another dozen." She still needed a single egg for the orange brownie soufflés she wanted to make that night at the treehouse. In a flash of inspiration, she declared, "I'm going to ask our waitress if I can buy an uncooked egg."

"You can't do that," Nova piped up. "It's against the law for a restaurant to sell you uncooked ingredients."

She wasn't sure if Nova was lying to avoid embarrassment or had some sort of inside information since she'd worked part-time in a restaurant for a year.

"Please don't," Nova begged, shrinking into the booth.

"Go out to the car and I'll ask her. What are you so worried about, anyway? We are never going to see any of these people ever again."

The waitress came to check on them, and Tessa seized the opportunity. "I have a weird question. Can I buy an egg from you, uncooked, and still in the shell?"

Confused, the waitress looked at her, dumbfounded.

"I know it's a strange request, but we are camping, and I only need one egg to make orange brownie soufflés."

"Huh," she said with a smile. "Let me ask my manager."

Tessa winked at Nova, who was sliding down into the booth clearly mortified. "Come on, it wasn't that bad."

Five minutes later, she came back to the table with a to-go container, and inside a nest of brown paper towels was one pristine white egg.

"He said to just give it to y'all."

"That's so kind. Thank you."

She placed the receipt on the table, and Tessa added a twenty-dollar tip and took it up to the stand to pay and thank the manager.

At the car, Nova said, "That wasn't fair. You said you'd ask *after* I went to the car."

"It was a life lesson. I wanted you to see how the world responds when you ask for what you need."

Nova threw her yet another eye roll. "You gave her a huge tip. That was like one hundred percent."

"I don't know if I've ever told you this, but Papa and I have a tradition. Once every year, we go out to eat and tip the server a ridiculous amount."

"That's pretty cool," Nova admitted. "We should start doing that."

"Technically, we just did." Tessa grinned.

They drove back to the treehouse as the sun burned into the warm summer day. Tessa spent time in the hammock while Nova hid inside, enjoying the air conditioning. She dozed off and woke up with a start almost an hour later. Going back into the treehouse, she made a dinner suggestion to Nova.

"How about we make campfire pies tonight?" Tessa asked.

"We can't do that. We need a pie iron."

"You mean something like... *this*?" Tessa grinned, pulling the pie iron she'd kept concealed in the Jeep from behind her back and waving it in the air.

"What?" Nova squealed and jumped up. "This reminds me of camping with Papa."

"That's why I got it! Those Pudgy Pies made quite the impression on you."

"They're so good!" Nova gushed as she handled the pie iron. "And you got the *double* pie maker. Good choice!"

"We have the ingredients for pizza pies," Tessa offered, and Nova jumped up to pull the ingredients out of the refrigerator. Her willingness to help without being asked and infectious excitement was a delightful change that melted Tessa's heart. Nova pulled four slices of bread from the cupboard and handed two over to Tessa.

"First you butter them up," Nova instructed, taking over the assembly process. "Place two slices face down on the pie iron. Then you add your sauce, some mozzarella cheese, and the pepperoni. Then top it with two more slices of buttered bread." Tessa followed her directions, and then Nova put the top on the pie iron and locked the handles together.

"Let's use our magical egg for the brownie soufflés." Tessa pulled out two oranges. She sawed the bottom off with a sharp knife so they would stand instead of roll, and then she scooped out the orange pulp. Nova mixed up the instant brownie mix with melted butter and the egg and poured the mixture into the hollowed-out oranges before wrapping them in tinfoil.

"I think we're ready," Tessa stated. "Let's go start the fire."

Now a pro, Nova built a fortress of logs around several thin sticks she gathered from the ground, and the fire roared to life within minutes.

"It's nice to see your survival skills bounced right back," Tessa complimented, feeling the warmth run up her feet and her shins from the flames nearby.

"Yep. If a killer solar flare hits the earth and its sheer electromagnetic power disrupts all the power grids, resulting in chaos and loss of world order, we can take to the woods and survive."

Tessa laughed. "Sounds like someone has been watching *Doomsday Preppers* again."

"It's mildly entertaining." Nova shrugged and stared

into the fire. After twenty minutes, the flames died down to glowing embers, and Nova nestled the pie iron into the coals. Then Tessa took tongs and lowered the foil-wrapped oranges a bit further away. Five minutes later, Nova pulled out the pie iron and opened it to expose perfectly golden brown pizza pies.

"Those look incredible!" Tessa praised with a huge smile, and Nova beamed. She plated them up on paper plates and offered one to Tessa.

"Let it cool down. They're like molten lava inside," Nova instructed. After another full five minutes, she finally said, "Okay, I think they're probably safe to eat now."

Tessa broke her pie in half, pulling it apart. "Wow. Look at the impressive cheese pull! Great job, honey!" The strings of mozzarella finally tore away, and Tessa bit into it, hearing a satisfying crunch. "*Now* I know why you couldn't shut up about these."

"Right?" Nova said with a contented smile as she tore into hers.

"The bread is so golden brown and crunchy, and the cheese inside! It's so gooey and good." They ate in companionable silence for a bit, and then Tessa said, "I think the soufflés might be ready." She pulled them out of the fire with the tongs and opened them carefully, putting one on each plate.

The brownie was cooked on top, but when she dug into it with her spoon, the center was still molten batter.

"It's like a lava cake!" Tessa exclaimed. "I wish we had some ice cream!" She took another bite and detected the delicate flavor of the orange combined with the choco-late. "What do you think?"

"It's pretty decent, but the Samoa S'more is still the winner for me."

"Our trip is more than halfway over," Tessa mused as the embers glowed faintly in the fire, mesmerized by the flickering flames.

For the first time, Nova looked sad at the prospect. "Already?"

"Don't tell me you're actually having fun." Tessa grinned.

"Maybe a little," Nova admitted.

Chapter Twenty

The next evening, Tessa set the GPS to the town of Elkmont and started the thirty-minute drive. Nova settled into the seat next to her and pulled up another true crime podcast. "Ooh, this will be a good one," she promised.

"I don't know if good is the right word for these podcasts," Tessa corrected. "Bizarre or outrageous seems more fitting."

A deep voice crackled through the speakers, spinning the tale of Julian Buchwald, a twenty-two-year-old man who'd fallen in love with an ultra-conservative seventeen-year-old girl. Besotted and horned up, she turned down all his sexual advances and insisted on waiting until they were married to consummate their relationship.

Tessa turned onto the highway, listening to the narrator explain Julian's twisted plan to get laid. He planted a deer carcass and then, in two separate locations, hid gloves, a balaclava, a jacket, a sleeping bag, ropes, duct tape, and military pants. He lied to his girlfriend, saying they were going to be hiking to a waterfall on his parents' property where he had a romantic picnic planned.

The day of the picnic, Julian left her in the car, claiming he saw an injured deer run off into the forest. Then he returned about thirty minutes later in the balaclava, pretending to be a kidnapper. Using the supplies he'd hidden on the property, he blindfolded and abducted her, cut her clothing off, and then forced her to kneel while he dug holes to hide the evidence. Terrified, she thought the hole he was digging was going to be her grave, and she begged for her life. He then took off his own clothes, hid them, and then called out to her weakly as if he'd been kidnapped himself.

"What in the hell are we listening to?" Tessa asked with a laugh.

"Shhh." Nova leaned forward and turned up the volume.

In the forest, they 'found' a sleeping bag and a jar of peanut butter right in the nick of time before starvation set in.

"Come on!" Tessa cried as she pressed the pause button. "You've got to be kidding me. This is absurd!"

"Have you ever heard about the Law of Attraction?" Nova grinned, her blue eyes sparkling with barely concealed mirth. "Maybe they *manifested* them."

"Hey!" Tessa frowned. "Manifesting works."

"If *we* were able to manifest a parking spot at Grotto Falls during the busy summer season, why is it so hard to believe *they* could manifest a sleeping bag and a jar of peanut butter in the middle of a forest?" Nova's tone was playful, poking holes in her mother's theories with glee.

She leaned forward and pressed the play button, and more of the ridiculous story spooled out of the speakers.

For the next week, Julian and his girlfriend hid in the woods, trying to outrun the 'kidnappers' and find their way to safety. In the evenings, they huddled together naked inside the sleeping bag for warmth. Julian put the squeeze on, trying to convince her to have sex with him by telling her they were already married in the eyes of God. She held out, clinging to her morals. After pressuring her for a week and realizing she would never give in, they miraculously 'found' their torn and dirty clothes and then stumbled out onto the highway where they were picked up by a trucker.

"That's officially the craziest story I've ever heard," Tessa said in shock while Nova laughed.

"We're here." Arriving at their destination, Tessa pulled into the parking lot.

"What is this?"

"This should be right up your twisted alley. Its the Elkmont Ghost town." Tessa explained, "In the 1900s, it was a logging community, but over time, it became an escape for wealthy families from Knoxville. They could hop on a train and spend the weekend in the mountains. When the national park was established, families who owned property had the option of selling their homes back to the park service or staying until the end of their lives. There wasn't enough money to maintain them all, so here they sit, rotting into the ground."

They got out of the Jeep and walked down a road with abandoned buildings lining both sides. Well-worn structures with wonky steps and rotted window frames sat vacant. Nova boldly entered a teal building with dirty white trim. Inside, a collection of rotted leaves gathered at the hearth smelled moldy. Tessa followed her, and the spongy wood floor was unsettling. In the kitchen, the cabinet doors were ripped off their hinges, and antique bulbs drifted down lengths of ancient wiring from holes in the ceilings.

"This is what thirty years of neglect looks like," Tessa said, afraid to take another step for fear she'd fall through the floor. She was grateful when Nova turned around and exited the building and they were both on solid ground again.

Then they followed a path deeper into the woods where every once in a while they would come across a tall stone fireplace and chimney in the middle of the forest. These lone hearths were the only evidence left standing from the opulent homes that used to exist in the now-abandoned Millionaire's Row.

Nova followed her mother further down the dirt path and let out a gasp that made Tessa whip around.

"Creepy," Nova remarked. "Do you feel that? There is a pocket of cold air here."

Tessa laughed. "It's ninety-two degrees, Nova, with a heat index of one-oh-seven. Where is this cold pocket you speak of? I want to stand in it!" She walked closer to Nova and pointed at a rickety set of posts several feet away, holding up a hand-carved sign that spelled out "The Old Elkmont Cemetery."

Nova groaned as she typed a search into her phone and began reading from it silently, her lips moving and her eyes widening. "Mom! This is one of the most haunted locations in the Smoky Mountains. Lots of loggers were killed or maimed here in logging accidents. And then there was a train wreck in 1909! We're talking about gruesome deaths from exploding boilers and trains derailing with massive logs slamming into people."

"It's Final Destination, the settler edition," Tessa mused, unfazed. "You know, I can't drive behind a semi full of logs because of that movie." She hesitated. "Should we go in?" The sun was lowering in the sky. "We don't have much time."

"Shhh!" Nova hissed. "I feel like we're being watched."

"Come on, you big baby!" Tessa teased as she decided for them both. She entered under the sign, then walked up a little hill and followed a dirt path that curved to the left flanked by moss that grew under dense green foliage.

Nova glanced over her shoulder, then rushed to follow Tessa under the arch. Tessa waited at the split rail gate and barbed wire fence. Just beyond it, crumbled gravestones and boulders marked over a hundred graves.

Tessa walked inside the fence and shivered as she read the dates on the tombstones. 1888. 1914. 1917. 1918. The grass among the graves was sparse, and the exposed topsoil was covered in yellow lichen and dead leaves.

Tessa stopped at a sunken stone where an infant rested. Next to it, a quartz stone was simply engraved in block lettering. "Sophia 1915-1917. Daughter."

"Why are there so many children buried here?" Nova asked, her blue eyes the size of dinner plates.

"The Flu Pandemic," Tessa answered as she followed Nova to a leaning headstone in decent shape.

"Did you know that quartz was used in graveyards because superstitious people believed it would hold their souls underground?"

"Where did you learn that?" Tessa asked.

"The internet. You can learn anything on the internet." Nova then froze in her tracks and hissed, "There. Again. Did you feel that chill?"

"Honey, it's all in your head." She continued to walk further into the field of gravestones.

"Can we leave? It's getting dark, and there are so many headstones around here, I don't know where to put my feet," Nova begged. "It's creeping me out."

"Maybe we need to cool it on the murder and mayhem podcasts for a while. You seem a little jumpy." Tessa glanced at her watch. "We need to meet our guide, anyway."

"Guide for what?"

"A surprise." She walked back to the parking lot with Nova in tow, whose anxiety dissipated the further away they walked from the cemetery. Closer to the parking lot, crowds of people began streaming into the forest.

"What's happening?" Nova asked, noticing the considerable uptick of visitors around them. There was a bus that dropped off sixty people who were carrying folding chairs and making their way on foot up into the forested area.

"I splurged on tickets for us to see a once-in-a-lifetime event."

"What is it?"

"The synchronized fireflies."

She'd had to book a tour with a guide since the lottery happened before she made the decision to come to Tennessee. Tessa scanned the darkened parking lot, looking for their guide.

A man in a white beard looking like a rugged Santa Claus was leaning against a truck that had the words

'Smoky Excursions' on the side. Tessa walked toward him and introduced herself and Nova.

"It's nice to meet you. I'm Chris." Tessa bit back the urge to laugh as she shook his firm hand.

"Your last name wouldn't happen to be Kringle, would it?" she heard Nova ask.

His deep belly laugh echoed and chased away the creepy residue that lingered from their walk through the cemetery. "Only around Christmastime when I volunteer at my church." From the back of his truck, he pulled out three folding chairs and a cooler that he slung over one shoulder.

"Do you want some help?" Tessa offered.

"Well, I reckon that would be breakin' the rules." He grinned. "You didn't come here to be loaded down like a pack mule. This is why they pay me the big bucks."

"Who's they?" Nova was confused.

"My wife," he answered with another laugh. "C'mon, I have the perfect viewing spot reserved for us." He handed them two flashlights covered in blue cellophane. "Keep them low and pointed at the ground in case the show starts early."

Tessa glanced around where the crowd was gathering. She followed behind Chris, who picked his way into the forest over fallen logs. "In the Great Smoky Mountains National Park alone, you can find over nineteen different species of fireflies, but there's only one species in America that synchronize their light patterns. Once every year, in early June, their mating ritual is a spectacular sight to see and draws thousands of people to witness it." He continued to lead them deeper into the forest as he explained.

"The pressure is on because, after a year of crawling

on the ground as larvae, the adults have only twenty-one days to find a mate."

"Wow," Tessa remarked.

"It's the males that have to do all the work. They fly around flashing, looking for potential mates, and if the females are interested, they respond from the ground with two quick blinks to mark their location."

Nova snorted. "How did the insect world get it right and humans are stuck in barbaric caveman land? Evolution failed us."

"Do we have a budding feminist in our midst?" Chris asked.

"Yep," Nova declared. "Just like my mom."

A proud grin tugged at Tessa's lips, surprised by Nova's response as they picked their way across the tree branches and to the top of a hill.

"This is our spot." Chris set down the chairs in the grass, busying himself with setting them up. Under a canopy of mature trees, the view meandered through a field of new-growth saplings. Spindly trunks popped up through the tall grasses, and wildflowers lived under their dappled shade. Tessa sat down on a chair and was embarrassed by a loud growl from her stomach.

"Don't you worry about that. The missus packed us a feast." He removed a single piece of ice from the cooler and used it to wash his hands. He then reached inside and pulled out glass bottles of root beer, and from a pocket on the side of the cooler produced a bottle opener and popped the tops off three bottles, handing one to Tessa and one to Nova. Tessa took a long sip. It was sweet and decadent.

"You're drinking high fructose corn syrup?" Nova

whispered with a smirk. "I thought it was the devil's poison?"

"When in Rome," she whispered to Nova under her breath, who shot her a questioning look. "Never mind."

He pulled out a tray filled with cheese and crackers. Pears and apples were already thinly sliced to nibble with ease. He also produced a wicker basket filled with fried chicken wrapped in a linen napkin. Chris offered it to Tessa, who pulled out a warm leg and bit into the still crunchy skin, moaning with delight.

"Delicious," she declared to a smiling Chris.

"She marinates it in buttermilk for two days and coats it in her special spice rub."

"This is the best thing I've ever eaten," Nova remarked.

"She's right," Tessa exclaimed. "You be sure to tell her so."

"It's getting ready to start," Chris said softly. "Shut off all the flashlights and your phones. It's best to witness this event in as much darkness as possible."

In the distance, Tessa saw a flicker of light. At first, she wondered if her eyes were deceiving her. But then, in quick succession, there was another flicker, and another, and another. Within minutes, the forest was ablaze with pulsating, bright lemon-lime flecks. Thousands of fireflies dotted all over the trees, circling in the air, and on the ground, as the forest sparkled in a wave of bioluminescent light that surged on and on. In awe, Tessa scanned the field in front of them, watching it be transformed by the twinkling lights of the male beetles looking for mates.

"Wow," Nova gasped, her jaded teenage jaw open wide, taking in the display. "It's so beautiful."

The blinking continued like the stars had dropped from heaven to twinkle in the forest. All at once, it was like nature's master switch had been thrown.

Nova was mesmerized as she leaned forward and whispered, "Remember my fifth birthday when the only gift I asked for was the Bug Bungalow?"

"I do." Tessa smiled. "You spent every night for a week out in the yard catching fireflies after dark."

"And every morning, I'd wake up to go feed them some grass, and they'd be gone," Nova recalled.

"That's because I freed them after you fell asleep."

"What?" Nova cried in sarcastic outrage. "How could you?"

"It was inhumane. Insects belong in the wild."

"You told me they were magic and Santa helped them escape with all the free time he had in the summer," Nova remembered Tessa's cover story with mind-blowing accuracy. "My entire childhood was a lie." A fake sob escaped her lips.

"And the Oscar goes to..." Tessa laughed.

In the forest, the lights blinked on and off, lighting up the sky with sparkling yellow glowing bits. Some far in the distance were a tiny pinprick of light. Others were larger and neon green from brave bugs flying closer to their chairs.

"What happens after they find a mate?' Nova asked.

"It's all downhill for them after the big show," Chris admitted. "They mate, lay eggs, and then they die."

"Lucky bugs," Tessa joked.

"Hey." Nova acted like she was taking it personally.

"I mean, poor things, not getting the chance to adequately mother the next generation."

"That's better." Nova scooted closer to Tessa and lay her head on her mom's shoulder. Tessa wrapped her arm around Nova and squeezed.

"Isn't this amazing?" Tessa asked her.

"Yes, it is," Nova said. "I don't think I'll ever forget this moment."

Tessa's heart swelled as they watched the rest of the show quietly, bellies full of fried chicken and soda. They watched for the next hour as the males worked to find their perfect match and the females flickered and flirted.

Insects had it so easy. They had a predetermined set of instinctual courtship rules to follow. He blinks. She blinks twice. They mate. Why couldn't it be like that for humans?

An hour later, they packed up their chairs and helped Chris carry them back to his pickup truck, where Tessa handed him a twenty-dollar tip. "This was almost a religious experience. Thank you."

"My pleasure," he said with a smile and then climbed back into his pickup truck and drove away as Nova and Tessa strolled back to the Jeep. The air was cooler and the waning moon was still full enough to light their way. They drove into the night toward their treehouse quietly. Nova had even given the true crime podcasts a break.

As the miles raced by, peace seeped deeply into the confines of Tessa's heart in the most remarkable way. The fear, anger, and frustration that dominated their interactions back home had been miraculously replaced by curiosity and love as their relationship shifted into fresh territory again. It was like a kaleidoscope, continuously transforming before her eyes, and for the first time, Tessa realized each combination was more beautiful than the last.

Chapter Twenty-One

The next morning, after eating breakfast, they drove back to the Smoky Mountains, where Tessa eased into a parking spot at Cade's Cove. "We're here! This is it! Our last hike of the trip!" She roused Nova, who was dozing in the seat next to her. The dawn was breaking, and the pink-tinged sunrise was giving way to a baby blue sky with puffy white clouds. "Wake up, sleepyhead." She grinned, shaking Nova's shoulder softly.

Nova yawned and then opened the door and stretched. Tessa glanced over at her, noticing her posture wasn't so rigid and her jaw wasn't as tight.

Tessa doused herself with bug spray and held it out to Nova. "Want some?"

"It's probably a good idea," Nova agreed and sprayed herself down. Tessa was taken aback by the shift. The negativity and defiance she'd exhibited earlier in the week had evaporated into ease, and Tessa was grateful.

They pulled their backpacks out of the Jeep, filled them with water bottles and Nutter Butters, and started down a path. Sticks cracked as they made their way down the tree-lined trail. The forest was still relatively cool since the scorching heat of the day would begin later. She'd planned it that way, getting an early start to avoid the crowded parking lots and masses of people. They steadily climbed up the trail, stepping up stone steps that were mounted into the sides of the path, then back down again as they scissored their way up the mountain. Tessa's sore muscles took a good twenty minutes to warm up, and she noticed Nova's sunburn was starting to peel.

They stopped to take a drink here and there and fell into a peaceful silence. Tessa was grateful the suppressed rage that had followed her up into Grotto Falls was gone. She slowed down her pace, and they walked down the trail shoulder to shoulder. A squirrel darted out of the grass and then up a tree. Tessa took a deep breath in, inhaling the humidity that hung heavy, cloaking the air in the damp scent of fallen trees and wood shavings.

"Forest bathing," Tessa said, then sucked in another long breath. "This is good for the soul."

"That's that Japanese thing you were talking about, right?"

"Yeah."

"You know what else is in Japan?" Nova asked, then without waiting added, "The Suicide Forest."

"You're going there already? Straight to the heavy topics at," she glanced down at her watch, "the crack of seven-twenty-seven?"

When Nova was little, Tessa made the conscious decision that no topic was off-limits for a spirited discussion. She'd read in the parenting books that when your child talked to you about mundane things, like why Cinnamon

Toast Crunch was their favorite cereal, they would feel safe enough to come to you with bigger issues or problems they were facing. As a result, they'd fallen down many conversational rabbit holes together.

Nova grinned and continued, "At the base of Mount Fuji, there is a forest that is considered sacred."

The name jogged Tessa's memory, and she snapped her fingers. "I think I heard of it, the Aokigahara Forest."

"That's the one. It's such a magnet for suicides that Japanese officials don't publicly release the official number anymore, but it's rumored to be in the hundreds every year. They even have signs posted at the entrance, telling people who have suicidal thoughts to turn back or seek help."

"Oh my God, really?"

"It wasn't even a phenomenon until the last eruption of Mount Fuji. Apparently, the lava hardened and created these chambers in the earth that people just crawl into and die, and authorities find their skeletons years later."

"Whoa," Tessa said.

"I wrote a paper about it in sociology last year," Nova offered and kept going. "The Aokigahara Forest is completely silent, no birds chirping nor other forest animals making any noises at all." Nova shivered. "Isn't that creepy?"

"Hold on." Tessa held up a finger and listened for a moment. Hearing the birds calling in the trees that engulfed them was a relief. "Looks like we're safe here."

Nova shot her a playful eye roll and then continued, "Apparently, you'll find strings of ribbon all over it. People who are undecided will tie a ribbon at the entrance and unspool it as they walk through, so they can find their way back out if they change their mind." She paused on the trail, thinking, then asked, "Do you think certain places are evil or hold darkness?"

"Anything is possible," Tessa admitted. "You said you felt cold air at the cemetery yesterday."

"They say the volcanic rocks found there have some sort of electromagnetic material that generates electromagnetic fields and affects brain activity, especially the parts of the brain that are triggers for depression and suicidal thoughts."

"Hmm." Tessa thought it through. "That's an interesting theory. The brain is very complex, and mental illness is a mystery that has been difficult for doctors to understand." The subject was heavy, but Tessa was thrilled her daughter could research topics she was interested in and could carry on intelligent conversations about them.

Nova picked up her pace and walked ahead to where the trail narrowed to a single path. "There's this YouTuber I follow, Logan Paul, and he actually went there," she chattered on. Tessa found herself riveted, despite the morbid subject. It was always interesting to hear what stuck in her daughter's mind. It was like Nova was handing her pieces to a puzzle Tessa could put together to learn who she was becoming.

"He wasn't even supposed to be filming there, to begin with, but, apparently, he was wandering around the forest and saw a body hanging from a tree and filmed it. Then he released it on YouTube to share it with his fifteen million followers. In the video, you can hear them cracking jokes and being disrespectful. Isn't that sick?"

"Um... Yeah, that's terrible," Tessa agreed with a

heavy sigh, then asked, "Why are you so drawn to the macabre?"

"All teenagers are, Mom," Nova responded matter-of-factly.

"That's probably true." Tessa remembered her own strange fascination with the Jeffrey Dahmer case when she was in high school. It was all anyone talked about for months.

"Isn't it interesting that the same country that is famous for forest bathing also has a haunted forest famous for suicides?" Nova asked.

Tessa was stunned at the connections she was making, as accurate as they were. "Have you ever…?" Tessa asked, afraid to finish the sentence.

"…had suicidal thoughts?" Nova finished. She stopped and pulled her water bottle out of her backpack, taking a long drink before answering. "I think it would be hard to find a teenager who hasn't," she admitted, "but I never had a plan."

The honest admission was hard for Tessa to hear. She knew Nova had been struggling for the last three years, but it hurt that she never recognized how deeply.

"You know you can always come to me," Tessa offered.

"I know, Mom."

Tessa sat down on a thick log and patted the spot next to her. "It's not easy being a teenager. Your brain is still developing, and when you add in the hormones…"

"Mom," Nova cautioned, afraid of where this heart-to-heart was headed.

"I know, I know, but let me finish." Nova nodded, and she continued. "It is normal for you to feel overwhelmed and afraid right now. And I know you've been coping with accepting the disappointment you've faced where your father is concerned. It is okay for you to be angry at him for not giving you what you needed. Your needs are valid and should never be minimized."

"I keep getting stuck daydreaming about the life I could have had with him."

Tessa reached out and squeezed her arm. "I do that, too. Lately, I've been stuck in that same place with Jason."

Nova gulped.

"It's so destructive, the lies and the fantasies we tell ourselves." She looked down. "But the thing is, it's never about you. It's *always* about them, yet it can leave you scrambling for worthiness."

Nova exhaled a heavy breath. "How do I…?"

"Fix it?" Tessa finished, and Nova nodded. "You let go of the fantasy and you love yourself. You fill your own well instead of waiting for someone else to do it for you."

"How?"

"Think about how you treat someone you want to date. You gush about them. You buy them gifts and treats. You consume your days looking for little ways to connect and make them smile," Tessa explained, then paused before summing it up in four words. "It's simple. Love yourself."

"Love yourself." Nova nodded, considering the suggestion.

Tessa held out her pinky finger. "Pinky promise me. From now on, we will find ways to love ourselves, and when we slip up, we will hold each other accountable." Nova wrapped her pinky around her mother's. "Lock it up," Tessa said, and then felt Nova tap her thumb against hers.

They stood and continued up the mountain, and Tessa was exhilarated with the newfound stamina in her legs. The week of hiking strengthened her muscles and made the hills easier to climb. Nova was stepping more lively, too, swiping her walking stick in front to ward off forest creatures. They picked their way back to the trail and climbed ever higher. The dense green foliage packed in tight around them as more morning light bathed the area. Up ahead, she could hear rushing water that intensified as they got closer. On the other side of the fast-moving stream was a waterfall, and Tessa was determined to have one more waterfall experience.

She stopped in front of the stream, assessing the best path. Next to her, the furious water was rushing by so loudly they had to shout at each other.

"You want to cross *this*?" Nova asked. Tessa nodded, then sat down on a rock and took off her socks and boots. Nova let out a sigh and yanked her socks off, too, knowing there was no way she was going to talk her mother out of it. Nova crossed first. Cutting through the rushing water like a boss, she never hesitated. Her steps were sure and solid. Within minutes, she was standing on the other side, waiting for Tessa to begin her trek.

Tessa tightened the straps on her backpack and began to pick her way across the rocks. Three feet from shore and submerged in thigh-high water, her vision blurred for a minute as the water rushed by, making her dizzy. She couldn't see through the water to figure out where to put her foot. As she took another small step into the unknown, a sharp stray rock cut into her foot, stopping just short of drawing blood.

She was too far away from Nova and too far in the

stream to turn back now. Deciding, Tessa glanced over at Nova and gave her a forced smile before she boldly took one huge step forward, trying to cross the stream in as few steps as possible. Her foot connected with a slimy surface that sent her plunging deep into the water with a yelp. Ice-cold, white water rushed up the length of her body to her neck. It carried her a couple feet until she wrenched her foot against a boulder and popped up, soaked from the neck down. Trails of water dripped down her thick thighs, back into the stream. On the other side of the bank, Nova laughed while she waited. Tessa took four more agonizing steps and finally made it to the shore.

"Was it worth it?" Nova asked with a smirk.

"No regrets!" Tessa responded with a grin. "Come on!"

The lime-green moss was like plush carpet under her feet as she climbed closer to get a better angle for one last photo. Nova picked her way behind her, crawling up the boulders in their path when the first strangled bellow came from several yards away. Tessa's eyes shot like a rocket over to where it came from, scanning the thick foliage for movement. The branches on a spindly tree shook, and then she heard it splinter and crack.

Still scanning the area, her eyes met Nova's. She quickly stepped closer and pointed. "Bear!" Nova whisper-yelled, her tanned skin blanching with fear. Tessa's heart began to hammer as her eyes followed Nova's gaze to the wooded spot she was pointing at. She saw a flash of fur and then accidentally made eye contact with the animal, who reared up on her hind legs and bellowed a second time. It was an ominous warning that spooked Tessa. The bear swiped at the foliage aggressively, and the trees rustled and cracked as branches caught the brunt of her rage. Further up the hill, a flash of movement in the trees caught Tessa's attention where two small cubs were chewing on leaves. Another roar came from the mother, a terrifying declaration Tessa recognized they must heed.

Quickly, she shielded Nova's body and shouted, "Go back the way we came! Shout at the top of your lungs!"

Paralyzed, Nova didn't move, her face white as a sheet and her eyes locked on the mother bear.

"Look at me!" Tessa said, forcing her daughter's chin up to make eye contact. "She's just protecting her babies. Cross the stream and wait for me on the other side. Go now!" Pulling the backpack off, she dug inside and was grateful when her hand connected with the bear spray she'd had the foresight to pack. "Go, Nova!"

Tessa took a few more steps back, waving her arms above her head and screaming at the bear while she slowly retreated. "Back off, Mama!" she shouted. Tessa removed the safety clip, hoping she wouldn't have to use it but still gripping it in her hand. It was locked and loaded, and if the bear charged, she'd have one shot to use the spray.

The mother bear advanced closer, and Nova let out a scream. "Mom!"

"I'm okay. NOVA! GO!" she screamed at Nova, who finally stepped into the creek. Tessa was relieved to see her scamper to the other side out of the corner of her eye. She continued backtracking, her feet stumbling on the rocks. She winced as sharp rocks cut the bottoms of her feet and she tripped backward, running out of dry land to stand on. The black bear roared and reared up on her hind legs. Over seven feet tall and unencumbered by the rough terrain, she bellowed at Tessa, a menacing sound that made her heart-beat blast through her ears.

"I'm not going to hurt you! Go away!" Tessa shouted, holding out the can of bear spray. The bear was closing in fast, now only ten feet away. Tessa's brain recorded the shaft of sunlight that illuminated its paws and the flash of white teeth. Over the thunder of the rushing water, Tessa heard Nova's screams as the bear closed in. Tessa closed her eyes and pressed the button, squirting the spray into the air as she waved it around in a circle. The bear yelped in pain as the capsaicin came in contact with its eyes. Tessa squinted, feeling the sting as she took the only opportunity she had to cross the stream. Eager to put distance between her family and theirs, she didn't even hesitate this time. Tessa quickly picked her way across the rocks in a rush of adrenaline to land in Nova's arms on the other side. Tessa wrapped her arms around Nova, who was trembling as she clung to her mother.

"Let's go." She dragged Nova back on the trail and began their descent as blood rushed through her, forcing them to walk faster. After ten minutes, Tessa finally stopped and sat on a rock, struggling to catch her breath. The stinging of her feet forced her to sit, and a long shaky exhale escaped her lips.

"You're bleeding," Nova said as she unzipped her bag and pulled out their first aid kit, handing it to Tessa. "I thought you were going to die." Nova started to cry again as the adrenaline dissipated.

"It was just a conversation from one mother to another," Tessa said, trying to lighten the mood. "She was protecting her babies, and I would have done the same for you." She wiped the blood away from her foot and applied super glue to the cut. After it dried, she wrapped it in gauze and downed three Advil as Nova handed over her socks and boots.

"Thanks, sweetheart." Tessa forced a smile, then tucked her head down while she pulled her boots on to hide her pained expression from an already distressed Nova.

"I think that's enough excitement for one day." She stood and found two more walking sticks and handed one to Nova.

"First the snake, now a bear. It's official. Nature is trying to kill us," Nova waxed dramatically. "Let's get out of here."

Nova picked up Tessa's backpack and carried them both back down the mountain. She followed Tessa closely as they navigated back to the Jeep, apologizing profusely when she misstepped and landed on her mother's heel and Tessa let out an anguished yelp. "I'm so sorry, Mom."

"It's okay." Tessa breathed through the pain, grateful they were the only injuries either of them sustained that day.

Chapter Twenty-Two

T he sunrise the next morning was an exceptionally beautiful one. Tessa wasn't sure if it was really more striking or if their recent brush with death was the cause, but either way, she sat on the deck and savored its beauty. Having just enough creamer to enjoy her last few cups of coffee, she stirred and sipped while Nova slept. Pale peach morphed into bright orange as the sun made its ascent higher in the sky, casting a warm glow on the mountain range behind their treehouse. The smoke on the mountains seemed especially thick that morning as she planned their last full day.

Around ten o'clock, Nova made an appearance, her face creased from the pillows, and her eyelids swollen and sleepy.

"You let me sleep in," she said as she balled her hands into fists and rubbed her eyes.

"I figured you deserved it after the exhausting adventure we had yesterday," Tessa said. Nova closed the distance between them, and Tessa stood and hugged her tight, feeling her daughter relax in her embrace. Her heart swelled with emotion. Every touch was intensified as she welcomed this new version of Nova into her arms.

"So, that's what we're calling it? An adventure?" Nova asked, pulling back with a smirk.

"It's always a choice, how you interpret the world and the experiences you have in it." Tessa smiled. "So, I guess the answer to your question is yes."

"What are we doing today?"

"We need to pack up our bags because this evening we're heading to the final treehouse, and I saved the best one for last! Tonight, the Donahue women are going to indulge in the most luxurious treehouse experience this side of the Mississippi."

"I like the sound of that."

"We can't check in until four, though, so I've got something special planned."

"Oh, no." Nova's reaction made Tessa laugh.

"I think you'll be pleasantly surprised."

"Is there any hiking involved?" she asked, her tone strained.

"Technically, no."

Nova grimaced at the word technically.

"It'll be fun. You'll see. That's actually one of Papa's catchphrases, but when *he* said it, it usually involved unloading a trailer full of firewood or vacuuming out his truck."

"I miss him," Nova admitted.

"I'm sure he'd love to see you more. When we get back, we'll start inviting him over for dinner on Sundays again." She glanced at her watch. "Get dressed and get your suitcase packed. We need to leave in about an hour."

233

Nova stood and Tessa added, "And make sure you wear comfortable shoes."

Tessa took a quick shower and rebandaged her feet. She tossed back a few ibuprofen, pleasantly surprised the pain was more of an inconvenience and wouldn't hamper their last day. They made quick work of reloading the coolers and packing their suitcases, as they were professionals by now, and loaded them easily in the Jeep.

Tessa got behind the wheel and drove back down the mountain, and then they were on the curvy roads headed to Sevierville. Keith Morrison's voice was now as familiar as family, and Nova pressed play on the latest podcast he'd narrated. About twenty minutes later, Tessa turned into Foxfire Mountain Park. Nova let out a little whoop of excitement. "We're going zip-lining? I thought it was your worst nightmare?"

"It is, but it's time to practice what I preach." Tessa grinned. "And I figured after what transpired yesterday, you deserved the adrenaline rush you crave in a safer delivery system."

Tessa signed liability waivers for them both, and then they were outfitted with safety harnesses and hard hats. They followed a small group of people into a shuttle that led them up the mountain. At the top, the view was spectacular. Tessa whipped out her phone. "Come take a photo with me," she called out to Nova, whose cheeks pinked up at Tessa's request made in front of the small group.

"I'll do that for you," one guide piped up. "I'm Ben."

"Thanks, Ben." Tessa smiled, handing over her phone. They posed, and he took three quick snaps. On the last one, Tessa turned toward Nova, registering the beaming smile on her face. It was focused on their lanky guide, who was over six feet tall with long hair and tattoos, but Tessa still considered it a win. Her daughter's face radiated happiness, and Tessa was filled with joy to see it there.

Nova fell in step with Ben, and they made small talk as they climbed up the steps to the first platform. There, Ben gave them a quick safety lesson with his partner, Connor. Their delivery was a rehearsed back-and-forth banter that reminded Tessa of the few times she'd flown and had stewardesses with a good sense of humor. She watched Connor clip in and then step off the platform and disappear into the canopy of trees shouting out, "Aye, aye, aye!"

Next, she watched Ben clip Nova in. When he tugged at the harness to confirm it was secure, he yanked Nova closer to his chest, which elicited an even bigger smile. Then, with a puppy dog grin that even Tessa had to admit made him handsome, he said, "You're good!" Without hesitation, Nova boldly stepped off the platform and zipped into the trees.

Then Tessa tiptoed to the edge of the platform. Taking a glance below, she felt her knees buckle. Her heart accelerated in her head and her stomach flipped.

"Are you okay?" Ben asked.

"Heights aren't exactly my favorite," she admitted with a tight smile. "How long have you been a guide?"

"This is my second year," he said with a grin, "and I've only lost one."

Her eyebrows shot up, and she swallowed a metallic burst of fear with a gulp.

He yanked on her carabiners and said, "I'm kidding." He grinned. "You're in great hands. Are you ready?"

"Ready enough." She swallowed and then closed her eyes and took a tentative step off the platform. There was a sensation of falling before the cables tugged up to support her weight. Her screams of terror turned into peals of delight as she realized she would not die. Tessa zipped through the tree line for nearly a minute before the next platform was visible. There, Connor waited with open arms to slow her down. She was ecstatic when her toes touched the wooden planks.

"How was it?" Nova asked.

"Terrifying… then incredible," Tessa answered, finally able to exhale.

"I'm proud of you. Look at all that growth happening outside your comfort zone!" Nova's mocking grin was infectious.

"Yeah, yeah, yeah," Tessa dismissed with a satisfied smile, thrilled Nova was listening. She was proud of herself, too. It *was* fun, she had to admit. Now that the initial fear was conquered, she looked forward to the rest of the tour.

At each platform, Ben and Connor took turns throwing out a pose challenge to the group. Nova was fearless and tried them all—The Starfish, The Usain Bolt, the Floppy Salmon, and the Body Builder. Tessa, on the other hand, clung to the bar at the top, her body rigid, as she zinged from tree to tree.

Seven different zip lines shot them through forest views and over the top of a rushing waterfall, and she screamed like a banshee through all seven of them. Tessa never got used to the free-falling sensation and the loss of control. Each time she successfully landed on the platform, her legs still wobbly from terror, was life-affirming. Seeing Nova's wide grin, her eyes sparkling, and her windswept ponytail bobbing up and down reinforced it had been a great decision to face her fear.

At the end of their two-hour excursion, when they had gotten back to the locker her purse was stored in, Tessa handed Nova some cash. "Give this to Ben and thank him for keeping us both alive."

Nova grinned and walked over to where Ben was standing, speaking to a family of four. She waited for them to move along. Finally, having him to herself, Ben turned toward her with a big open smile, and she reached out with the cash. Tessa saw Nova stick her thumbs in her pockets and rock side to side, dragging one toe in the dirt, clearly smitten. A few minutes later, she skipped back to Tessa with a huge smile.

"What a rush! That was so much fun, Mom. Thanks."

The compliment made Tessa's heart fizz up with joy. She wrapped an arm around Nova's shoulders and pulled her in for a side hug. "I'm glad you enjoyed it."

They walked down a wooded path and then under a rough-hewn wooden sign that read "America's Bridge to Prosperity." The suspended bridge rocked gently from side to side, a quality that normally would have made Tessa anxious, but compared to the zip-line she'd just ridden, was small potatoes. She'd already suffered through two hours of exposure therapy in the treetops and now found the rocking sensation oddly comforting. She followed Nova down the bridge, holding on to one side. It had wood plank flooring and chain link fencing on either side that made it feel more secure. In a single file line, they comfortably walked the length of a football field, eventually walking through a wooden archway. A message was carved into the wood overhead that read, "May all your wishes come true."

Nova waited for her at the opening of a covered bridge where the underside of the roof was covered in a thick thatch of ribbons. On each ribbon, a wish was written in Sharpie and attached to the ceiling. The roof was so full of wishes, visitors started to attach them to the sides. It was a gorgeous rainbow of color covering the bridge, giving it a festive look that captivated them both.

"What is this place?" Nova asked, her voice filled with wonder as she looked up at the ribbons in every color of the rainbow.

"It's called Whispering Winds Covered Bridge," Tessa answered, and Nova's fingers brushed across the ribbons softly and she leaned closer.

"That my mom is cured of cancer," Nova read out loud from a green ribbon that was attached to the side of the structure. "That my daughter gets into Harvard" was written on a red one. "That the polar bears stop starving" was inscribed on a yellow ribbon.

"Should we?" Tessa asked.

Nova nodded eagerly and followed her into the museum to purchase the ribbons. Nova chose red, her favorite color, and Tessa a sensible blue. She took a moment to scribble her wish and, just out of eyeshot, Nova did the same.

"What's your wish?' Tessa asked.

"Wait. Are these like birthday wishes? If you say it out loud, it won't come true?"

"I highly doubt it," Tessa replied. "I'll go first. You don't have to share yours if you don't want to." She held up the blue ribbon between her fingers. Written in her perfect penmanship was, "That my daughter goes out into the world and creates a big, fat, juicy life for herself."

A sweet smile formed on Nova's lips. Awkwardly, she held up her red ribbon. "That I become someone who makes my mom proud."

The sentiment choked Tessa up, and she pulled Nova into her arms. She held her tight and whispered into her ear, "Wish granted. You already do."

Nova grinned and pulled back. "But just think how much more proud you'll be when I'm a world-renowned tattoo artist?" Still holding her mother's forearms, she said, "But for real, thank you for giving me the space to find my own way. I know it's not the career path you would have chosen for me, but I am grateful for your support."

"You *always* have my support, Nova. Never forget that."

"Alright, you sap factory, what do you say we go hang these before you start scaring little children with all the wailing?"

"Good idea." She followed Nova to the bridge, and then they attached their ribbons side by side. In the center of the bridge, a long rope dangled from a bell they'd heard ring out several times during their walk to it.

"Let's ring it together," Nova suggested. They each grabbed a length of the rope. It was scratchy in Tessa's hand, and when they tugged it together, the metallic bell clanged high above them and out into the air. The deep jingle of metal on metal reverberated deep into the forest and mountains, but never compared to how deeply it resonated in Tessa's heart.

Chapter Twenty-Three

"Ready to head to the last treehouse?" Tessa asked when they were settled back in the Jeep.

Nova's bottom lip jutted forward into a forced pout. "I'm sad to see our trip coming to an end."

"Me too, honey. It exceeded any expectations I had."

"Agreed," Nova answered. A long pause filled the Jeep that both of them were hesitant to break. They'd reached such a tender place of understanding and felt the gravity of this new terrain they had fought their way to, and neither of them wanted to jeopardize it.

Finally, Tessa spoke. "This last one is a literal tree-house mansion. It's called Whimsical Treehouse, and I know you're going to love it."

"Alright, let's go." They drove twenty minutes down a curvy two-lane highway that wrapped around a mountain. Following the pin down a narrow gravel road, they finally arrived and parked the Jeep in a parking pull-out. From the back of the Jeep, they retrieved the backpacks they'd re-jiggered to hold toiletries, pajamas, and clothing they'd need during their stay. Together, they meandered down a tree-lined path filled with quaint stepping stones. At the end of the trail, they entered a small clearing, and it was love at first sight.

"It's so cute!" Nova cried.

Tucked into the trees, it had a spectacular view of the mountain range beyond. The treehouse was a multi-level dwelling with catwalks surrounding it and a cedar-lined bridge that led to the front door. Tessa tapped in the code on the app on her phone and it unlocked. Nova turned the handle and swung the heavy handmade door into a light-drenched kitchen with an adjacent living room. The main area was spacious enough to fit a full-size white leather sofa in the living room and a larger kitchen with bar stools. The adjoining bathroom featured a luxurious rain-style shower head, and the floor of the shower was a natural surface of polished river stones. A vessel sink sat on top of a thick slab of black granite with a natural edge, and the window tucked into the wall offered a view of the mountains in the distance.

Double glass doors in the back of the house washed the treehouse with natural light and opened out onto the deck that was tucked into the trees. On it sat a fire table and a charcoal grill. Tessa followed Nova, who was walking down a short cedar walkway to the left. They passed two chaise lounges and then Nova let out a squeal.

"A hot tub? *And* a stripper pole?" Nova gushed.

Tessa laughed as she corrected her. "That's a *totem* pole." A thick tree trunk featuring a carving of birds and deer popped through an opening in the deck.

"Potato, Po-ta-toe," Nova shrugged waving off her mother's explanation.

They walked back inside and up the staircase that switched up and back several times until they entered a spacious loft that held the bedroom. Suspended from a real tree trunk that spanned the length of the entire ceiling, two canvas swing chairs were connected with a strong silver cable system.

"Whoa." Nova was impressed. "Are those indoor swings? You can do that?"

Tessa laughed. "I guess you can." She'd never seen anything like it either. It was a whimsical touch that made the treehouse even more magical.

Never one to be cautious, Nova jumped into one of them, and it made a scissoring sound as she settled in. She pumped her feet back and forth a few moments with glee, then turned from side to side, taking in the features of the rest of the room.

One-third of the loft-style bedroom was covered in stretchy bungee cording that gave the floor a see-through hammock effect. On either end of the hammock floor were piles of decorative pillows with sweet sayings about adventure and relaxation. Opposite the floor hammock area was a king-size bed.

"Careful," Tessa said, hearing Nova's swing screeching as it swung from side to side. Tessa sat down on hers a little more gingerly. To her left, Nova's swing made one final protest, then settled. "Look, there are fairy lights." Tessa extracted herself and went to the outlet to plug them in. They twinkled in the low light of the treehouse as the late afternoon sun waned, adding a soft glow.

"How romantic," Nova said.

"I'm sure we're probably the first mother and daughter who've ever stayed here."

"Really?"

"I would think with the steep rental fee, it's more popular with newlyweds or people celebrating an anniversary."

"Wait, do you think people used these as sex swings?"

Tessa laughed. "I highly doubt it. The geometry just doesn't work."

"Gross, Mom." Horrified, Nova dismounted from her swing and then belly-flopped on the bed. It was plushly appointed with snappy white linens and layers of white textured throw pillows. Behind the wooden live-edge headboard was a wall of stone with several niches. Tucked into each niche was a flameless luminary. The overall effect was romantic, rustic, and warm.

"Actually, I think you have a higher chance of coming into contact with body fluids on that bed. It's a good thing we don't have a black light."

Nova popped up like she'd been burned. Disgusted at the thought, she started to make gagging noises that made Tessa laugh harder.

"I'm sure it's fine," Tessa said as she flopped down on the bed, looking straight up at the wooden ceiling. "Isn't it beautiful?" The ceiling and walls were covered in reclaimed barn wood. Weathered browns and warm grays hugged every angle and peak. The back wall was mostly glass that framed a mountain view, and triangular windows were tucked into every corner, bathing the room in the last bit of natural light of the day. "It's so charming," Tessa remarked.

They cooked up the final two hot dogs over the grill and ate the last of the fruit. After a twenty-minute dip in the hot tub, they took showers and settled in for the night.

Knowing this was her last chance, Tessa pulled out the deck of cards from her suitcase and called through the hammock floor to Nova resting on the couch below.

"How about one last game?" Tessa asked.

"Yeah." Nova was much more agreeable, bordering on excited.

They drew twelve cards and played until their hands were empty, and learned discovering vulnerable truths about each other was easier when you could dispel the awkward energy by rocking. The sun's rays lowered and washed in through the wall of windows, and a prism of rainbow color brushed across Nova's cheek. In the last rays of golden hour light, Tessa was struck by Nova's natural beauty, without the theatrical makeup that had been her security blanket. Her skin was pure and her eyes were dancing, and the vision took Tessa's breath away. A fact she tried to hide as she gathered up the cards and tucked them back into the case.

"There's one last thing I'd like to do tonight before we head home in the morning."

"What's that?"

"I wanted us each to write a letter about the one thing we want to leave here in Tennessee, and then we'll burn them in the fire pit."

"Are you serious?"

"I think it would be good for us."

"As much as I love you and think that would be good for *you*…" Nova started in.

"I think I would be good for you too," Tessa said tentatively.

"I don't really subscribe to forcing symbolic moments on a false journey of self-discovery," Nova protested.

"Just humor me this one time, and I'll let you choose the music all the way home tomorrow." Tessa held out her hand. "Do we have a deal?"

Nova contemplated it carefully, it was a compelling offer as there were twelve long hours of driving ahead. Finally, she gave in. "Okay."

Tessa pulled her notebook out and gave them each a pen and a sheet of paper. The sun set as they wrote their messages. It dropped behind the trees, and the clouds became outlined in vibrant colors. Then the Edison bulbs outside of the treehouse illuminated the catwalks in a sea of color.

After fifteen minutes, Tessa had written her letter. "Are you finished?"

"Yeah," Nova answered from below.

"Let's do this." They left the treehouse and walked to the fire pit tucked into a clearing. Nova gathered sticks while Tessa stacked up their remaining firewood and lit it with the lighter she'd packed. The fire struggled with a single ember and a puff of smoke, but Tessa fed it thin sticks and pieces of dry bark until its flames licked the logs and lit up the enveloping darkness. The logs cracked as they began to char and glow.

She pulled her paper out. "I want to share what I wrote with you, but you can choose to keep your letter private." Nova nodded, and Tessa cleared her throat and began to read.

Dear Nova,

Ever since the moment I knew you existed, I loved you, but I haven't always been proud of the way I've shown it, especially lately.

If I could leave one thing behind here in Tennessee, it would be our old relationship. I've hovered, I've scheduled, I've projected, and I've controlled. It took coming here for me to understand that kind of domination, even if I do it out of love, is not healthy nor sustainable for either of us.

You are almost an adult, and it is time for the reins to move from my hands to yours. I know you aren't going to be able to see around every corner, and I know you are going to make mistakes. But I want you to know that no matter what, I am always by your side.

I believe I can support you best by taking the back seat and letting you figure things out from now on. You are strong enough and smart enough to face any challenge you encounter in this life. Believe that, because I do.

I can't wait to see how your life unfolds, and I can't wait to build on what we've learned here. I want our relationship to grow into one that fits us both, and it is time I acknowledge my part in tearing us down. I am sorry for parenting out of fear, and I am sorry for letting my ego get in the way of the authentic relationship I want us to have.

I vow to work on myself and address my own shortcomings, so I can be a better support system for you. You will be entering a brand new stage called adulthood soon, and so many wonderful things await you here. You are a beautiful, intelligent, talented young woman, and I look forward to the next evolution of our relationship.

As she read the letter, Tessa's eyes glanced up from time to time to focus on Nova, where tears gathered at her lash line and then spilled down her cheeks. When she was finished reading, Nova balled up the sleeve of her sweatshirt and swiped at her eyes, and Tessa shifted forward and placed the letter into the fire pit where it burst into flames. The fire danced and illuminated Nova's face for a single moment before the paper transformed into ash and drifted into the sky.

"I think I want to share mine, too." Nova sniffled as she pulled the folded sheet of paper out of the sleeve of her sweatshirt. She cleared her throat and began in a small voice.

Dear Mom,

I know I've made life difficult for both of us lately. If there is one thing I want to leave behind, it's my anger. I don't even know where it comes from. Maybe it's a delayed reaction from every time Dad blew me off or refused to make me a priority. Probably. But you didn't deserve it. I'm sorry for the way I've treated you, for the phone calls you've received in the middle of the night, for the mistakes I've made, and for being the reason you and Jason are having problems. Maybe on some level, I was acting out, wanting to have you all to myself again. Reverting back to childhood to fight off the fear, knowing I'd be forced to be an adult soon and not feeling anywhere near ready.

The only person who has ever shown up for me consistently has been you. I see that now. I know you've been doing your very best in a really difficult situation.

It's you and me again against the world. It's always been that way, even though I refused to acknowledge it.

I love you, Mom. I want us to have more fun together and to even go on more adventures like this, and yes, play your stupid games because I want a deeper relationship with you. One where we talk about real things that matter.

It's taken me a long time to appreciate you, but I promise I see you now. I see the sacrifices you've made to give me a great life, and I love you more than anything.

Nova sniffled and swiped away the tears freely coursing down her face and let the paper fall into the fire, where it exploded into flames within seconds. Tessa stood up, took a step toward her daughter, and wrapped her in her arms. Her heart was so full of love; it threatened to burst wide open.

Chapter Twenty-Four

The next morning was bittersweet as endings often are. Eager to begin the long journey home, Tessa rose in complete darkness and, while Nova slept on the couch, brewed a cup of coffee. She walked out to the back deck to sip it. Fog hugged the ground and wrapped the world in a theatrical softness. It was thick in the mountains, and she was contemplative as she took in the final morning view she would enjoy of the Smokies. She hugged the warm cup of coffee in her hands and felt gratitude flood her.

She glanced back over her shoulder through the patio door at Nova as she slept, her lighter roots beginning to show, and wondered if Nova had been as affected by the journey as she'd been. They'd arrived hostile and frustrated, each stuck in their own stubbornness, unable to find middle ground. But the journey had changed them both in subtle and more substantial ways. Tessa finally learned that parenting wasn't all about discipline and control. It wasn't effective to white-knuckle a child into bending to your will. It was a lesson she'd refused to learn until it forced itself upon her, and now she was grateful for it. Life always had a way of repeating a lesson you needed to learn until you learned it.

Through the door, she heard a soft knock on the glass. Tessa turned to see Nova wave and stifle a yawn with her balled-up fist and offered her a warm smile. Twenty minutes later, they'd packed their bags and locked up the treehouse. They wandered back down the cobblestone path when Tessa stopped and turned around. She pulled Nova close for a side hug, and they both stole one last glance at the treehouse.

"This is it," Tessa said, squeezing Nova in closer. "Of all the days we've spent together, these last eight have been my favorite."

Nova glanced over with a grin. "Mine too."

With her heart full, she said, "Let's go home."

When they reached the Jeep, Nova set the GPS and offered Tessa a donut from the box they'd gotten at the gas station when they filled up.

"Let me get us out onto a real highway and then you can drive," Tessa offered. "You should try to get some sleep while you can." Nova nodded and put her earbuds in, and set the seat back. Two minutes later, she was asleep again in the seat next to Tessa.

In the early morning, the fog burned away as she drove the winding road that led back to the highway. Absent-mindedly, she recognized she'd almost become comfortable driving the curves of Tennessee at the speed limit. The highway was empty as the sun climbed higher, and she set the cruise for nine over.

Around noon, she pulled into a gas station to refuel, and Nova stretched like a cat. She ran into the store to use the restroom and Tessa did the same, handing off the keys to Nova when she headed back to the locked vehicle. When she reached the Jeep, she saw Nova had already claimed the driver's seat. Tessa paused briefly, then opened the driver's side door, formulating an excuse in her mind, but Nova beat her to the punch.

"You said you wanted to take a back seat and let me drive," Nova said with a smirk, her eyes glittering with mirth.

Tessa laughed. "That's not fair! You're using my fireside confession against me?" She had to admire her daughter's audacity and eventually came to the same conclusion. "You know what? You're right, I did." With that, she shut the door, walked around the front of the Jeep, and slid into the passenger seat without another word. She helped guide Nova back to the interstate, forcing herself to face forward and relax. No more micromanaging and pumping the invisible brake. She compelled herself to breathe in through her nose and out through her mouth, and to prove it to Nova, she pulled the lever and reclined the seat.

"You're taking a nap?" Nova's confused glance darted to her mother and back to the road. Her voice rose an octave in panic.

"I'm going to try." Tessa pulled her pillow from the back seat, balled it up against the window, and closed her eyes, knowing she wouldn't sleep a wink. It was progress though, and progress was progress, no matter how small.

"But what if…"

"You've got this. Stay on this road for an hour, then do what the GPS says," Tessa encouraged and closed her eyes, turning up the music on her earbuds as she heard the first bars of "Look Down" cue up on the Jeep's speakers, grateful to have escaped the seventh ring of show tune hell.

Part 3

Chapter Twenty-Five

A week after returning home from their treehouse tour, Tessa darted around the townhouse, fluffing pillows and making sure she made the bed. She glanced at her watch. Five more minutes until Jason would walk through the door. His eight years spent in the military guaranteed his punctuality. In her belly, a tingle of anxiety had taken up residence while she waited. She brushed blush on her cheeks and swiped some fresh mascara upward on her lashes, not for him, but to add to her own confidence. A few minutes later, she heard his knock at the door. She pushed her long curtain of smooth hair back and let out a deep breath, circling her shoulders a couple times before plastering on a bright smile and opening the door.

"You have a key, silly." Her eyes landed on his broad shoulders in the suit and her stomach flipped. "You could have let yourself in."

"I wasn't sure," he admitted. "I didn't want to overstep."

"Do you want a glass of wine or something?" she

asked as she laced her shaky hands together and led him into the kitchen, not wanting to reveal to him how nervous she was. He took a seat at the island while she stood behind it, leaning back on the counter for support.

"Sure," he agreed, and she pulled out a bottle they'd picked up at a local vineyard they'd visited last summer. They'd planned a trip to Napa a year ago but had to cancel it at the last minute when Nova tested positive for influenza A.

"Remember this one?" She held it out to him, and he took it from her, studying the elaborate gold label on the bottle.

"I do. I thought we were saving it for a special occasion." His dark eyes searched hers, looking for clues, and she shuttered them.

"Being alive is a special occasion," Tessa answered as she pulled out two wine glasses and poured the pinot noir into them. She handed one to him and watched him swirl it around the glass, then take a small sip. He swished it around his cheeks. It reminded her of the day they'd bought it, when he showed her how to properly taste wine and then quizzed her on what she detected. Plummy. Oaky finish. Smokey notes. It was as if she was walking through the memories of a stranger now, and the disconnection she identified made her legs tremble.

"Where's Nova?" he asked.

"She's still at school."

"But it's after four." He glanced down at the impressive timepiece on his wrist.

"She's working with a tutor to get her grades high enough to get accepted to the University of Nebraska."

Jason's wide eyes revealed his shock. "What happened to her big dream of becoming a tattoo artist?" he asked.

Months ago, when Nova changed her career plans to become a tattoo artist, he'd told Nova she was making the biggest mistake of her life. At the time, Tessa had agreed and was grateful for his support, but now she saw it differently. Two days after they returned from Tennessee, Nova shared her plans to revisit her art teacher dream and to take on an apprenticeship for tattooing in her free time.

"She decided to pursue it on the side."

Surprise registered on his features, and she rubbed her lips together in the awkward silence that followed. He took a longer sip of the wine, and she decided to broach the reason for his visit. Typically, she would have let him lead the conversation, but she didn't want to be a bystander in her own life anymore.

"What are we doing here?" she asked. "Is there anything left between us?"

"I don't know how to answer that," he confided. His usually deep, booming voice was quieter. "I thought this time away would solidify things for me and give me some clarity."

She nodded and took a sip of the wine, grasping the delicate stem in her hand.

"I think you're great," he admitted. "We get along well, we have the same goals, and want the same things out of life."

"But?" She said the one word he was too afraid to say.

"But Nova," he admitted. "I never really saw myself as a father figure. It's the reason I never had children in the first place. I've tried, but she makes life so difficult around here for all of us. You have to at least admit that."

"There's no doubt she's been struggling lately."

"I don't know if I have the bandwidth for it."

She gulped, the lump in her throat strangling her, making her stomach tighten. Her gut responded, putting into words what she should have said long ago. "We're a package deal, and you knew that going into this relationship." Her eyes rested on his.

"I did. I just didn't expect it to be so challenging." His gaze locked on hers, and there was genuine sorrow in them.

"I got some clarity on my trip with Nova, and I know what I want now. Do you?" she asked, her voice steady.

"Let's hear it."

"I want a partner in every sense of the word, and I want someone who will invest in my daughter. Not just go through the motions, but really put time and effort into building a relationship with her."

This time, he gulped. His silence spoke volumes.

"I want someone to love us both, not look at Nova as a forced obligatory requirement to be with me," Tessa admitted. "But you can't give me that, can you?" The question hung in the air. Her voice trailed off at the end because she already knew the answer.

Tessa took a deep breath and let it out slowly. She set down the wine glass and squeezed her hands, focusing on the sharpness of her fingernails making half-moons in her palms. Determined not to cry in front of him, she decided she'd indulge her tears later.

He got quiet, and she found the strength to continue. "I want more, Jason. I want a big love or nothing at all, and the person who I choose to share my life with must also love Nova just as fiercely."

He nodded and took another sip.

"She needs a real example of what a good man is, someone who can show her how high to set her bar." Tessa's eyes beseeched his, and he was the first to break the glance. Jason cleared his throat, and time stood still as a small tingle of panic crept into her heart. He was a good guy, and she'd been with so many terrible ones. The idea of throwing away a decent relationship to start all over was a bitter pill to swallow. For a split second, fear made her want to take all her words back, then she felt a subtle shift in her heart that seeped out to her limbs.

"I don't think I'm that guy," he muttered softly. "I'm sorry, Tess."

A small gasp escaped as her heart broke in two. "I know. I am, too." Silence hung heavy and settled on her chest like a ton of bricks. She glanced around the town-house and assessed the hardwood floors and the white marble with delicate gray veins. She thought the house would make them a family, but it didn't. Tessa wanted to flee from it, knowing instantly that the faster they decoupled, the better off she and Nova would be. Her heart couldn't take a long goodbye.

"How do we move forward? I can't stay here." She didn't want to admit she'd quit her job. Tessa wanted to move forward with her head held high.

"I'd like to untangle our lives as respectfully as possible," he said. "I was the one who insisted on this place. I can take over the lease, and we can file the paperwork to release you from it."

"That makes sense," she mumbled. It did, but that didn't mean the logical way he was dismantling their lives didn't hurt. A small part of her yearned for him to take her in his arms, kiss her passionately, and beg for her forgiveness. For him to make good on all the promises he'd made when they moved in together, but the difference was, now she knew better. As much as it hurt, she had to move forward, and now she knew that meant without him.

On paper, he was perfect, but in her heart, she knew it wasn't enough. He finished his glass of wine and set it on the counter. Tessa swallowed and then formulated a plan. "I need a week to get things packed up. I don't want Nova to have to live here while we sort things out. It wouldn't be good for her."

"I agree." He stood to his full height. "I'll contact the property manager and get the paperwork changed over and give you as much time as you need to find a new place and get your things moved."

He was being gracious, and she swallowed her hurt and anger and said, "Thank you for understanding." He stood, and she quietly walked him to the door. She shut it carefully behind him and watched him get into his Lexus and drive away. That's when the tears came and she swiped them away. She was red-faced with swollen eyes when Nova came through the door a little while later.

"What happened?" Nova sat down on the sofa next to Tessa, her eyes afraid. She reached out to squeeze her mother's forearm.

"Jason just came by," she said and quickly swiped the tears under her eyes and pasted on a smile. "I need to talk to you."

"Okay." Nova bit the inside of her cheek, her face pensive. "What's up?"

"We have decided to go our separate ways," Tessa

started, then instantly explained, "You don't need to worry about anything."

"But... you don't have a job. Where are we going to live?"

"Let me worry about that."

"But why?"

"It's been a long time coming." She started to explain, "We don't share the same values, and the worst thing you can do is stay in a relationship that doesn't fit you."

"I think the worst thing is being alone," Nova admitted.

"You can be alone, even *inside* a relationship," Tessa said. "It will be freeing to focus on myself and on you for the next long while. It's time for me to build the life I want to live on my own, without making concessions for someone else. You'll see. Once we get settled, it will be the best thing we've ever done together. Come here." She pulled Nova into her arms and hugged her. "It's going to be amazing."

* * *

After a quiet dinner, Tessa dialed her dad's phone number. He answered on the first ring.

"I was wondering when you'd have time to call your dear old dad. Tell me all about the trip!"

Tessa filled him in on every detail over the course of the next hour. She'd discovered so much about herself and Nova, and it felt incredible to download the lessons she'd learned and share them with her father.

"Sweetheart, I'm so proud of you."

"You might want to wait before you pile on the accolades," she told him as she chewed on her bottom lip.

"What do you mean?"

"Jason and I have decided to part ways."

"I'm sorry to hear that." He sighed. "But I am sure you have your reasons. How can I help?"

"I want to go all in on myself. I did a lot of thinking while we were in Tennessee, and I think the relationships I've developed with my clients over the years give me the opportunity to take a big risk."

"I like the sound of that," he encouraged, and it emboldened Tessa.

"I want to start my own accounting firm, and I need to find a new place to live, but being self-employed, it's going to be difficult to meet the financial requirements to get a lease."

"How about you move in with me?" he asked. "If you're starting a new company, you are going to be gone a lot, and I can help with Nova. To be honest, I'd love the company."

Tessa considered it. He was right; she *was* going to be busy, and Nova needed a fresh start, too. The only obstacle in the way was her pride. "What does that say about me, that I'm moving back in with Dad at my age?"

He laughed. "It says whatever you let it say."

"Yeah?"

"Yeah," Ed assured her. "It's not forever, just until you get your legs under you. I wished I'd been able to do more for you when you were growing up."

Tessa teared up. "You did enough."

"Someday, Nova will know you did, too." His warm voice tugged at her heartstrings. "So, is that a yes?"

"That's a yes."

Chapter Twenty-Six

A month later, she was grabbing dinner with Kristie.

"You look *so* good," Kristie gushed as they sipped on margaritas and ordered tacos el carbon. "Dare I say relaxed?"

"I *feel* good," Tessa admitted with a convincing smile. "Dad has been great. He's set me up in a home office at his place so I can keep costs down as I get the firm started."

Kristie leaned in to reveal, "The partners are practically shitting themselves and scrambling for new clients to make up for the drop in revenue from your book of business. *And* they just changed the employment agreement, adding a non-compete clause after all your clients left en masse."

"Really?" Tessa grinned at the news and punched the air in victory. "It might be petty, but God, it feels good to kick those sexist bastards in the balls right where it counts."

"Enjoy your victory, honey. You earned it," Kristie said

with a smile. "Now, when you get to the place where you can afford an office manager, I'm your girl!"

"That's the dream," Tessa admitted. "Being able to go to work every day with my best friend?" She raised her glass and Kristie chimed hers against it, then she took a sip, enjoying the burn in the back of her throat. "I would love that."

Kristie paused for a moment, looking deep into Tessa's eyes, making her shift uncomfortably in the booth.

"What?" Tessa asked.

"Have you had any contact with Jason?" Kristie's voice was gentle.

"Not since we met at the townhouse office to break the lease," Tessa admitted.

"How was it?"

"Brutal but necessary. He wasn't the right one, but he did his best to make the process as easy as possible, and I will always respect him for the way he handled a delicate situation." She paused before revealing, "If I'm being honest, there have been a few late nights when I typed out texts and then deleted them."

"You loved him for a long time. If you didn't do that, I'd be worried." Kristie took a sip. "You invested in the relationship, and it didn't work out. I'm happy to see you taking the time to process the end of it."

"I don't want to go back anymore. I only want to move forward," Tessa confided.

"You'll get there."

"I finally figured out that I need to fix *me*. I've been like a used car driving through life with the check engine light on."

Kristie laughed at the analogy.

"Since we got back, I've been engaging in a lot of deep self-reflection. It illuminated a bunch of residual crap that I have avoided facing my entire life."

"It's easy to fall into a pattern where you focus outward instead of inward," Kristie commiserated. "Trust me, we all have our junk."

"I've been journaling and meditating, which I am truly terrible at, by the way." She laughed at herself. "And even though every time I lie down to do it, it's a battle to clear my thoughts and relax, I have to admit it *is* slowing down my brain in a remarkable way."

"Keep it up and it will change your life."

"That's the plan." She smiled. "I'm choosing to focus on the good and let go of the bad." Tessa took another sip, and her mind wandered, acknowledging the sprouts of fresh growth she was finally starting to see.

"How is Nova adjusting to the new school and living arrangement?"

"Surprisingly well, actually. She's been spending a lot of time with Dad out in the garage. He taught her how to change the oil in his car."

"Your Nova?" Kristie asked with a shocked grin.

"My Nova," Tessa confirmed with a smile. "On the way home after therapy last week, she told me she likes having boundaries. She said that even though she fights me on the rules, she knows they're good for her."

"Whoa!"

"I know! I was dying." Tessa laughed. "You were right. The trip was exactly what we needed to shake things up and discover where the next steps of our relationship will lead. She's graduating next year, and then she'll be an adult, making her own decisions and creating her own life.

Like it or not, I have to step back and let her take the reins. The difference is, now, I know I can trust her more with them."

"She's going to make mistakes," Kristie cautioned.

"Of course she is," Tessa agreed. "But they are her mistakes to make, and no matter what happens, I'll always be in her corner, cheering her on to shake it off and go after her dreams."

"That's beautiful," Kristie admitted.

"It is." Tessa thought for a long second. "My life is simpler now. I loved Jason, and we had a lot of great moments together, but it came with a required sacrifice. Now that it's gone, there's no push and pull for my attention anymore. Nova has calmed down, and all the effort I put into keeping him happy, I have reallocated into building myself back up." She took a sip and then added, "It turns out, all the dreams I had in my head when I graduated from college were still there waiting for me to wake up and actively participate in my life."

"I just got goosebumps." Kristie held out her delicate forearm, which was covered in chill bumps.

"There's no tug of war inside me anymore. It's just peaceful."

"That's amazing," Kristie said. "I am so happy for you. No one deserves it more."

"Thank you." Tessa felt tears gathering at her lash line and fanned her eyes with her hand. "You're making me tear up! We have to change the subject. If you say you're proud of me, I might start sobbing and cause a real scene."

Kristie reached out and squeezed her arm. "I *am* proud of you. But more importantly, are *you* proud of yourself?"

Tessa nodded and let out an exhale between her teeth.

"I am." After a long pause, she said, "And I'm training again. I'm planning on celebrating my fiftieth birthday at the Tahoe Rim Basin." Tessa let out a little nervous squeal. "It will be a solo trip, with hiking and camping along the way, and it scares the hell out of me, so I know it's my next grand adventure."

"Look at you!" Kristie exclaimed. "You turned into a total badass right before my eyes."

"You helped me get there."

"That's what besties do."

Chapter Twenty-Seven

Tessa stretched her arms high above her head. Standing, she bent forward and placed her hands on the ground in front of her in a downward-facing dog pose. Her hair fell to the floor, and she said out loud, "I am enough. I have always been enough. Goodness flows to me in all ways, and I use my gifts for the greatest good."

"Talking to yourself again?" Nova interjected.

Tessa straightened up, her cheeks pink from the rush of blood being displaced. "You're enough, too, you know. It would do you good to remind yourself every day."

Nova was a ball of jittery energy. She thrust her thumb into her mouth and chewed her thumbnail.

"Why are you so anxious?"

"I've got my PSAT today."

"Just think of it as another step toward the life you want to live."

"Agh, the pressure. You aren't helping."

She pulled Nova in for a quick hug. Since they'd returned from their trip, Tessa made a new habit of hugging Nova at least once a day, whether she needed it or not. At first, it was awkward, but now, it was a reflex. She pulled back and cupped Nova's face in her hands to deliver some last-minute advice. "Always go with your first answer. Second-guessing yourself leads to more errors. You've got this!"

"Ready to go to school?' Ed called out as his formidable frame filled the doorway, munching on a piece of buttered toast. He held out a banana for Nova. "How about some brain food?"

Tessa smiled at the thoughtful way her dad took care of Nova. Since they'd moved in with him six weeks ago, she and her dad had developed a parenting shorthand. When her beloved grandfather suggested sensible eating or studying for tests, it was an easier sell to Nova, and Tessa was grateful for his support.

"Let me grab my bag and we'll go," Nova acknowledged as she left the room.

"What's on tap for you today?" he asked.

"I have two new client meetings. If I sign one of them, I will have achieved my goal for the month," Tessa explained, the anticipation and drive evident in her excited tone.

"But it's only the fifteenth!"

A wide grin spread across Tessa's face. "I know, right? Then anything else is gravy. If they sign an agreement today, I'll spring for dinner tonight."

"Deal!" He took a step closer and swept her into his strong arms. "I'm so proud of you, honey." Tessa closed her eyes, feeling the safety of his embrace envelop her.

She pulled back to look into his sparkling blue eyes. "It feels really great to stand on my own two feet, with a little help from you, of course. It won't be long before I can afford to get a place on my own." She was eager to be independent again, not wanting to overstay their welcome.

His face fell at the suggestion. "Don't throw your money away renting. Save up a proper down payment for a house. Besides, I enjoy having you two around. The silence when you live on your own is deafening."

"You don't mind all the extra running around and noise?" Tessa asked.

He laughed. "That's the beauty of getting older. Your ears don't work as well." He looked down at his feet. "I like having people to come home to." Until that moment, she'd thought they had been a burden, and Tessa was working around the clock to rid him of it. "This arrangement has benefitted me as much as it has you."

"I doubt that," Tessa said. "But you're an excellent roommate, so if you'd like to keep this living situation for a while, that would really take the pressure off."

"I'd keep you here forever if I could," he said with a smile that made the skin by his eyes crinkle.

"Thanks, Dad. For everything."

The praise made him uncomfortable, and he quickly left to take Nova to school. Tessa sat back down at her computer, looking at the screensaver. The photo made her smile and transported her right back to the moment it was taken. It was her favorite photo from the trip, but not because either of them looked great in it or the location was the most beautiful. In actuality, Nova's smile was forced and hid the angst she'd felt while hiking to Grotto Falls, and Tessa's frustrated smile never reached her eyes. It became the most precious because it had been a turning point for both of them.

Having an hour to walk down memory lane, she swiped through all the photos and videos from their trip together. It was strange how the passage of time made each moment they shared more magical. She stopped at a photo of the two of them smiling in front of the GlampVentures sign. It was the beginning of their journey back to each other.

It's funny how your memory isn't perfect or impartial. It's easily influenced by outside factors, and as time goes by, the little frustrations minimize and drop away and all you are left with is the aftertaste of sweet nostalgia. A highlight reel you can return to any moment the mood strikes.

Two women got in the Jeep together who didn't understand each other and had a tendency to butt heads. Two different women emerged. They had taken down the walls they hid behind brick by brick and used them to build a new bridge to each other. Tessa had a new appreciation for the bright and creative spirit that was her daughter. Nova was finding her way on her own terms and had seemingly matured overnight.

When they returned home, Nova dove headfirst into the diversion program. She scheduled her own community service and reported to her appointments with Mrs. Clifton. She volunteered at a local food pantry and loved it so much that she continued to volunteer long after completing her requirement.

Nova amazed Tessa with her initiative, for the first time really taking responsibility for her future and making amends for her mistakes. For the first few weeks, Tessa had to force herself to take a step back and let Nova do the heavy lifting. As she successfully completed important tasks independently, Tessa encouraged her to take on more. Now, Nova was making her own therapy appointments and setting up college visits.

She waffled back and forth between going to college and seeking out an apprenticeship with a tattoo artist. Working herself up into such a tizzy one night, she'd had a breakdown. Sobbing and shaking, she ranted, "What if I make the wrong choice? There is so much pressure. People keep asking about my future. Where I'm going to school, what I'm choosing as a career, and I don't know how to answer any of these questions. I am freaking out."

"Come here." Tessa patted the seat next to her on the sofa. "You are putting too much pressure on yourself. Did you know the average person changes careers over five times in their lifetime? So, even if you become a teacher and then decide it isn't for you, and then become a tattoo artist but realize that isn't right either, you can still find a better fit."

Nova was listening. She jerked her chin over her right shoulder and then her left, and Tessa heard her neck pop. "But I don't want to waste time and make the wrong decision. I just want to make one decision and be done."

"That's not how it works, honey," Tessa said. "Life is not a one-way track you take to be successful. Think about how dull it would be if we didn't freak out from time to time, fall in love, see our greatest wish come true, or live through the most painful loss of our life." She was quiet for a minute. "The contrast makes life worth living." She smoothed Nova's hair back. It was an ultra-short pixie cut in her natural color which Tessa favored over the goth look. A week ago, Nova cleaned out her closets and donated her spiked chokers, and had begun adding more color to her wardrobe. She was changing again, right before Tessa's eyes, finding her way to her authentic self, step-by-step. It was inspiring to witness.

Tessa covered her daughter's hand with her own, taking a second to appreciate the intricate brown design that looked like a henna tattoo surrounding her wrist and jutting up her forearm. "You're going to be okay."

"Promise?"

"Always," Tessa said. "Because you have me."

Chapter Twenty-Eight

Eight months later, on a picture-perfect day in May, Tessa sat on the bleachers of the football field, and her father sat next to her in the only dress shirt and tie he owned, fanning himself with the program in his hand. Wearing heels and a navy blue dress cinched at the waist, beneath it were the powerful muscles she'd honed in the gym preparing for her upcoming hiking trip to the Tahoe Rim Basin. Her arms were strong and tanned, and she relished the feeling of strength she felt in her body. Still a year away, her fiftieth birthday adventure was going to be a gift to herself.

She carried herself differently. At least, that was what Kristie told her when Tessa offered her a job last week.

"Of course, I'll accept a job offer from the fastest-growing female-led accounting firm in Omaha."

Tessa was building up every part of her life. Now the owner of a thriving accounting practice, she had more work than she knew what to do with and was considering hiring her first associate.

Nova had even convinced her to try therapy. After seeing the undeniable transformation in her daughter, she decided to listen. She was on a mission to make positive changes in every way.

The school band started playing the first few notes of *Pomp and Circumstance*, and the crowd got to their feet as the graduates filed in row by row. Tessa craned her neck, searching for Nova, who she easily recognized from the customization she applied on the top of her cap. In Nova's world, every surface was a canvas for self-expression. She'd used thin pieces of boldly colored Washi tape to spell out her name and graduating year.

"There she is!" Tessa pointed her out to Ed as Nova walked to her seat, giving Tessa a little wave in the stands. Her face broke out in a huge smile.

"That's our girl," Ed said, wrapping his arm around her. They shared in Nova's accomplishment equally.

"She's walking on that stage right now because of you, Dad," Tessa said as her eyes filled with happy tears.

"I can't take credit for that. You did the raising, and Nova did the work."

"She did," Tessa acknowledged. "I can't believe how far she's come."

"How far you've *both* come," he corrected.

Tessa basked in the warm glow of her father's praise.

The ceremony took over an hour, and Tessa found her mind wandering. There were days she never thought she'd see this moment. Her heart swelled with the sweetness of the battle they'd waged together and won. The little girl they placed in her arms in the hospital was now an adult. Eighteen years had whipped by in a blink. She saw the little baby who wanted to be carried everywhere and refused to roll over until she was almost nine months old. Then the toddler, who could find the tiniest onion in the food she was fed and who would throw it on the floor and giggle hysterically. She saw the kindergartner who ordered the boys around in her class, telling them what to do. Her fierce independent streak had been something the teachers at school fought to tamp down, and which led to many arguments between them, but now its existence thrilled Tessa. It would become Nova's North Star.

The vice principal rolled through the students' names, and each graduate crossed the stage to accept their diploma. Tessa's eyes were glued to Nova following the line and inching up closer, waiting her turn.

"Nova Delilah Donahue," he announced, and Tessa and her father leapt to their feet, clapping until their hands were stinging and red. Nova beamed as she reached out her hand to shake the principal's. Taking two steps to exit the stage, she waved the leather holder in the air in triumph. Then she grabbed her tassel and pulled it to the other side of her cap and made her way back to her seat, waving at Tessa and Ed.

Two hundred names later, the service concluded. The graduates stood and, with a whoop, took off their caps and flung them into the air under thunderous applause from their loved ones in the bleachers. Families stomped their feet and cheered until they were hoarse. After a final processional song by the band, Tessa and Ed followed the sea of parents down to the field, scanning for their graduate. A few minutes later, Nova flung herself into her mom's strong arms. Tessa lifted her off the ground and spun her around like she had when she was little.

"You did it!" Tessa kissed her cheek, giving her another squeeze.

"Papa!" She turned to Ed and hugged him tight.

"We're so proud of you kiddo." Ed said, "Now, you can take the world by storm."

"Oh, I plan on it."

One Year Later

Tessa glanced at her watch and smiled. Any minute now, Nova would burst through the door, home for the summer after completing her first year at college. Tessa couldn't wait to lay eyes on her daughter.

She opened her carry-on and filled it with her hiking clothing, stuffing it with gray wool socks and layers to peel off when it got warmer in the canyon. She was leaving in the morning for Tahoe, and excitement zinged through her body, electrifying her nerves. She'd never undertaken a solo hiking trip like this before, and the idea of it still terrified her.

In college, she'd always been part of a group or had taken trips with friends. But this time, there was no one to consider but herself, and she vacillated between euphoria and terror. She'd planned for every potential challenge and had done her research. All that was left was to go.

She checked her watch again and walked to the kitchen as Nova burst through the door.

"There's no place like home!" she declared, setting an

overflowing basket of dirty laundry on the ground, then turned toward Tessa with a huge smile.

Her hair had grown out and was scissored into a dramatic, razor-sharp bob. Long silver earrings hung from her ear lobes to land on her clavicle. Her fitted t-shirt was tucked into a black lace-up corset and showed off her trim waist, where a holographic skirt darted out. To Nova, dressing was an art, a way of communicating her aesthetic to the world without words. Tessa looked down at her Land's End shorts and her moisture-wicking pullover, enjoying the contrast.

"I thought I heard your voice," Ed bellowed as he strode into the kitchen to hug his only granddaughter. "Let me look at you." He pulled back and drank her in. "Is that a nose ring?"

Nova laughed. "It's a magnet. I'm trying it out."

"I kinda like it." He smiled.

"You're an enabler," Tessa scolded Ed with a grin.

"Hey!" He raised his hand in defense. "That's not true. I've always been a fan of self-expression."

Nova grinned at his answer. "Well, now all we have to do is get this one on board." She hiked a long, red, stiletto-shaped thumbnail toward Tessa.

"Are you two ganging up on me already?" she cried in mock protest. "You've been home all of thirty seconds!" Tessa loved the easy relationship they had together. Nova and her grandfather simply adored and understood each other.

Tessa learned a lot about letting go over the last year while Nova flew from her empty nest under the power of her own wings for the first time. Not being able to lay eyes on Nova daily was a huge adjustment for Tessa. It cued up fears during the first few months they were apart. To truly let go and trust her child to make life-changing decisions on her own was brand new territory. Tessa had to force herself not to inundate Nova with phone calls and texts. She'd erased a hundred of them.

Are you eating breakfast?
Never leave your drink alone in a bar.
Don't dig yourself a hole signing up for credit cards.
Are you wearing flip-flops in the shower?

Going from the daily concern and care of another person to radio silence was a tough adjustment for Tessa. Nova embraced the change fully, only calling home on Sundays, and sharing tidbits of her life that were appropriate for her mother's ears. Tessa was smart enough to know there were likely big things being left out in an effort to keep her mother's fears in check and so she didn't interrogate her daughter on the calls.

It had taken a few months, but they'd gotten into a good rhythm, and by the time she'd come home for Christmas break, Tessa's fears had turned a corner. Their independence had done good things for both of them. Nova was fierce. College was forcing her into autonomy, and she wore it well. Nova was shedding the fragile girl she'd been and stepping into her own power, and Tessa marveled at the drastic change every time she visited. Throughout Nova's childhood, her daily changes were incremental, but now, with the distance and the passage of time, her transformation was astounding.

This huge influx of free time gave Tessa the luxury of working out at the gym daily to train for her solo hiking trip. She often had dinners with Kristie and went on the occasional date to have fun, but she wasn't ready to delve into something more serious. She liked who she was without a man.

Her practice was thriving. After hiring Kristie, she brought on two more female associates, and word quickly spread about the new all-female badass accounting firm, Donahue & Company. The local news had done a story on her, and that's when the business really exploded. Last month, she'd signed a lease on an office building downtown within walking distance of the Old Market. Kristie dove into planning an incredible grand opening party, complete with cupcakes with their logo and champagne. The ribbon-cutting ceremony was scheduled around Nova's classes so Kristie could stream the event for her.

Getting a bigger piece of the pie came with more responsibilities, but Tessa was more than capable and, with proper management, found she could actually work less. Her mindfulness training made every minute of her day more effective. Although the living arrangement with her father wasn't financially necessary anymore, she stayed. Tessa simply loved his company and cherished their nightly dinners.

Tessa was in control and building financial security, knowing the day would eventually come when she would live on her own again. The climbing number in her bank account empowered her, building a sense of ease deep in her soul. It gave her options, instead of having to rely on a partner, her spirit was filled with a state of contentedness she'd never experienced before.

Looking at Nova now, she saw a bit of the same spirit echoed in the calm countenance of her daughter. Nova was maturing and stepping into her own. Seeing her daughter create a life she loved for herself gave Tessa such a sense of pride she had a hard time articulating it. Eventually, she came to realize that everything was as it should be. Your children are supposed to go on to live their own lives separate from yours. It was good to see Nova step up for herself and go after what she wanted. Tessa adored the woman she was becoming.

"I've got an internship set up at the Omaha Center of the Arts starting in two weeks. It's not paid, of course, but it will look great on my resume."

"That's fantastic! Way to take initiative and make things happen for yourself. I am so proud of you."

"Thanks, Mom," Nova answered. "I also found a serving job at the diner."

"Sounds like you've gotten your life all figured out."

"As much as you can when you are nineteen." Nova changed the subject. "So, are you ready?"

"I think so." Tessa admitted, "Two weeks is a long time, but I am ready for the challenge. To really push myself and see what I can do."

"Look at us," Nova said. "The Fabulous Donahue Women, unstoppable adventurers going after what we want in life."

Tessa nodded with a smile. "We've come a long way."

"We have." Nova stretched, cracking her neck, then yawned. "What's to eat? I'm starved!"

"You're in for a treat." She walked to the fridge and pulled out a Ziploc bag filled with chicken parts bathing in buttermilk and spices and waved it in the air. "I might have gotten in touch with Chris Kringle for his wife's secret recipe."

Nova squealed with delight. "Seriously? Wait, are we talking about the real deal? Or are you going to make it keto by breading it in pork rinds?"

Tessa laughed. "It's the full-carb version. I would never stoop so low as to serve you healthy fried chicken on your first night home. Now, tomorrow? That's another story."

"You'll already be on your way to Tahoe," Nova corrected. "It'll be pizza and ice cream every day over here while you're gone."

"Hear, hear!" Ed said with a grin. "Now, let's go unload your car."

* * *

Four days later, Tessa was exhausted at the top of Spooner Summit. She'd fought her way up over seven thousand feet, surrounded by ancient fir trees and dramatic granite outcrops, and her legs and calves burned. She found a rock to sit on and pulled out a granola bar and a bottle of water from her backpack. Catching her breath, she wiped her forehead with the back of her arm and looked out onto Lake Tahoe. The vibrant blue of the still water seemingly went on forever until the mountains in the distance curbed it.

She looked down at the boots on her feet, her lucky ones she'd worn in Tennessee, and was grateful the soles now contained earth from Spooner Summit. It was the most challenging hike she'd ever taken. She'd even had to climb in places, and it tested her endurance, but she'd made it. Fighting her way to the summit only made her appreciate the stunning view even more.

"Would you take a photo of me so I can send it back to my daughter?" she asked one of the women gathered in a cluster of hikers near her.

"Of course." The woman clicked away and returned her phone. Tessa looked down at the photo. Her hair was pulled back into a ponytail, and she was rocking a head-band. She was sitting on a rock, beaming, with the beau-tiful blue water behind her. The photo belied the amount of focused effort it took to get there. It wasn't much different from when she looked at a recent photo of Nova. The absolute strength and happiness radiating from Nova's eyes didn't display the struggle it had taken to grow up. But now, when they were individually standing at the next summit of their lives, the view was so magnificent it took her breath away.

* * *

Thank you for reading "Up in the Middle of Nowhere." If you loved the Donahue Family, you'll enjoy meeting the Churchill's in "When Wren Came Out." Please enjoy chapter one below:

It only takes the snag of one thread to unravel the tapestry of a seemingly perfect life. You never know what event will cause that snag to happen, when the illusion of the public façade you've carefully built crumbles, and you are forced to see your world stripped bare and with fresh eyes.

The unraveling of our lives began with a phone call from the event coordinator, Marcy, desperate to fill a last-minute volunteer opportunity at my daughter's Catholic high school. St. Augustine's always hosted the Annual Show Choir Showcase for eight schools in the Minneapolis suburbs we'd lived in for the last four years. When the first email call for volunteers landed in my inbox, I was expressly forbidden by my daughter to sign up.

"It's so embarrassing when you come running up to school to volunteer every chance you get," Wren grumbled. "Why can't you get a real job like Sammie's mom?"

"I *have* a job," I'd remind her, "taking care of my family," while I folded John's white t-shirts into perfect squares. "But it would be nice if my coworkers would try to make it a little easier on me," I teased her, and she rolled her eyes and stormed away. Discounting traditional roles of womanhood was as easy as casting off dirty socks in the corner for her. I knew I was a dinosaur, about as far away from a card-carrying feminist as possible, and in Wren's judgmental teenage eyes, this fact was offensive. It diminished my value. Until she was hungry, and then my love for cooking, baking, and homemaking became more palatable qualities.

Now that she was sixteen, Wren was painfully aware of my presence and had started loathing my penchant for volunteering at her school functions. Not wanting to rock the boat, I gave in. Sure, it stung when she was so vocal about blocking my participation, but I chalked it up to the inevitable growth cycle of all teenage girls united in their shared mortification of their mothers. I remember mocking my own mother for her fashion choices and inferior make-up application techniques, and now Wren was doing the exact same thing to me. It was the circle of life.

During the first twelve years of our marriage, we moved seven times. We were an Army family, and her father was frequently deployed for long stretches of time, climbing the ranks to Master Sergeant. While he was away, I was Wren's constant companion. I was the chef and the taxi and the playmate. I was the confidant and the giver of hugs and the trusted advisor.

Then, around thirteen, our relationship shifted when Wren's coltish first steps toward adulthood carried her further away from me. She delegated me to the sidelines, where I gazed at her with my eyes brimming with hope and longing for an engraved invitation to slip back into her life. I probably should have insisted and interjected myself into her life more, but it wasn't my way.

It was a challenge, but I tried not to hover, instead branching out in the community and volunteering at our church. Making friends as an introverted adult is brutal. I'd rather be at home infusing bone broth and figuring out ways to sneak it into Wren's diet. Or gardening or reading, anything that didn't require wearing lipstick or pants with an actual zipper. When John retired and we first moved to Eden Prairie, for Wren's sake, I decided to put myself out there more. After the initial awkwardness and my social anxiety lessened, I had to admit it was starting to feel like home. A *real* home for the first time in our marriage.

Home was a weighty, elusive concept while we lived the nomadic life imposed upon us by the military. I was enmeshed in the duty of motherhood so fully I didn't realize what was missing until we moved to Eden Prairie, and I felt peace envelop me for the first time. There is a stillness in your heart where tranquility grows in the fertile soil of stability. It was a resounding steadiness and baseline contentment that let me breathe deeper and relax more fully, and in record time, Eden Prairie became our own little Garden of Eden.

With the thrill of fresh purpose unfurling in my belly, I ran up the stairs humming a jaunty *"When the Saints Go Marching In"* and threw on some bedazzled Converse sneakers I'd found at a garage sale. From a hanger, I pulled on the maroon St. Auggie's Show Choir t-shirt I had purchased at the beginning of the season over high-waisted mom jeans that covered a multitude of sins. A little soft in all the wrong places, I made peace with my body that enjoyed chocolate caramels a little too much and a little too often.

God bless the first designer who introduced spandex to denim. You, sir, are a saint.

With dainty features, a smattering of freckles across my nose and cheeks, and big brown eyes, I was labeled cute as a child, a descriptor that I never shook. I didn't think it was terrible company to be in. After all, puppies and babies are cute. I raked my fingers through my shoulder-length, brown hair, noticing a few glittery white strands catching the light from the fixture above the bathroom mirror. Trying to smooth them down with water a couple of times, I gave up after they stubbornly popped right back up.

I tugged the gold St. Christopher's medal I always wore to free it from catching on my sports bra—I was convinced underwire was a torture instrument of the devil —and centered it on the chain around my neck. I liked to keep my jewelry simple and utilitarian.

Who has the time to swap out earrings to match their outfits? God knows I don't.

I always wore the simple gold band John presented to me a month before he got called for active duty in Iraq, and on my ears, the conservative diamond studs he splurged on when he returned. They were a complete surprise gift to soften the rock-hard edges he developed from living in a war-torn country without us for nearly two years. I wasn't fussy, or someone who spent money or time on handbags or shoes. I was practical and prided myself on my frugalities. Where it was hard to buy myself a new pair of jeans unless the ones I was wearing developed significant holes, I doted on Wren, whose closet was bursting at the seams with jeans and sundresses. Many of them still with tags on.

Why is it so easy to spend money on your children, but infinitely harder to spend it on yourself?

Guilt colored most of my decisions my entire life. I was steeped in it. I know I shouldn't speak ill of my own religion, but even as a little girl wearing a plaid skirt at my own Catholic elementary school, I remember its source of origin. Guilt and Catholicism go hand in hand and travel together. I'm pretty sure it was the first official pairing to cross the gangplank on Noah's Ark.

Glancing at the stainless-steel watch that ringed my wrist, I had to hustle. My shift was starting in twenty-five minutes. I hesitated briefly, thinking I should probably send Wren an obligatory text to fill her in on the change of plans, but my desire to be punctual, and by punctual I mean ten minutes early, outweighed the need to inform her of the change.

Ten minutes later, I was guiding my sedan into a lucky open parking spot next to the wall of yellow school buses emblazoned with local school names. With a grin, I pulled the gold medal to my lips and kissed it, acknowledging my good fortune. The lot was packed, but I'd scored a spot only a few feet from the door.

St. Christopher for the win again.

St Auggie's was a typical school built in the eighties, olive green and drab with a bricked façade. A blanket of fresh snow covered the old roof that our parish priest disclosed we were going to have to replace next year at the last elder's meeting. Inside, ancient painted radiators tucked between the rows of lockers clanged and burned the dust, leaving a charred earthy smell behind. St. Auggie's Catholic School was an old girl—a clean building, showing her age, but lovingly cared for by the shoestring staff. We didn't have the influx of property tax income the public schools did to pay for shiny upgrades and the latest technology. The school and church were supported by the tithes collected every Sunday in the gold church plate that was passed from aisle to aisle by our balding ushers.

Not even stopping to glance at my reflection in the rearview mirror, I hoisted my enormous black leather purse to a shoulder and hurried to the entrance. Peaceful snow floated to the ground as I navigated thick tracks of slushy trails in front of the entrance in an attempt to keep my feet dry. Once inside, I unbuttoned my coat, shook off the flakes like a dog coming in from the rain, and hurried toward the source of the sound, the rubber soles of my shoes squeaking on the speckled epoxy floors. Pop music pumped through the PA, and the roar of cheering and singing intensified with each step I took. At the entrance, the metal doors of the gym were a mouth gaping open wide as I merged into the controlled chaos, waving at acquaintances every few steps. The gym was packed wall to wall with people—parents relegated to the stands and teenagers sprawled across chairs and standing in rows closest to the makeshift stage. I picked my way through the crowd and up the wiggling bleachers to find a seat hidden in the mass of humanity that filled the maroon vinyl seats. Scanning the room, I searched for Wren's thin frame and long, dark blonde hair.

Sweet Caroline cued up on the PA system, and the crowd began to sing in unison. The notes bounced off the wooden floors with such intensity my heart thrummed and the bleachers I was sitting on began to vibrate. It was a song I knew by heart and had sung to Wren to calm her down when she was a colicky baby. I'd dip and dance around the pale green nursery, crooning into her ear with the perfect pitch singing voice I was blessed with and had passed down to Wren.

My heart ached to return to those sweet, heady, exhausting days where nothing mattered except keeping a tiny human alive. When you are in it, deep in the trenches of motherhood, sleep-deprived, and with hours passing without accomplishing anything tangible, people will tell you to hang on, it will get better. I never understood why they said that. Sure, I'd have sold my soul for four hours of sleep in one stretch, but I savored every moment. Wren even had the dreaded colic, unable to get comfortable in the evenings, her tiny belly distended and red. The inconsolable screaming didn't even phase me; it actually gave me purpose. I'd buckle her in the car seat and drive until she'd finally give in and sleep would overcome her. Her long, curled eyelashes and fat baby cheeks finally still, her mouth slack and then sucking a phantom nipple, then slacking again as she finally relaxed, as I drove down dark streets, warm and snug in the car with my sleeping babe.

John and I decided together when Wren was on the way that I would be a stay-at-home mom. It was a title I adored. I didn't shrink from it or feel unfulfilled like the talk shows always told me I should feel. I took my job of shaping this tiny life seriously. The days converged and melded from one into the next, her babyhood a mashup of library story hours and lazy afternoons at the park where I'd push her for hours in the baby swing. The wind rushing into her face would make her giggle and her eyelashes flutter from the breeze. Kicking her chubby legs in unison as she got closer, I'd sing out, "Wheeeeeee!" and grab her baby toes to tickle them while laughter bubbled up over us both. She'd ricochet back up into the air, looking like she was an angel baby floating in the clouds, only to return to me. I cherished the time spent holding her in my arms in the spring when the lilacs were in bloom. The sweet scent of them filled my lungs as she reached a chubby arm out to grab onto a stalk, her eyes crossed in concentration.

"Pretty," I said, talking to her like an adult, naming her world and taking great pride when her squeaky little voice repeated back a discernible, "T-t." Those days passed in a blink and seemed so far away now as I sat in the gymnasium.

"Bah, Bah, Bahhhh," I sang out from my perch on the

bleachers in the throng of parents I was cocooned in. Rocking from side to side to the music, my singing voice was strong and steady, using my diaphragm to project it cleanly out into the chorus. Singing was an activity I enjoyed and a gift I felt compelled to share as one of the musical worship leaders at St. Auggie's. I occasionally made a little extra pocket money singing for weddings and funerals. It was squirreled away into the college fund I created for Wren before she was born, and I took pride in seeing that number grow a little each month and knowing it would give Wren options. I never went to college, but gosh darn it, my daughter would.

Singing the words loud and proud, I stood on my tiptoes and scanned the crowd, my eyes searching for the face it always craved—the beautiful face of my daughter. The one I lived and breathed for. The truth was I knew there were only two years left. She would go on to do great things, taking the world by storm, while I was left behind wondering how the heck the time went so fast. I'd then wait for her to grace us with her presence, accompanied by the expected loads of dirty laundry hauled from her dorm.

I loved being a mom. You could say I was made for it, begging for dolls for Christmas since I could speak. I always dreamed of being surrounded by a large, rambunctious family. Being raised Catholic, it is a fate almost expected of you, that and the result of relying on the rhythm method as the standard of birth control.

Motherhood is an exquisite study in contrast. While pregnant, you are biologically fused together with your child, but every single day outside the warm cocoon of your womb, there is a subtle tearing away. Even though the

291

pull to separate is natural and part of the journey, it still hurts like all get out, this bittersweet symphony of life.

Every stage of childhood had something great to love about it, but then, before you could settle in or get used to the way things were, they would shift and change again. Leaving you forever grappling with figuring out where you fit in. Scrambling to establish your value repeatedly to this new version of your child. Parenthood is a million tiny endings to grieve. The day the crib and baby swing leave your house after sitting idle for a few months while you denied that you didn't need them anymore. Every day in tiny, almost immeasurable increments, your child is leaving you and embracing their autonomy. They are becoming their own independent being.

My eyes finally landed on the recognizable long, thick shock of curly blonde hair. Show Choir demanded the female performers' hair be styled identically in order to participate. Part of the uniform, it was required to be pulled back from your face and curled into long ringlets that cascaded down your back. It paired perfectly with the sparkly, floor-length, flared dresses each girl was asked to wear with heels. The overall look was cohesive, embracing the feminine, and every time I saw Wren in costume on stage in full hair and make-up, my heart swelled with delight. She was growing into her beauty, the awkwardness of the pre-teen years fading away to uncover the beautiful woman she would soon become.

Curling her hair for competitions was one of my favorite rituals. Spending the hour before the event with Wren held captive, perched on the edge of one of our sturdy dining room chairs while I got to work sectioning her satiny hair into even chunks. She had such thick hair it always took over an hour to curl it. I was proud she took after her father in the hair department and had successfully avoided the genetic weakness of my own limp, darker locks. Wren's delicate features and upturned nose paired with the layers of beautifully curled hair made her look angelic.

Today, my eyes landed on her with a smile that rapidly morphed into embarrassed confusion. A prickle of irritation needled up my ribs, watching her carousing with my best friend's daughter, Sammie, without a care in the world, oblivious to everyone around her.

She knows better than to sit on someone's lap at a school function. It is completely inappropriate. What will people think?

I glanced quickly around the crowd, feeling exposed as the first sliver of parental shame walked up my spine. I felt a flush of warmth rush up my cheeks and rubbed them with the palms of my hands. This latest stage of development had a willful Wren pushing boundaries and buttons harder and faster the closer she got to adulthood.

I made a mental note to discuss it with her on the way home, but I couldn't tear my eyes away from the interaction. Just a few feet from the stage, Wren was singing and swaying in the throng of teenagers. Her skinny arm, all elbow, was slung around Sammie's thicker shoulders. I saw Sammie's arms wrap around her waist, pulling her in tighter as a faint alarm sounded. In complete denial yet unable to look away, time slowed as I continued to study them from afar.

Wren's thick, curly hair fell forward as she leaned in closer to whisper something to Sammie that made them both laugh. It was a brazen act that my intuition understood and cataloged instantly. The exchange was *intimate*, unveiling a shocking affection that formed a lump in my throat and made my mouth an instant desert. My breath quickened and I felt myself flush again with shameful warmth. I looked down, giving myself an internal pep talk.

You're crazy. Wren would die if she knew you were thinking like this.

I forced my eyes back up, and they landed on Megan Stonewell. Her eyes narrowed and her head tipped and tilted toward Wren in such a tiny, nearly imperceptible movement I initially thought my mind was playing tricks on me. When her lips settled into a scowl, I couldn't deny her disgust. I pried my eyes from hers and wrenched them back to Wren, examining the interaction with Sammie, not wanting to rush to judgment. Wren was laughing and carrying on in a massive assembly of her friends and peers, completely unaware that I was watching from my perch on the bleachers. Lately, she had been hostile and sullen, hiding in her room under the pretense of studying for her upcoming SATs. Here, she was lighter and carefree, smiling widely and energetically engaged. The song ended, and Wren jumped to her feet with the rest of the audience, clapping and cheering along with the entire gymnasium.

The crowd rose around me as I sat stunned for a long second, unable to move. Panic and fear surged through me as I grappled to accept what my eyes had seen. Going through the motions, I finally found my feet and applauded, knowing it was what was expected of me, but internally, my mind churned. Reliving the last five minutes over and over in slow excruciating detail, I shook it off. As the crowd dispersed, I walked to my post at the coat check and busied myself with the task at hand, glad to have something else to focus on. There was a tingle of truth I refused to acknowledge. I stuffed it down along with the anxieties and worries that come with raising a child in this day and age.

She's just cutting loose, just having fun. You are losing your mind.

Available on Amazon, BN Nook, Apple iBooks, Kobo, Google Play.

Order now at: https://tealbutterflypress.com/products/when-wren-came-out

* * *

Like FREE Books? Enter to Win a Gift Card to My Bookstore   https://tealbutterflypress.com/pages/join-our-email-list-and-win

There's a new winner every week!

Acknowledgements

I am eternally grateful for my partner in life, Patrick. It seems weird to call someone your boyfriend when you are pushing fifty, but until man friend hits the mainstream, partner it is. He embodies the word. Patrick has supported and encouraged this dream for three years, even though the fruits of my labor have been meager. It's rare to find someone who suits you so well, actively looks for ways to improve your life, and who steps into a stepparent role with ease.

Thank you for bringing calm and peace into my life for the first time. You have held me together during some devastating moments and made me laugh hysterically through others. Thanks to your love and dedication, the only drama in my life currently is found on the pages of my books. Life for us is just getting to the good part, and I can't wait to go on our first adventure together.

I also want to thank his sister, Kristi. She has been an alpha reader for me for the last three years. I bet she didn't know that was in the cards when she heard her brother met someone, but she has graciously been a first reader of my work. Kristi is unafraid to tell me the unvarnished truth, even when it hurts, and in the sweetest way. I value her opinion and trust that, when she tells me something isn't working, she's probably right. Kristi, I truly love you like a sister.

Kristin and Anthony from the GlampVentures were delightful. The off-grid experience in their tree tent is one I will never forget. Our host at Walland Forest also went above and beyond to make our treehouse tour memorable in every way and deserves my kudos as well.

Last but never least, I'd like to thank my editor, Kendra. She makes every word I write better. I am grateful you are on my team. Who knows where this road leads? We've come too far to turn back now.

Read more about the Hellavue Tree Tent Experience in Kristin's Own Words

In 2017, Kristin was diagnosed with an aggressive form of breast cancer. During her treatment, she would hike the property and sit and watch the wild world around her—the birds chirping, the squirrels gathering nuts, the deer grazing—and it brought her peace. She decided to quit her stressful sales job and open up the property for others seeking peace and adventure. When treatment ended, her husband and father-in-law (Pops) started clearing a few spots and milling the lumber that came from the property to start building tiny cabins. In the spring of 2021, Kristin, Anthony, and Pops started building their first cabin—the Cedar Sun Catcher. Then they built the deck for a large canvas Bell Tent, Royal Rest, then a spot for a Tentsile Tree Tent for the really adventurous types. They opened their glampground, named GlampVentures, on Sept 1st of 2021.

Meeting many great folks, listening to their awesome stories, and receiving incredible feedback, their dream had become a reality. In 2022, they started construction on their tiny A-frame, Lady A, located where the tree tent hung the year before. After searching the property, they found the perfect spot to relocate the hanging tent. "Helluvue" was cliffside, offering a view of the Nolichucky River and seven mountain ranges. This is a special spot on the property and Kristin's favorite view. The views of Leconte, English, Snowbird, and Mt Cammerer mountain ranges, just to name a few, stand prominently in the background as the birds from the nearby Rankin Bottoms Wildlife Refuge can be seen fishing the river below. Birds that are found at Rankin Bottoms include: Double-crested Cormorant, Great Blue Heron, Great Egret, Black-crowned Night-Heron, Killdeer, Semipalmated Plovers, Least, Semipalmated, Western, Pectoral, Spotted, Solitary, and Stilt Sandpipers, Greater and Lesser Yellowlegs, Short-billed Dowitcher, and several species of swallows. Eagles have been spotted fishing the river from "Helluvue" while the deer cross over to the mile-long island that is visible when the Douglas Lake that floods the Nolichucky River is drained after Labor Day.

Giving folks a place of peace and abundant nature to hike, kayak, lounge in a hammock, and relax is what they always dreamed of. A place where the simple things are important. A place in this crazy world where they can breathe in the fresh air while listening to birdsong and slow down for a bit.

The Real Life Treehouse Adventure

This book was inspired by a real-life adventure and a desire to reconnect with my child, J, who was on the cusp of becoming an adult. In the middle of a relentless Iowa winter in 2021, I woke up in a panic when I realized their childhood was almost over. Fueled by coffee in the early morning hours, I schemed my craziest adventure yet —a treehouse tour in Tennessee. Over the course of the next month, I booked four treehouses, and we set off for our grand adventure in June 2022.

Tennessee was beautiful. A curvy southern belle that welcomes new beaus with open arms. The drawl of the native tongue had such a warmth to it, I wish it would have stuck to my staunch midwestern syllables. It was lyrical, combining words together yet shortening them at the same time. The roads were dizzying, spinning us through hollers and chugging up peaks while we baked in the sun of a decadent summer.

It was the last summer of J's childhood, and I was deeply grateful for the opportunity to press pause for a moment, to recalibrate, and to shake things up. Our normal life had gotten into a rut of frustration and survival, and I wanted the dynamic to change.

I cannot express how much closer together this trip brought J and me. We had outgrown the mother-child relationship and had gotten to a place of stagnation and misunderstanding. Our treehouse adventure changed everything. We came home refreshed, re-centered, and ready to take the next steps of creating a healthy mother and adult-child relationship.

I walked through the events and revelations for months after. My mind wandered as it often does, sorting and shifting, looking for meaning in the quiet moments. That is the gift of travel, especially traveling with those you love.

There were several takeaways from the journey for me. I realized that although my nest will be empty soon, a mother's heart never is. Over the course of your children's lives, you get the chance to transform over and over in tandem with them as they shift into adulthood. If you've done the work, your children will return to your empty nest, begging for the chocolate chip cookies you used to bake when they were little.

I am looking forward to watching the next stage of their lives unfold. I hope I've modeled the courage required to persevere through tough times and go after their dreams. No matter where life takes them. Mistakes will be made, that much is expected, but life is long and endlessly forgiving when you approach it with an open heart. I vow to not give advice unless expressly asked for it, and to encourage and support whatever their heart calls them to do. Even if it means being a full-time tattoo artist. Now, I can say without fear, GO FOR IT!

I can't wait to see them soar and someday build their own nest and hatch an egg or two. I've learned so much from parenting my children. It's tested my strength and brought my weaknesses to light and forever changed me from the inside out.

This book was inspired by true events, and here are a few that made it into the book. The S'mores Cook-off. Yep, that was real, and I am telling you that putting candied bacon on a S'more will change your life. I'm drooling right now thinking about it. #2 was the Reese's Cup, #3 was the Original, #4 was Fudge Stripes. The orange brownie soufflé was a total flop, and I did embarrass the hell out of J when I asked to purchase an uncooked egg from our waitress at the Pancake House. J was mortified.

And my final confession, yes, I did in fact rip my swim shorts during the river float and then proceeded to flash entire families floating by on inner tubes. J couldn't stop laughing long enough to stop me, and I am certain children were scarred that day. In case you were wondering, no, the water didn't feel any different. I truly had no idea my cheek was on full display. It was my Janet Jackson at the Super Bowl moment.

The characters of Tessa and Nova differ *vastly* from us and are true figments of my imagination. The treehouses, however, were very much real.

The Treehouses

1. Hellavue GlampVentures in Newport, Tennessee
Kristin and Anthony were amazing. Truly wonderful hosts

and we had a once-in-a-lifetime experience in their tree tent living off the grid.

2. The Bark Treehouse in Sevierville, Tennessee

Best exterior and weirdest flooring choice. Maybe it's just me, but Astroturf is not carpeting.

3. Walland Forest in Walland, Tennessee

My dream is to re-create this treehouse on a piece of land someday. It was incredible! It featured the ideal layout in the smallest square footage I've ever lived in, but with the huge deck, it never felt small.

4. The Whimsical Treehouse in Sevierville, Tennessee

Over-the-top luxury is the only way to classify this one. Those indoor swings and fairy lights were magical.

Thank you for reading! Be sure to check out exclusive photos and videos from the trip using the QR Code below.

Always choose adventure.

XOXO Blair Bryan

Read More By this Author

Use the QR code below to access my current catalogue. **Teal Butterfly Press is the only place to purchase autographed paperbacks and get early access.** Buying direct means you are supporting an artist instead of big business. I appreciate you.

https://tealbutterflypress.com/pages/books

Also available at Barnes and Noble, Kobo, Apple books, Amazon, and many other international book sellers.

Find My Books at your Favorite Bookseller Below.

Books by Ninya

Books By Blair Bryan

About the Author

 I've always been a risk-taker, so at 44 I decided to write and publish my own books. It has been a roller coaster ride with a punishing learning curve, but if it were easy, everyone would do it. I write under the pen names of Ninya and Blair Bryan.

I love to travel and a trip to Scotland with a complete stranger was the inspiration for my memoir. I also seem to attract crazy experiences and people into my life like a magnet that gives me a never-ending supply of interesting storylines.

If you love a good dirty joke, a cup of coffee so strong you can chew it, and have killed more cats with your curiosity than you can count, I might be your soulmate.

Let's connect in my facebook reader group, **The Kaleidoscope: Teal Butterfly Press' Official Author Fandom**